W9-DHR-716

He couldn't stop thinking about Cheri

Sky didn't like to admit it, but in a way she was right. The timing *was* lousy. He was finally on the verge of gaining a national reputation. In this business that would mean eighteen-hour days, extensive traveling and a single-minded focus on his career.

Right now he wasn't sure that was what he wanted.

He'd seen from the beginning that Cheri was a naturally sensuous woman, but he'd been surprised by the intensity of his response to her. It had gone far beyond the merely physical into something almost spiritual.

Sky smiled. That was an odd term for someone in his line of work to use.

Besides, he was concerned about Cheri and Tad. Actually, Sky had never much believed in ghosts, but he did believe there were phenomena that scientists couldn't explain. Some of those phenomena could be helpful, others amusing, but some could be dangerous....

ABOUT THE AUTHOR

Jacqueline Diamond, who lives in La Habra, California, with her husband and son, loves flowers, chocolates, bargains and long naps, and hates exercise. She has had several letters published in the *Los Angeles Times* in which she identifies herself as president of Softbodies of America and extolls the virtues of the most adorable body shape in the world, that of the teddy bear.

Books by Jacqueline Diamond

HARLEQUIN AMERICAN ROMANCE

 79–THE DREAM NEVER DIES
196–AN UNEXPECTED MAN
218–UNLIKELY PARTNERS
239–THE CINDERELLA DARE
270–CAPERS AND RAINBOWS

Don't miss any of our special offers. Write to us at the following address for information on our newest releases.

Harlequin Reader Service
901 Fuhrmann Blvd., P.O. Box 1397, Buffalo, NY 14240
Canadian address: P.O. Box 603,
Fort Erie, Ont. L2A 5X3

Ghost of
a Chance

Jacqueline Diamond

Harlequin Books

TORONTO • NEW YORK • LONDON
AMSTERDAM • PARIS • SYDNEY • HAMBURG
STOCKHOLM • ATHENS • TOKYO • MILAN

For Clara Hieronymous

Published January 1989

First printing November 1988

ISBN 0-373-16279-0

Prologue

The real estate agent was taking down the For Sale sign when a woman in her late forties stopped to ask him who had bought the old Granger house.

"Young couple from Los Angeles," he said. "You one of the neighbors?"

"Not exactly." She had a plain face, but there was something striking about her eyes, as if they saw beyond this world into another dimension. *No.* That was just his imagination. He was glad this listing was off his hands; even without the ghost stories, there was something spooky about the place. If he'd had to show it much longer, he'd have started thinking he saw ghosts himself. "This young couple," the woman said. "Do they have a daughter?"

He shook his head. "No. A boy, little kid. First-grader, I think."

The woman looked puzzled. "I keep seeing a girl, or maybe a young woman, but she isn't married."

"Someone hanging around here?" the agent asked.

The woman smiled. "I'm sorry. You see, I'm a sensitive. What some people would call a psychic. I—get impressions about things."

"You oughta love this place." The agent carried the sign to his car. "They say it's haunted."

"So they do."

He considered asking the woman if she'd seen any spooks around, but he was already late for an appointment. Besides, she might be some kind of nut, and he didn't want to encourage her.

Vinnie Dumont watched the agent drive away and wished she'd kept her mouth shut. People usually thought she was crazy when she mentioned being a psychic, or else they began plying her with questions about their future, questions she didn't always want to answer.

She'd been on the point of asking him to warn this couple, but what good would it do? There was tragedy ahead for them, but it wasn't related to the house. She couldn't save them, no matter where they lived.

And after them, the girl would come.

Vinnie shuddered in spite of the late-afternoon Southern California sunshine. Some things couldn't be stopped, but she didn't have to like it.

She walked along in front of the house, keeping to the sidewalk as she examined the shuttered windows, the Victorian gables and the overgrown bushes. It had been empty for months, since the last owners had decided they'd be happier at the beach.

It wasn't an evil house; she could feel that. But a dangerous one in its own way.

For me, too.

Vinnie didn't usually get psychic insights about herself, but she felt drawn to the Granger house in a way she couldn't explain. Whoever the young woman would be, she had a role to play in Vinnie's life, as well as in the future of this house.

Reluctantly Vinnie turned away. She had to tape a show in Santa Ana in half an hour, and it would take her nearly that long to get there from Orange in rush-hour traffic.

But she knew she would come back. Whether she wanted to or not.

Chapter One

When Tad woke up, the house was dark and silent around him. He hugged his teddy bear tight; it still smelled a little like Daddy, and that made him feel braver.

Then he heard it again, the noise that had woken him up. Someone crying softly, way up in the attic. Or in the wall somewhere. Like one of the Borrowers that Aunt Cheri had read to him about, a little person who lived here with them and stole things.

He'd heard the crying before, ever since Mommy and Daddy died, but he hadn't told anybody. He kept hoping maybe it really was Mommy, and that if he was very, very good, she'd come back. Only it was getting harder and harder to remember what she looked like. He kept seeing Aunt Cheri's face instead, and that made him feel as if he'd done something wrong.

The crying stopped; now the woman was speaking softly, like a radio turned down too low. Tad pushed Buster the teddy bear away from his face so he could hear better.

"I love him." He could make out those words very clearly. "I can't live without him."

Maybe it wasn't Mommy, or even one of the Borrowers. Maybe it was the ghosts. Mommy and Daddy had laughed at those stories about this old house being haunted. Aunt Cheri didn't believe it, either. But Tad had seen a video movie about ghosts coming out of a TV set, so he knew they really existed.

He waited, in case the ghost said anything more, but all he could hear was the whisper of a warm September breeze through the cypress tree out front. Soft teddy bear fur tickled Tad's cheek, and he burrowed deeper into the pillow. Soon he was asleep again.

SUNLIGHT WAS STREAMING through the kitchen window as Cheri tucked a package of raisins into the Cookie Monster lunch box. Tad didn't really need lunch, since he'd only be gone until noon today, but she didn't feel right sending him off to school empty-handed.

She wished he hadn't insisted on going alone today. She'd gotten him signed up for second grade and everything, but she felt as though she ought to be there for his first day back at school since his parents had died. But it seemed to be a matter of pride with him to go alone. Or maybe loyalty; he pushed her away sometimes, as if resenting her presence. Well, she knew she wasn't his mother, but she was doing her best.

A thump from upstairs startled her. "Are you all right?" she called, but there was no answer.

She was just deciding to go up and check on him when Tad clumped down the stairs and into the kitchen, where he plopped into his chair. In the morning light, Tad looked startlingly like Cheri's brother Jeff, with chestnut hair a shade lighter than her own and eyes the same bright green. She swallowed the tears that always seemed near the surface these days.

"I heard you banging around upstairs," she said. "You didn't hurt yourself, did you?"

"Wasn't me." Tad stuck out his chin. "Must be one of the ghosts."

"Right." Cheri leaned over to rebutton the top of his polo shirt, which he'd gotten crooked. "Want some eggs?"

"Mom always gives me cereal," he said.

With a sigh, Cheri lifted down a box of Strawberry-in-the-Middle squares from the pantry. "These okay?"

"I guess so." He didn't even say thank-you as she poured the milk, but Cheri didn't want to chide him. She wondered when she'd feel secure enough to act like a real mother. Well, there would be plenty of time to remind Tad of his manners later.

He finished in record time, grabbed the lunch box and headed for the door. "Tad—" Cheri stopped herself, on the point of telling him that his rudeness was hurting her feelings. "I suppose you've missed your friends this summer," she finished lamely.

"Yeah, I guess so." Facing her, Tad paused, his lips pressed tightly together. "There *are* ghosts here, you know."

"You don't really believe that, do you?" True, local legend had it that the house was haunted by one or more of its original owners, a peculiar family named the Grangers. But as far as Cheri was concerned, the only ghost on the premises was that of her overworked vacuum cleaner, which had died the day before. "Tad, there's no such thing as ghosts."

"There are, too!" He clutched his lunch box tightly. "You just don't want me to know."

Before she could think of an answer, Cheri heard the school bus chugging up the street, and Tad dashed outside without even a goodbye wave.

She stared after him for a moment before closing the door. He was so small and defenseless, and he'd been through a lot this summer. She just hoped she'd be able to penetrate the wall he'd built around himself, to help him learn to love and trust again. And that she wouldn't lose her temper along the way and spoil everything.

Feeling a bit lost without her nephew, Cheri wandered into the living room. The high ceiling and large bay window were cozily offset by the rose-patterned carpet and antique oak furniture. She'd been surprised when Jeff and Donna found such an old home here in Southern California, but that was before she'd visited Orange and seen its old-fashioned neighborhoods, looking solid and unruffled by the nearby freeways and shopping centers.

Donna had spent most of last spring redecorating the house, even installing the golden tile in the kitchen herself. Jeff, absorbed in his work as an assistant professor of art at Chapman College, hadn't had much time to help, but for Donna's birthday he'd put in the oak cabinets. How they'd loved this century-old house; they'd planned to live here forever.

But first they'd rewarded themselves with a long-awaited vacation in Italy, and Cheri had been delighted at the chance to spend the month of June here taking care of Tad. It was hard to believe they'd all hugged each other and said goodbye in this house less than three months ago. It had been only two weeks later that the phone call came from Rome, telling her Jeff and Donna had been killed in an automobile accident.

Cheri paused before a wall of photographs. There was a sepia-toned shot of the house back in the 1890s with nothing but farmland around it. In another photo, a Model T stood in front of the wide porch that ran the length of the front. That was from the era when the Granger family had lived here.

The people in the pictures looked stiffly formal, as if they'd forgotten how to smile. They didn't seem like real people at all, more like plastic figures in a store window.

Maybe people who'd died before you had a chance to know them always seemed that way. As if they couldn't be real. It hurt to think that Tad's children would think of their grandparents that way, that new people would come into his and Cheri's lives who would never know Jeff and

Donna as they'd been when they were warm and vibrant and full of laughter.

It was almost enough to make Cheri wish there really were ghosts, so the people she loved could come back to her again.

She shook her head. The last thing she wanted was to say anything to reinforce Tad's fantasies about ghosts. He needed security, not tall tales and groundless fears.

Of course, in the dark of night, lying upstairs in her bed, Cheri sometimes thought she heard a scrape or murmur that couldn't be readily explained. In the small hours, when dreams seep into waking thoughts, didn't everyone believe in ghosts just a little bit?

A script lay on the couch, and Cheri forced herself to sit down and open it. She'd promised to report on its merits for her friend Elaine, who was starting a production company. She'd asked Cheri to join it, both as actress and producer, but even though she had a great deal of respect for Elaine's talents as a director, the answer was no.

I'm a mother now, she'd told Elaine, but they both knew that wasn't the only reason.

Cheri read the description of the heroine:

Belle: a French maid in her early twenties, a gamine with a girl-next-door smile. She's romantic, sexy in a healthy, down-to-earth way, and full of mischief.

Yes, it sounded appealing. A year or two ago, Cheri would have jumped at the chance to play Belle. But now there was too much hurt and bitterness for her ever to go back to acting.

Cheri had grown up on a television series and had made a number of lightweight TV movies. Then, as she reached her mid-twenties, she'd been restless for new challenges. Besides, although she'd always looked younger than she was, she couldn't pass for a teenager any longer.

Her agent had insisted she had to perform nude scenes if she were ever to establish herself as a serious actress. Cheri had refused. Then, last year, as she was still reeling from the breakup of her first love affair, her agent had come up with a feature film that didn't require nudity.

At first it had seemed like a godsend. But the director had been moody and erratic, her co-star turned up drunk more often than not, and the critics had trashed the picture. Audiences stayed away in droves.

Suddenly her phone calls to her agent weren't returned. Trendy restaurants seated her in the back. Producers ignored her, and people she'd considered friends forgot to invite her to their parties. It had brought home to Cheri the shallowness of the life she was leading.

At twenty-seven, Cheri was tired of struggling to be taken seriously as an actress, tired of worrying about whether she was thin or pretty or talented enough to make the transition to adult stardom. Even though the flop was gradually being forgotten and she'd begun getting TV offers again, just thinking about going back to work tied Cheri's stomach into knots. So she'd decided to live quietly on her savings while raising Tad. If only the house didn't feel so empty just now...

Something scraped overhead, and Cheri sat bolt upright, her heart thudding.

Her mind raced through the possibilities. It couldn't be Tad; he'd left for school. Yet surely she would have heard if someone had broken in.

She listened for a repetition. All was silent.

You're worse than Tad! she scolded herself. *You've lived in apartments for so long, you've forgotten what houses are like. It's probably just settling.*

Snuggling against the arm of the sofa, Cheri dug into the script. It was a lively romance about Belle going to work for a family in a ritzy L.A. neighborhood, and the dialogue was zippy. It might be just the light comedy Elaine needed to establish her new company.

As she read, Cheri kept one ear cocked for the doorbell. Her lawyer had phoned to say he was sending his junior partner over today with some estate documents for her to sign. The law firm was friendly and informal, and she appreciated that the man could drop by on his way to the office.

Overhead a board creaked, as if beneath a footstep. Cheri froze.

Maybe she should call the police. No; the report might find its way into the newspapers, and then she'd have the last thing she wanted: gossip writers turning her life and Tad's into a circus. She'd experienced more than enough of their cruelty during her ill-fated love affair with an actor the year before.

Cheri walked to the foot of the stairs. Her voice caught in her throat, but she forced it out fiercely. "I've called the police and I've got a gun, so why don't you get out the same way you came in!"

Nothing stirred.

She paused with her foot on the bottom step. She was almost certain now that the noise hadn't meant anything, and she didn't intend to cower downstairs all day worrying about it. Resolved to act firmly, she fetched the portable phone from the kitchen and carried it up the stairs with her. The police were only a call away.

At the top of the steps, Cheri stopped to listen again.

A faint rustling came from the direction of her bedroom. The only other sound was the thudding of her heart.

Slowly, clutching the phone, Cheri advanced down the hall, her sneakers making almost no sound. Near the door to her room, a blast of cold air startled her. She gazed around for the source of the draft, but didn't see it. There couldn't be any such things as ghosts, but maybe there *was* something odd about the way the house was built, something that had given rise to the legends. . . .

Swallowing hard, Cheri stepped into the room. Out of the corner of her eye, she saw something white billow toward her in eerie silence.

It was too much for her strained nerves. With a shriek, Cheri dropped the phone and raced out of the room, down the stairs and through the front door. Once outside in the safety of the September sunshine, she grabbed a column on the porch for support.

"Are you all right?" A man was coming in through the gate, a tall man wearing a crisply tailored three-piece suit and carrying a briefcase.

"Oh—oh, thank goodness you're here." There was nothing like a lawyer to drive nonsense out of your mind, Cheri thought as she gulped in the fresh air. Suddenly she felt terribly embarrassed to be seen in such a state, especially by this self-possessed man with lively gray eyes. He must think she was a real basket case. "I—I did have sort of a scare. I thought I heard someone upstairs, and then I saw something move, but I'm not sure what it was."

A firm hand reached out. "Take my arm. Really, Miss Louette, I make a great leaning post."

"No—I'm all right." But as she let go of the column, Cheri felt herself sag against him.

"Not quite all right," he corrected, slipping an arm around her waist for support. Without waiting for a reply, he guided her into the house.

Although Cheri was a little above average in height, she felt slender and light to Sky Welton. He'd seen her on television many times, of course, but in person she looked somehow fresher, with her curls brushed back loosely from the delicate cheekbones and her eyes shining from exertion. Of course, actresses were supposed to look good. It was their business. But he was finding her unexpectedly appealing, and Sky wasn't sure whether to trust his reaction or run like crazy in the other direction.

He'd imagined any number of ways Cheri Louette might greet him, from slamming the door in his face to demanding a hefty fee. He certainly had never imagined anything like this, but then, she obviously didn't know who he was.

If she knew he was a TV host, would those delicate features form a mask of calculated interest? Would she ask about ratings, trying to find out if his Orange County show could help boost her sagging career? He'd heard that Cheri Louette had withdrawn from Hollywood for personal reasons, and had wondered if that wasn't just a cover-up for a case of wounded ego.

But he hadn't expected someone so vulnerable, so artlessly in need of help. Damn it, he didn't want to get close to a woman right now, particularly not an ambitious one. On the other hand, his show needed her. She was still Cheri Louette, practically a household word. Besides, there was a delicious softness about her mouth and a hint of fragility in her jawline that he couldn't quite bring himself to ignore.

"Something to drink?" Sky asked.

"Maybe some coffee." Cheri moved reluctantly away from the comfort of the man's arm and led him into the kitchen. She hadn't had anyone to lean on these past few months; she hadn't realized until now how much she missed it.

"Would you like me to go upstairs and look around?" The man set his briefcase to one side and poured her a cup from the half-filled coffee maker. "My hands are registered as deadly weapons."

Cheri smiled for the first time since she'd met him. "Actually, I'm feeling kind of foolish." She took a sip of the coffee. "I'm sure you're in a hurry...."

"As a matter of fact, I'm not. Finish your coffee." He waited until she did, then collected the cup and put it into the sink. The simple, considerate gesture struck her as endearing, something her onetime lover would never have thought of doing. "Why don't we just go up together and see what's there?"

"I suppose we might as well." Cheri pushed back her chair and stood, inexplicably relieved when he came to her side.

"Now, tell me first about the noises you heard." His voice was deep and reassuring.

This is odd, Cheri thought as she described the creaking board and her aborted investigation. She didn't usually feel so self-conscious about her lack of makeup and the faded jeans she wore around the house. Why should she care what this lawyer thought of her? But for some reason she wished she'd at least put on some lipstick this morning.

As he listened intently, Cheri wished she could remember his name. Had the senior attorney mentioned it? He seemed solid and confident, but in the way he studied her face as she spoke, she sensed something else, too, a tough, penetrating intelligence, as if he were looking beneath the words, gauging the depth of her soul. As if he wanted to learn more than a lawyer had any need to know.

"Did you feel anything in particular? A chill, for example?" he asked as they started up the steps side by side. Sunshine flooded the upstairs hall from one of the bedrooms, and Cheri's fears of a few minutes ago struck her as preposterous. And so did her reaction to this man. He was just being polite, trying to help.

"Well—there *was* a draft of cold air. I couldn't figure out where it came from. Do you suppose there are cracks in the walls, behind the wallpaper?" She turned to look at the lawyer, but his expression was hard to read. Somehow he'd changed since they left the ground floor, had become more focused on what lay ahead.

"Maybe. It is an old house, after all." They reached the hallway and she pointed out her bedroom. "Why don't you wait here and I'll take a look?" he said.

"Thanks, but that's not necessary." Ashamed of her earlier cowardice, Cheri led the way. "There..." She stopped. The bedroom window was open halfway, and gauzy white curtains flared into the room. "I don't believe it. I didn't even think about the curtains...but I could swear I closed it this morning."

The man stepped over and shut the windows firmly. "You haven't noticed anything else strange since you moved in, have you?"

"Some noises at night," Cheri admitted. "But I thought it was just my nephew." The man's presence steadied her, but after all, he'd come here on business, and she had no right to take advantage of his kindness. "Look, I really appreciate your help, but maybe I'd better sign those papers so you can get on to the office."

"I beg your pardon?"

"The estate. Didn't you bring—?" The question hung in the air as Cheri stared at the man.

She'd been so preoccupied with her own fright that until now she hadn't questioned her assumption that he was the lawyer. He certainly was dressed for the part in his three-piece suit, but ...

At that moment, she became acutely aware of how large the house was, how isolated they were, and that they were standing in the middle of her bedroom.

"You—you knew who I was." She tried with only moderate success to disguise her discomfort. "You called me Miss Louette."

"Of course I know who you are." His tone was mildly teasing. "Doesn't everybody? You were the girl on *Young and Eager*."

"Then what are you doing here?" Cheri defiantly folded her arms in front of her.

"Helping a lady in distress." His smile was touched with irony. "Or so it seemed at the time. But I'll admit I came here for another reason."

"You weren't just passing by?"

"Not exactly, no." The light from the window highlighted the shape of his body, more muscular than she'd realized at first in the tailored suit. "Allow me to introduce myself. I'm Sky Welton." He held out his hand and, torn between annoyance and curiosity, she shook it.

"What can I do for you?" She had no intention of letting him see how intimidated she felt. Now the peculiar way he'd studied her downstairs made sense. The world was full of kooks and hustlers, and unfortunately, he might be one of them.

"You can appear on my television show here in Orange." At her puzzled look, he added, "It's called *Sky's the Limit*. But most people around here call it something more descriptive."

"What's that?" She felt herself held by his gaze.

"They call it *Ghostbusters*." He paused to measure her reaction and then added, "I'm here to see about your ghosts, Miss Louette. There's a possibility they may be real."

Chapter Two

"You've got to be kidding!" Cheri turned toward the bedroom door, years of painful experience in dealing with snoopy reporters coming to her rescue. "I think this has gone far enough. Who do you really work for?"

"The CIA," the man said promptly. "My show is part of a covert operation to flush out KGB agents posing as mind readers."

His response was so outrageous that Cheri found it difficult not to smile. But life, at least in Hollywood, was full of charming manipulators and personable con men. "And CIA stands for, let me see, Confessions, Invasion of Privacy and..."

"Apologies." Sky Welton lounged against the door frame, his lazy air belied by the thoroughness with which he was examining her. "I always apologize after I take advantage of someone's blind trust. I do have a conscience, you know."

"What did you say your name was?" Cheri wasn't about to let this intruder get the upper hand, and her question was designed to put him in his place.

"Sky. Short for Schuyler." He was obviously unfazed by her tactics. "And yours is actually Cheryl Lewiston, or at least it used to be. Your agent changed it. Former agent, the one you fired last spring after he stuck you in that lousy movie. You're a good actress, Cheri; it's too bad your agent couldn't see it."

So he *had* researched her past. Whatever he really wanted, he took his work seriously. Cheri just wished she didn't feel so inexplicably disappointed at finding that Sky Welton was no better than all the other opportunists she'd fended off for years.

"I can see that you've done your homework, Mr. Welton. However, you came into my house on false pretenses and I'll thank you to leave, right now." With as much dignity as she could muster, Cheri scooped up the phone she'd dropped earlier, brushed by him and marched downstairs.

She heard footsteps following but didn't turn around until she was safely at the bottom, when Sky said, "Doesn't the condemned man get a chance to defend himself?"

He was resting one arm on the newel post, awaiting her response. How did he manage to look so much at home? It was almost as if the house were welcoming him. *Whatever game he's playing, he's good at it.* "Look, Mr. Welton, I appreciate your helping me check out the upstairs, but right now I'd like to be alone."

Sky shook his head slowly. "Not until we talk more about this house. Besides, running into a ghost and meeting me in the same morning are enough to throw anyone into shock. I think another cup of coffee is in order." Before Cheri could protest, he moved past her into the kitchen.

"Look, I know all about the Grangers." Trailing behind him, Cheri returned the telephone to its place on the counter.

"For instance?" Sky poured out two cups of coffee.

"Well..." Darn it, had she really thought she could get rid of him so easily? Donna *had* told Cheri a little of the story, but she hadn't paid much attention. "They made carriages. And... and there was an old maid who outlived the others."

"That's it? You've been hearing suspicious noises at night and you don't even care whose ghost might be marching through your bedroom?" Sky relaxed onto one of the chairs. With a tightening in her throat, Cheri realized that she liked the sight of a man here in this warm kitchen. This house was too big for just a woman and a small boy.

"You're not trying to tell me I'm in some kind of danger from these so-called ghosts?" Reluctantly conceding that Sky wasn't about to be dislodged, she took a seat opposite him. "I'm not one of your gullible viewers—or maybe I should say readers." Which tabloid did he work for, anyway? "I don't even believe in horoscopes."

"That's all right with me." Sky grinned. "I only read my horoscope every morning so I'll know what isn't going to happen." With a fluid movement, he snapped open the briefcase he'd left in the kitchen earlier and pulled out a press kit. "Here's what the CIA put together for me."

Cheri flipped open the glossy folder and found photographs and press releases bearing the letterhead of a local TV station. Despite her reservations, she was impressed by the pictures of Sky with several prominent psychologists, anthropologists and authors. "All right." She closed the folder. "I guess you really do host a TV show on the paranormal, or whatever you call it. But Mr. Welton, I don't want publicity. As far as I'm concerned, you might as well work for a tabloid, because I'm not giving you an interview."

Sky tucked the press kit back into the briefcase and pushed it aside. "Hey, it isn't my fault you moved into the Granger house. No offense, but I was interested in this place long before you turned up."

"Then why haven't you done a show on it before?"

He helped himself to a chocolate chip cookie from the jar she kept for Tad. "You tell me: why should the last couple of owners all refuse to let me go through the house with a psychic to find out what's really here?''

''Because they knew what was really here: they were. And I suspect they didn't want *their* privacy invaded, either.'' Cheri couldn't resist taking a cookie for herself, even though she'd sworn not to put on weight just because she wasn't an actress anymore.

''May I ask you a personal question?''

Startled, she blurted, ''No.''

''That's too bad. I was going to ask for your cookie recipe.'' His gray eyes widened in pretended innocence.

''Don't tell me you're the domestic type, because I won't believe it.'' Was there a Mrs. Welton? Cheri wondered suddenly. He wasn't wearing a ring, but that didn't mean anything.

To her dismay, she saw Sky register her glance at his ring finger. ''No, I'm not married, although why you should want to know that could raise some interesting speculation.''

She took a quick swallow of coffee to hide her embarrassment. ''Just trying to get the lowdown on the opposition. As you did before you came here.''

''Which brings me to the personal question I was going to ask.'' Sky selected another cookie. ''It's none of my business, but how come it took you so long to figure out your agent was a nerd?''

''You're right; it *is* none of your business.'' Cheri sneaked a second cookie and promised herself to atone for it later by jogging around the block a few times. ''I'll take a look at your show if you like, but that's as far as I—'' She broke off as the phone rang and lifted the receiver from the counter. ''Yes?''

Although he pretended not to listen, Sky eavesdropped shamelessly. The call, he gathered, was from that lawyer she'd been expecting, apologizing for not having dropped by. Nothing important was said, nothing he could use as a lever to get Cheri to agree to an interview.

Damn it, taping a show on Cheri Louette and the Granger house could be exactly the boost he needed to get *Sky's the Limit* syndicated. He'd expected, when he came here, that she might refuse his invitation because his show was small potatoes; he hadn't expected that she'd turn out to be so publicity-shy.

The fact was, Sky admired her for taking on the responsibility for her nephew, and he sensed her brother's death must have been a severe blow. But appearing on his show wouldn't really do any harm. Celebrities were always being interviewed at their homes. It went with the territory.

Well, it appeared he might have to work to get around her defenses. He just wished he didn't find himself instinctively wanting to protect her. Not only was it against his own interests; his reaction also sent up warning flares.

Don't get involved. Cheri might be nursing her wounds now, but sooner or later she'd get hungry again for the spotlight and the attention. He'd tried marriage once to a woman as ambitious as he was, and even though he'd been willing to meet her halfway, it hadn't worked. He wasn't going to put himself through that again. But damn it, this lady had a special magic about her that wasn't going to be easy to resist.

Cheri hung up the phone and sat there tapping her fingers on the counter, as if debating the best way to get rid of him. Sky knew he'd better press on quickly. "Since you apparently plan to be a member of our community, I think you should meet some people around here. Not television people—real ones."

"Don't worry. I intend to join the PTA and—and—whatever people usually join." Cheri smiled ruefully. "I suppose I am out of touch with the real world, aren't I?" She glanced out the window and a startled expression came over her face. "Is it noon already?"

A young boy was coming up the walk, his face too thin and serious for his age, Sky noted as he followed Cheri to the front door. And the electric-green eyes held the same reserved expression as his aunt's.

"How did it go?" Cheri asked.

"Okay." The boy handed some books to Cheri and then noticed Sky. "Hey! Aren't you that guy on TV?"

"You must be Tad." Sky reached down and shook the boy's hand. "I'm glad to find I'm not entirely unknown in this household."

"Dad used to say your show was a bunch of bunk."

"Tad!" Cheri reproved.

"Well, that's what he said." Tad surveyed Sky with interest. "Do you know a lot about ghosts? Like, what do they talk about?"

"Talk about?" Sky looked puzzled, but at least he was taking Tad seriously. Cheri liked it when adults treated children with respect.

"When they wake you up," Tad pressed on. "And they kind of groan to each other. What does it mean?"

"It means you're still asleep," Cheri cut in firmly. Darn it, she didn't want Tad retreating into some fantasy world. Was it possible he even imagined the ghosts were his parents, come back to protect him? Maybe that was a comforting thought, but she felt instinctively that Tad needed to grieve and to say goodbye before he could get on with his life.

"Have you heard voices, Tad?" Sky looked as if the boy's questions bothered him, too.

"Well..." Tad glanced at Cheri. "No, I guess not. But—I mean, if you went through here with a psychic like you do on your show, if there *was* anything here, you'd find out, wouldn't you?"

"I'm sorry. I can't allow any cameras in here," Cheri said firmly—and was startled at the anger that flashed onto her nephew's face.

"But it isn't your house!" Tad lashed out. "It's mine! And my Mom's and Dad's!"

Cheri froze for a minute, her heart skittering wildly. She hadn't realized how much Tad resented her. Maybe it was only natural, maybe even healthy that he was letting it out, but she didn't know what to do. If she put her arms around him, he'd push her away. She wanted so much to help him, to hold him close, but right now she felt useless and clumsy.

"I'll tell you what." Sky laid an arm around the boy's slim shoulders, and Tad didn't seem to mind. "We could have an informal tour right now, and I'll tell you what I know about the house. Maybe that will help."

"Okay," Tad agreed, looking somewhat placated.

Cheri nodded, grateful that Sky hadn't tried to use the boy's anger to manipulate her into granting the interview. "But first you're going to have a bite to eat. It's lunchtime." Firmly she escorted the two males into the kitchen and fixed tuna salad sandwiches. Tad's lunch box went into the refrigerator; he hadn't touched the raisins or the apple juice.

The boy relaxed during the meal as Sky regaled him with stories about hoaxes he'd uncovered. Cheri, still shaken by the way her nephew had flared up, tried to remind herself that his anger was a good sign. Up to now Tad had repressed his emotions, acting almost like a little robot. She only wished she knew how to avoid being seen as an enemy.

"Are there a lot of ghosts in Orange County?" Tad asked as Cheri passed around glasses of juice.

"Not too many, but I range as far afield as San Diego and San Francisco." Sky finished his second sandwich. "Frankly, my initial interest was in other cultures and their spiritual beliefs—voodoo and that sort of thing. In my younger days I made a few documentaries in South America. Won a couple of awards and nearly went broke."

Cheri swallowed a bite of avocado from the small salad she'd fixed for herself. "Tell me honestly. Do you believe in ghosts?"

He regarded her with amusement. "Do you think I'm going to answer that and jeopardize my professional objectivity? If you watched my show, you'd know that I try to find natural causes for so-called psychic phenomena. Still, there are a few cases that defy explanation. I work with a psychic named Vinnie Dumont, and while I'm not one hundred percent sure I believe everything she tells me, I don't exactly not believe her, either."

"How did you get started?" Tad took a gulp of apple juice. "Did you ever see a ghost?"

"Well, I spent part of my childhood in England, before my family moved to Southern California, and haunted houses are a lot more common there," Sky said. "But I don't have any ghosts among my close friends, no."

He helped Cheri clear the dishes, and then guided them to the living room, where he studied the photographs with interest. "The Granger family. What do you know about them, Tad?"

"They were some weird people who used to live here, right?" The boy stood with his legs apart in his customary tough-guy stance, but to Cheri he looked small and touchingly childish.

"Weird—yes." Sky turned to Cheri. "Someone ought to write a book about them. They could call it *The Curse of the Grangers*."

"A curse?" Cheri wasn't sure she wanted Tad to hear this. Suppose he started believing his parents' deaths were somehow the result of moving into this house?

She was relieved when Sky said, "Of course, the curse died with the last of the Grangers. But it caused a lot of trouble while it lasted."

"Who cursed them?" the boy asked. "A witch doctor or something?"

"Legend has it that it was an old man, a pharmacist named Perry Dotson." Sky led the way from the living room into the adjacent dining room as they continued their tour. "Supposedly one of the Granger brothers wronged his daughter, Jane."

Cheri watched Tad to see if the story was upsetting him, but he was listening raptly as if to an episode of *The Twilight Zone.*

The Granger brothers, Sky explained as they walked, had made a small fortune in the carriage-manufacturing business. The younger brother, Charlie, a real ladies' man, abandoned Jane and married a socially prominent widow named Marcella Cray. His older brother, Mack, had a reputation for being a ruthless businessman.

"We don't know exactly what the curse was," Sky said. "We do know that of Charlie and Marcella's two sons, one died in childhood of diphtheria—children are vaccinated against it today, Tad, but then it was a common disease. The other son was killed in France in World War I."

As he spoke, Cheri felt the veneer of the present peel away. She visualized the walls still papered with the formal flower design Donna had found before redecorating, and she could almost see the flare of gaslights illuminating stately figures in Edwardian dress. Figures in mourning for their son.

"What about the older brother?" Cheri asked as they climbed the steps. "Mack?"

"Mackenzie, yes. He had one daughter, Alice, whom everyone called Allie," Sky answered as they checked the walls for signs of cracks, but didn't find any. Tad ran up and back, full of restless energy, not wanting to miss a word of the tale.

"What became of her?" Cheri asked.

"Well, she was quite a blithe spirit in the Roaring Twenties." Sky opened the door that led to the attic. "She used to have costume parties and scavenger hunts with friends who came down from Los Angeles, according to the newspaper society reports I've been able to dig up."

"Did she get sick, too?" Tad bounced up the steps ahead of Sky and Cheri.

"No, not Allie." They emerged into the dusty attic, the ceiling sloping sharply to the floor on either side. There were old trunks here that Cheri was planning to go through; but they were locked, and she couldn't find a key. Donna and Jeff hadn't pried them open, probably because there hadn't been time. They'd lived in this house for less than six months before their deaths.

"Allie had some kind of disappointment in love," Sky said. "After that, she shut herself up in this house and rarely came out. May I?" At Cheri's nod, he fiddled with the lock on one of the trunks, but it resisted him stubbornly.

"Did she turn into a ghost?" Tad held up a blue china shooting marble he found in one corner. "Was this hers?"

"Could be. It's probably lain in that corner for better than half a century." Sky intoned the words gravely, and Cheri had to suppress a shiver. It was easy to see that Sky's show must be fun to watch. "Allie Granger lived here until she died, almost twenty years ago. And that was the end of the Granger family."

"She died here?" Tad shivered. "In this house?"

"I think she was taken to a hospital," Sky reassured him. "But it was after her death that the stories about ghosts began. The next owners reported strange noises, lights, voices, even occasionally a bit of mischief, as if Allie Granger had come back as her youthful self again. I suppose that means there's some kind of unfinished business. Maybe she wants to live her life over again, to make it come out differently."

"Was it because of the curse?" Tad asked.

"Maybe." Sky held the door open for Cheri as they left the attic. "Or maybe she was just an ornery lady who put pride ahead of common sense."

"What a sad story." Cheri hurried down the stairs, glad to be away from the dusty half-light that filtered through the attic's yellowing windows.

"I'll bet she did come back as a ghost," Tad declared as they descended to the first floor. "I mean—it could be true, couldn't it, Aunt Cheri?"

"There's no such thing as ghosts except in fairy tales, sweetie." Cheri stopped in the front hallway. "Sky, thank you for entertaining us. I'm sorry, but I still can't allow you to bring your cameras here."

"Aunt Cheri!" Tad protested.

"We'll just have to help your aunt change her mind, won't we?" Sky said. His gaze met Cheri's in an open challenge. "Before Tad came home, I was about to invite you to a picnic my family's giving on Saturday. You might meet some interesting people, and there'll be lots of playmates for Tad."

That wasn't fair, Cheri thought. Sky was playing on her concern for the boy. And yet she felt instinctively that he wasn't the type of person to exploit others. Or maybe she was allowing herself to be misled by the unexpected effect his teasing manner and masculine self-confidence were having on her heart rate. It had been a long time since she'd dared to trust a man. And this was the wrong time and place to start. "I'm afraid . . ."

"All the more reason to get out of the house," Sky said promptly.

"No, I didn't mean—"

"Oh, come on, Aunt Cheri." Tad wrinkled his nose. "It's boring, sitting around here all the time."

Cheri had to admit the boy had a point. Jeff and Donna hadn't kept him isolated, so why should she? And she really didn't know anyone in Orange yet. "All right, Tad, if you really want to go, I suppose it couldn't hurt."

"I'll pick you up at noon." Sky caught Cheri's hands firmly in his as he said goodbye. Darn it, she didn't need a man to lean on. She didn't want to be this aware of a man's touch, of the power in his arms and shoulders, of the gentleness in his eyes. She was managing just fine by herself, thank you.

Sky ruffled Tad's hair and then, before Cheri could change her mind, he whistled his way out the door.

A FEW MINUTES LATER, as he slid behind the wheel of his car, Sky looked back at the house.

The old place was peaceful in the sunshine, its peaked roof recently reshingled and its wooden sides painted pale gold, trimmed with chocolate. In the yard, rosebushes bloomed a deep pink, and the waxy leaves of a giant camellia bush shadowed one side of the porch.

Coming here today, he'd expected to find someone both tougher and shallower than Cheri Louette had turned out to be. Someone with an unassailable ego, someone he could charm into helping him, and then leave behind without worrying when his career shifted into the next phase. But he wasn't at all sure he would want to leave Cheri behind, if he ever got close to her.

This was dangerous ground. The wisest course would be to find some other way to win over the New York-based syndicate that Sky had been courting for months. And maybe he'd do that.

One thing he knew: regardless of what happened with his show, it would be a crime to let Cheri Louette shut herself up here, the way Allie Granger had done fifty years before.

Chapter Three

On Thursday night, Cheri saw Sky Welton again. This time, though, he was speaking from her television set instead of standing on her front porch.

She and Tad were lounging on the couch, eating popcorn and drinking orange juice, when the commercials ended and the title *Sky's the Limit* flashed across the screen, to the accompaniment of a faintly eerie melody. The orchestral theme and sharply juxtaposed background shots of Sky, prowling through an old mission and interviewing a white-coated woman in a laboratory, looked far more sleekly professional than she'd expected from a local show.

Cheri found her pulse speeding up with anticipation as the camera panned across the front of an ordinary ranch-style house—ordinary except for the charred porch and fallen-in roof. She wanted to see Sky again, she realized with a mixture of eagerness and dismay.

But first, she heard his voice, deep and suspenseful yet without melodrama. He had a natural gift for holding an audience spellbound.

"Last July 2, more than thirty teenagers were having a party in this West Covina home at one o'clock in the morning when the house suddenly burst into flames, injuring eleven of them," Sky said as the house came into closer view.

Then the camera cut to a close-up of a teenage girl with large brown eyes and windblown hair, sitting on a park bench in front of a cypress tree. "And this is Annie Corona, who claims she predicted the fire and kept five other teenagers from attending. Had they gone, she says, at least two of them would have died."

Cheri glanced at Tad. He was chomping away at the popcorn, his eyes riveted to the screen.

The camera pulled back to include Sky. He was staring straight at the audience, straight at Cheri. She knew he wasn't really looking at her, yet she couldn't shake the nagging sense that he was watching her.

Or someone was watching her...

With a frown at her foolishness, Cheri returned her attention to the program as Sky interviewed the girl and then talked to several other teenagers, including those who'd stayed away from the party.

One young man insisted that anyone could have predicted the fire, because the teenagers were unsupervised and had planned to set off fireworks. A city fire official confirmed that firecrackers were believed to be the cause of the blaze.

Then Sky interviewed neighbors and friends of the girl's family. Several of them recounted other incidents, in which she'd predicted everything from a friend's unplanned pregnancy to the outcome of the World Series, all with amazing accuracy.

"Did Annie Corona foresee the fire in a dream, as she contends, or did she merely use common sense? Is she a psychic, or just a good guesser?" Sky stood in front of the fire-ravaged house, once again staring straight at Cheri. "Maybe it doesn't matter. Maybe the important thing is that she and five other teenagers stayed away, and that all the youngsters survived." A commercial blared.

"I think she foreseed it," Tad announced, picking half-popped kernels from the bottom of the bowl.

"Foresaw it," Cheri corrected. "But I don't think . . ."

Tad cut her off. "It's starting."

We're going to have to work on your manners, young man. But she didn't want to speak to him harshly, not yet.

The second segment of the show was conducted in a studio, where Sky and two guests discussed a piece of news just released by the Soviet Union. According to the report from Tass, two clairvoyants now undergoing intensive testing had predicted the Chernobyl disaster weeks before it happened, but had been ignored. In fact, it wasn't until long after the meltdown that anyone went back and confirmed the prediction.

The topics under discussion ranged from psychic research in the Soviet Union—where such matters were taken more seriously than in the United States, one of the guests said—to the reliability of disaster predictions and the danger of setting off mass hysteria.

Finally Sky turned to the camera. "Next week, we'll talk about earthquakes. Can they be pinpointed in advance? We'll examine some new information from China about animal behavior before major quakes. Until then, this is Sky Welton, thanking you for watching *Sky's the Limit*."

The phone rang. Cheri grabbed the empty orange juice pitcher and deposited it on the kitchen table as she picked up the receiver. She knew even before she heard his voice that it had to be Sky, calling to find out if she'd watched.

She didn't wait for him to say hello. "Yes, we saw you."

"And what did you think?" His voice sounded warmer than it had on television.

"I don't think she's any more psychic than I am. I could have predicted that fire, too." She leaned against the table, looking forward to a rousing dispute.

But it quickly became clear that he wasn't about to argue the point. "You know what? So could I. But I couldn't have predicted the outcome of the World Series, and neither could you." Sky changed the subject. "How are you and Tad, Cheri? Any more bumps and grinds in the night?''

"The ghost of Jenny Lind sang the entire score of *La Traviata* in my ear the other evening. Other than that, no.''

Sky chuckled. "Maybe I should have you on my show as the resident skeptic.'' Behind him, she could hear the soft jazz of a Chuck Mangione record.

"Your viewers would hate me. They want to believe, Sky.''

"We all have to believe in something.'' Then he added softly, "I'm looking forward to Saturday.''

For a tantalizing instant, Cheri found herself wishing he were here, sitting across the table from her, munching on a chocolate chip cookie. There'd been something reassuring about his presence, and something tantalizing in the way her body responded to his. She almost wished they were going on a real date Saturday, just the two of them, talking and teasing and finding out where the chemistry between them might lead.

Then she heard Tad giggling in the living room along with the canned laughter of a TV sitcom. It brought her firmly back to reality. "We'll see you then. Goodbye, Sky.''

"Call me if you need anything.'' His last words echoed in her mind as Cheri hung up. How kind and inviting he sounded. And—tempting.

Just as anyone could have foreseen the house fire, she didn't have to be psychic to know it would be easy to set off a blaze between Sky and herself. But, Cheri told herself firmly, she was old enough to know how to avoid touching a match to a fuse.

It had been different last year, when she'd fallen in love with a rising star named Terence Omara. She'd been terribly naive for a twenty-six-year-old woman, Cheri could see now, but up to that point she'd been dominated, first by her mother and then by her agent. This had been the first test of her judgment as an adult, and it had turned into a disaster.

It hadn't occurred to her that their much-publicized romance was boosting Terence's career, nor that when he landed a plum role in a new adventure movie he would no longer need her.

Six months after their affair began, he went on location to Spain for the film. Committed to shooting a movie in Los Angeles, Cheri hadn't been able to go with him.

She would never forget the moment six weeks later, when she'd wheeled her shopping basket into a line at the supermarket and seen a tabloid's headline—screaming that actor Terence Omara had just dumped her for the Swedish model who was his latest co-star. And there she stood with a basket full of fruit and cottage cheese, her heart shattering into fragments. One thought had penetrated the pain: what a rotten way to live this was, with your private life splashed across a tabloid for the amusement of strangers.

Maybe that was what had set her thinking about ending her career, although if Cheri's film had been a success, things might have turned out differently. She couldn't entirely blame Terence for the turn her life had taken, nor for her naiveté. Like a lot of people in show business, he was just self-centered and immature.

Including Sky Welton? Maybe not, but Cheri didn't intend to find out, she told herself firmly as she mixed up more orange juice and rejoined Tad in the living room. She had more important things to take care of right now, and she couldn't imagine a dynamic man like Sky settling comfortably into her life of quiet domesticity.

THE HOUSE WAS FULL OF PEOPLE, laughing, talking, clinking their glasses. The women wore their hair short and sleek and trailed clouds of perfume whenever they moved. The rustle of silk-fringed dresses and the brittle laughter reminded Cheri of films she'd seen of the Roaring Twenties.

No one seemed to notice her as she walked through the house. It was the Granger house, but the patterned carpeting was bright and new. The parlor furniture had a blond Art Deco flair; she'd never seen anything quite like it before. And the curtains were made of fine lace, like something left over from the turn of the century.

A woman slipped her arm through Cheri's. She was young, with a merry face, yet there was a trace of sadness in her eyes. "Nora," she said. "I'm so glad you joined us. I don't care if you are supposed to be my companion, you're my friend, too. Thanks for being here."

Somehow Cheri had become someone named Nora, a hired companion. The woman had to be Allie Granger, judging by the style of dress and the proprietary way she greeted the guests. Cheri did her best to smile and nod and play the role she'd somehow dropped into.

When they had a moment alone, Allie said, "I'm glad you're getting to meet all these people, so you'll know who they are when I talk about them. That's Sammy over there—he's lots of fun, you should hear him play the piano—and that's Mary; she always knows where there's a party going on."

You have a lot of acquaintances, Cheri thought, but are they real friends?

She must have spoken the words aloud, because Allie looked startled, then shrugged. "Who knows? Does it matter?" Abruptly she stopped speaking as a man entered the room.

He wore his dark hair slicked down and parted in the middle, like Rudy Vallee. The man was handsome in a large-boned, blustery kind of way, but she didn't like his habit of smiling vaguely while studying the furniture and the decorations, as if trying to figure out how much they'd cost.

"Jeremiah Hunt." Allie whispered his name almost reverently. "He's the one I told you about." Then, as if Cheri

had replied, she went on, "Well, Papa wouldn't have approved, I guess; not of a plain old traveling salesman. I guess he's broken a few hearts in his time. But he's ready to settle down now. Isn't he divine? I love that man so much."

She waved across the room, Jeremiah turned, and Cheri thought she saw that shrewdly assessing look cross his face again before he smiled in return. As if he were trying to figure out how much Allie would cost, too.

Cheri tried hard not to think, because apparently Allie could read minds. Or maybe, in this familiar-unfamiliar world, thoughts were the same as words. Cheri didn't like this man. She wanted to protect Allie, to save her from getting hurt, the way Jeff had once tried to warn Cheri about Terence. But she hadn't wanted to listen, and neither did Allie. But it couldn't be Allie, not really, because Allie Granger had been dead for twenty years. This couldn't be the 1920s, either, and Cheri wasn't someone named Nora.

"Someday I'm going to marry him," Allie said. "But he doesn't know it yet."

Doesn't know it.... Doesn't know it....

Half rising into wakefulness, Cheri heard the words fade slowly into an echo. Then her eyes flew open and she was staring into the darkness of her bedroom. The clock on the bedside table said it was 2:40 a.m.

Had it been a dream? *Of course,* it must have, and yet everything had been so clear. Allie had worn lily of the valley; Cheri couldn't remember ever smelling anything in a dream before. And it had all been so real: the rustle of silk when Allie turned, the laughter of the guests, the transparent greed of that man named Jeremiah.

The dream was gone, but something rattled lightly overhead, like a mouse scampering across the attic floor. This was ridiculous. She was letting those absurd stories about ghosts work on her nerves. But at this hour of the morning it was hard to be rational.

Uneasy, Cheri swung off the bed and pulled on her robe and slippers. She padded down the hall to Tad's room and looked in on him, relieved to see the boy sleeping quietly with one arm encircling his favorite teddy bear. Thank goodness, he wasn't having one of his nightmares tonight.

Cheri suppressed the urge to take a flashlight and walk through the house. It was an old place with some squeaky floorboards, and she might wake Tad. Besides, if there really were mice running around, she certainly didn't want to run into them at this hour.

Returning to bed, she curled into a ball beneath the covers and tried to think of pleasant things. She'd talked to Elaine the previous day, Friday, and had been glad to learn her friend had been able to lease some office space in Century City for only a moderately outrageous amount. Elaine had been eager to discuss the movie script with her, and they'd agreed to meet for lunch on Monday. Cheri was looking forward to the break in her routine.

Beside the bed, the numbers on the digital clock flicked over to show 3:00 a.m.

Today was Saturday, and they'd be seeing Sky. Cheri hugged her pillow tighter, electricity dancing across her nerve endings like lightning in a summer sky. Why had he called on Thursday night? How much of his interest in her was business and how much was personal? What would happen if she took a chance, if...? The subject didn't bear examining closely, especially at this hour.

Cheri forced her mind to go blank, and lay listening to her own regular breathing. After a while, her eyelids closed of their own accord.

VINNIE DUMONT drove slowly by the Granger house on her way to the Weltons' party Saturday morning. Sky had filled her in on the new occupant, with an enthusiasm that had piqued her curiosity.

She hadn't imagined the young woman would be someone famous. Vinnie didn't watch much television, but she vaguely recalled from a newspaper photo that Cheri was quite young, with delicate features and large eyes. Someone obviously attractive to Sky. She couldn't recall him ever showing so much interest in a woman. It was time he got involved again, but the circumstances made Vinnie uneasy.

She stopped her car across the street from the house. Someone brushed by the curtains in an upstairs room, but it was impossible to see inside. Not that Vinnie intended to turn into a Peeping Tom. She wasn't even sure why she'd driven by here today, except that she felt drawn by some force she'd never encountered before.

Why are you going to be so important in my life, Cheri Louette? And why do I feel a disturbance, as if something in the house has awakened?

Vinnie was reminded of a film version she'd seen once of the Sleeping Beauty story, of a slumbering castle covered with cobwebs and dust suddenly coming alive again, people stretching and yawning and rousing themselves, wondering how long they'd been asleep. It troubled her; if there were ghosts refocusing their energies on this house, some of them might be dangerous. Perhaps the young boy was inadvertently stimulating them, or Cheri was, or both together. There was a restless energy about certain young people that could bring on a poltergeist.

I'll have to keep a close watch on things, Vinnie thought. *If they'll let me help. For Sky's sake, if not for my own.*

She didn't usually let herself get caught up in her work this way. In her adolescence, when the psychic impressions began to intensify, they'd been overwhelming at first, but she'd learned through training to control them. Now she could usually shut them out if she really wanted to.

It was Vick who had helped her gain the stability she'd needed, who had steadied and reassured her through their nearly thirty years of marriage. He'd been only fifty-five when his heart gave out without warning. Why hadn't she been able to foresee the one thing that threatened her most?

Now she was alone, with only her work as a psychic and her dabblings as a painter to keep her occupied. If only they could have had children—but it hadn't turned out that way. It had seemed like an omen, somehow, and Vinnie had decided not to adopt. Looking back, she could see that she'd been afraid. Afraid of losing a child she would have loved more than life itself, or of failing as a mother the same way she'd failed as a painter.

Uneasy, she put the car into gear. She had an urge to protect the woman and the child in that house, and Sky, who had become a close friend during the years they'd worked together. Well, she'd do whatever she could, when the time came.

Chapter Four

Tad was so keyed up about the picnic that he awoke at 6:00 a.m. Cheri went down to fix him breakfast, baked a batch of chocolate chip cookies and then climbed back upstairs to soak in a hot bath while her nephew slew invaders from outer space on the computer in the library.

Later, as she selected a sundress from the closet, Cheri realized this was the first time in months that she'd dressed to go out with a man. Of course, this wasn't exactly a date, and yet it was fun to feel flirtatious again.

As she slid the cotton dress over her head, last night's dream suddenly came back to her—the guests in their 1920s garb, the painful intensity in Allie Granger's voice as she spoke about the man she loved. Cheri could remember details—the harsh cloud of cigarette smoke in the air, the flashy embroidered jacket one of the men had been wearing—as if she'd been there. As if somehow she really had been that hired companion named Nora who'd wanted to protect Allie against the heartbreak that lay ahead.

Crazy. This whole thing is crazy. Cheri frowned into the lighted mirror as she brushed her hair into place and began applying makeup. Maybe her subconscious mind was rebelling against the losses of the past year, trying to escape into a make-believe world. It was harmless, she supposed, so long as she didn't let herself get carried away, but at the same time she felt troubled. Were Tad's dreams as intense as hers? If so, it was no wonder he believed in ghosts.

Cheri was just coming down the stairs when the doorbell rang. Since Tad was still in the back of the house, she answered it herself.

"Hi." She took a deep breath to calm her pleasure at seeing Sky. In a navy-blue cashmere sweater over gray slacks, he looked younger than on television, and his hair was ruffled as if he'd let it blow in the breeze on the drive over. But what touched her was the hint of uncertainty in his eyes, as if he wasn't quite sure of his welcome.

"I thought you'd enjoy these." Sky produced a bouquet of dark red roses in a jar. "They're the old-fashioned kind. Take a sniff."

Cheri inhaled deeply. "English gardens and French perfume. Wonderful." The florists' arrangements that once had crowded her dressing room had never even approached this rich summery scent. "I'm almost afraid to ask. Did you grow them or steal them?"

"I stole them." He smiled. "But my mother's a good sport."

As she turned to take the flowers into the kitchen, Cheri heard the squeak of sneakers in the hall and then Tad appeared. He studied Sky for a moment before admitting, "I wasn't sure you'd come."

"Of course I came." Sky's deep voice rang through the hall. "I said I would, didn't I?"

"Yes, but—people don't always keep their promises."

The rest of Tad's words were lost in the rush of tap water into Cheri's best crystal vase, but she'd heard enough. She remembered feeling that her own father had abandoned her when he died, as if he'd had a choice. She'd been only eight then, a year older than Tad. Maybe he, too, had taken his parents' death as a kind of betrayal. It would be important to show him that the people he loved weren't going to make a habit of disappearing from his life.

Except that the people I loved have made a habit of disappearing. A knot of pain twisted inside Cheri's chest. She tried to steel herself against it, but it took a while to ebb. Darn, she'd always despised self-pity as a useless emotion, and she wasn't going to give into it now.

After setting the flowers on the table, she carried the box of cookies into the hall, trying to focus on the pleasurable day ahead of her. "I wasn't sure if we were supposed to bring something."

Sky gave the box an appreciative glance. "No reasonable offer will be refused. Especially if it has chocolate chips in it."

"What has chocolate chips besides cookies?" asked Tad, taking him literally.

"Ice cream. And—you could put some on your breakfast cereal. And how about in your salad?" Sky scooped the boy up and swung him around. "You'd like that, wouldn't you? Come on, admit it!"

Tad giggled as the two of them spun about. Cheri wished she had the same free and easy manner with him that came so naturally to Sky.

Then she caught a measuring glance from those gray eyes and pulled herself up sharply. The man's amiability was part of his television personality. She mustn't forget that his goal was to drag her and the Granger house before the camera. Perhaps today's invitation had been a thoughtful act, but after growing up in the self-serving milieu of Hollywood, Cheri wasn't about to let herself be charmed into gullibility.

Still, she enjoyed the drive through town en route to the party, with Sky pointing out an old-fashioned traffic circle, freshly painted cottages converted into antique shops, and the picture-postcard campus of Chapman College.

"I feel as if I'd been dropped into a small town in the Midwest." Cheri gazed intently out the window, drinking in the sights as if to fill up the empty places left from a too-rushed childhood. "It's hard to believe we're only an hour's drive from Hollywood."

"There are advantages to being so close to L.A.," Sky said. "But it's nice to have a real town to come home to."

His eyes met Cheri's over Tad's head as the boy sat contentedly between them. Sky laid one arm across the boy's shoulders and his hand brushed Cheri's wrist. She missed the warmth the instant it was gone.

Before she could sort out the reasons for her reaction, the car halted in front of a handsome old house, probably built in the twenties. Showers of purple and pink petunias spilled across the front flower bed, and roses twined up a trellis near the door. Everything looked perky and fresh, and from the dampness of the sidewalk it was clear the lawn had just been watered.

"My mother has never gotten over the fact that she can garden all year in this climate. She's always outside puttering with something." Sky helped Tad unbuckle his seat belt and came around to open the door for Cheri. "We tease her about her herb garden; I suspect she's got belladonna and deadly nightshade there in case anyone in the family gets out of line."

Stepping out of the car, Cheri felt her foot slip on the wet pavement, throwing her off balance. Sky's hands caught her waist lightly but firmly, and she swayed against him before steadying herself. "I'm sorry. I'm not usually so clumsy."

"Not clumsy at all." His voice sounded a bit hoarse, and he released her quickly. *Maybe he doesn't want to get too close to me, either.* The thought should have been comforting, but it wasn't.

From around the back of the house, Cheri heard the hum of voices intermingled with the clink of glasses. Tad's grip tightened suddenly on her hand. "I changed my mind. Let's go to the mall instead," he said.

"Scared?" Sky bent down to the boy's eye level. "Meeting a lot of new people isn't my favorite thing to do, either."

"I'm not scared." Tad's mouth tightened. "It just sounds like they're all grown-ups."

"Well, I know my nephews are going to be here. I'll bet they've never met anyone who lives with ghosts," Sky said.

Tad squared his small shoulders. "Oh, that's nothing. We hear them creaking around all the time, don't we, Aunt Cheri?"

"Well, we hear *something* creaking once in a while," she conceded.

"Probably my jokes." Sky escorted the two of them around the corner of the house, without giving Tad a chance to realize he'd been conned.

The aroma of barbecued chicken wafted toward them, honing Cheri's appetite, but she too felt a quiver of something almost like panic as they neared the crowd of people on the broad, shaded patio. How was she going to deal with all these strangers without her manager and her publicist, without the knot of protectors she'd grown used to?

Then Sky caught her eye, and Cheri felt herself flush, embarrassed by her thoughts. She was a grown woman, in charge of her own life. She didn't need to lean on anyone. And, when she looked again toward the other guests, the faces began sorting themselves into small groupings, couples and parents with their children, nothing to be intimidated by, after all.

A boy darted toward them, his freckled face alight with curiosity. "Hi, Uncle Sky," he said before turning to Tad. "I'm Joey, and I'm eight. How old are you?"

"Seven." Tad planted his feet apart, as if to withstand an attack.

"Tad, this is my nephew Joey." Sky made introductions as gravely as if the two boys were important diplomats. "Joey, Tad lives in the Granger house."

"You do? No kidding?" Joey bounced up and down. "Is it really haunted?"

"You bet." Tad shot a quick look at Cheri. "I mean, we hear some strange stuff at night."

"Like chains clanking and people screaming?"

"Well, more like creaks and, you know, voices." Before Cheri could correct him, Ted darted away to try out Joey's new skateboard and, she had no doubt, to brag some more about their resident "ghosts."

"Voices?" Sky lifted an eyebrow. "He mentioned something about that before. What do you think it means?"

"It probably means I talk in my sleep." Cheri moved toward the patio, determined to change the subject. She wasn't ready to tell anyone about her dream last night, particularly not Sky. "I'd better say hello to your family before they think I'm antisocial."

Although he looked as if he would have liked to discuss the subject further, Sky followed her lead and presented Cheri to his parents.

It would have been impossible not to like them. His mother was a robust, outspoken Englishwoman who might have stepped from an episode of *Masterpiece Theater*. His father was thin and quiet, with a dry sense of humor that showed itself just often enough to deflate any hint of pomposity in the conversation.

Cheri especially liked Sky's sister Kate, an unflappable woman whose calmness belied the fact that she had two rambunctious young sons. In addition to Joey, there was six-year-old Malcolm, Sky explained.

Kate endeared herself immediately by her concern for Tad, and told Cheri the boy was welcome to visit at her house whenever he liked, especially since he and Joey seemed to have hit it off so well.

As Kate headed in Malcolm's direction to extricate him from a quarrel over a bright red wagon, Sky led Cheri toward a woman of about fifty, her brown hair touched with gray. She was looking at Cheri as if they knew each other.

"Here's someone I want you to meet." Sky kept one hand lightly on Cheri's back, as if to give her courage. "This is Vinnie Dumont, the psychic I told you about. Vin, this is—"

"Yes, I know." The woman took Cheri's hand and shook it firmly. "I take a keen interest in the Granger house." She smiled to soften the words. "Don't be intimidated. People sometimes think psychics can read minds, but I assure you I can't."

And yet, Cheri had the uncomfortable feeling the woman understood things no one else could. "You actually believe houses can be haunted?"

"Sometimes I wish it weren't so." There was a down-to-earth quality about Vinnie that reminded Cheri of her late grandmother. "I didn't choose to receive impressions, and sometimes they're painful. Especially when I can't do anything to stop... well, never mind about that. It's a lovely house. I suppose the colorful history adds something to the charm."

"You'll have to drop in sometime and see how beautifully it's been remodeled," Cheri said, then realized a visit from a psychic was the last thing she wanted. Still, there was no point in appearing ungracious. "Not in your official capacity, of course."

"I never tell people things they don't want to know," Vinnie assured her. "And don't let Sky browbeat you into anything that doesn't feel right. We're delighted to have you in our community, and I hope you feel right at home here."

"I'm beginning to, thanks," Cheri said before Sky steered her away in the direction of the food.

The warm welcome brought up a surge of nostalgia. When Cheri was small, there had been large family gatherings for Christmas and birthdays at her grandmother's house in Santa Barbara. Then her grandparents had died and her father had suffered his fatal heart attack. A year later, her mother had taken her to audition for a part in a new television series, and Cheryl Lewiston had become Cheri Louette.

As Cheri and Sky found places at a card table and got down to the business of consuming heaps of chicken and roasted potatoes, she luxuriated in the cheerful babble of the party around them. It was fun to be with people who ignored the fact that she was a celebrity, although she could tell from their glances that several of the guests recognized her.

"I like your family and your friends," Cheri said.

"We're a close-knit group." Sky's gaze lingered on Tad, who was playing some newly invented form of kickball with the other youngsters on the lawn. "I'm used to being part of a family. I suppose that's why I stuck with my marriage for so long.... But I didn't mean to bring that up."

"Why not?"

He shrugged. "It's not exactly a cheerful subject."

"How long have you been divorced?" Cheri was glad of the chance to learn more about what lay beneath Sky's easygoing surface.

"Eight years." Sky hesitated, tempted to veer to a safer subject. On the other hand, it was hardly fair that he knew all about Cheri's much-ballyhooed breakup with Terence Omara, while she knew next to nothing about him. "We were too young to get married, I suppose."

"There had to be more to it than that." Cheri was watching him thoughtfully.

"We are both ambitious. That brought us together when we were in college, me talking about how I was going to set the world on fire making brilliant documentaries, Arlene planning to discover a cure for cancer or how to halt the aging process." As he talked, Sky could feel again the excitement of their early relationship, when everything had seemed possible.

"But your ambitions ended up pulling you apart?" Cheri guessed.

"I used to believe two ambitious people could have a good marriage." Sky tapped a drumstick against his paper plate. "Now I'm not so sure, at least, not without tremendous sacrifices. We tried to maintain a long-distance marriage for a while, but it didn't work. Finally I offered to move to Stanford, where she had a research grant, but only on the condition that we both devote more time to each other. Arlene wasn't willing to give up much of her research time, and that was the end of it. I suppose it was inevitable sooner or later; I could only put my dreams on hold for so long, and then I would have begun to resent her."

"I'm sorry." There was genuine regret in Cheri's eyes. "I wonder how many of us would make the same choices about our dreams if we could see what we'd have to give up along the way."

"How about you?" he asked. "Would you make the same choices?"

She rested her chin on her palm as she searched for an answer. "The truth is, I never really chose. I was only nine years old when my mother took me to try out for *Young and Eager*. Acting in television was the only life I knew. At times Emily, the character I played, seemed more real to me than I did to myself."

Sky pulled another can of root beer from a nearby cooler. "You had a stage mother, then?"

"In a way." Cheri folded her hands on the table. "Not that she ever meant to force me into anything. She just loved the excitement of Hollywood openings and parties; we went everywhere together, and I was glad to make her happy. I felt responsible for her, in a way, not just financially, but emotionally, too. Sometimes I felt as if I were the mother and she was the child."

Sky was beginning to understand more of this challenging young woman, who seemed so fragile at times and yet fiercely self-possessed at others. "But underneath, she was the one in control."

Cheri nodded reluctantly. "Looking back, I can see that I let her make all the important decisions. And after her it was my agent. The only person I could really relax with was Jeff. He was my best friend as well as my brother, even though he was away at school a lot of the time. And then Donna and I were so close...." She stopped abruptly.

Sky fought down the impulse to take her delicate heart-shaped face in his hands and soothe the sorrow away. Damn it, he was letting himself get involved. That wasn't what he'd intended. Yet he wasn't sure he could avoid it.

There was an unconscious sensuality about Cheri that drew him in a way no other woman had, not even Arlene. It was more than the glow of her skin or the instinctive grace with which she moved, or even the glints of fire that flashed sometimes beneath her cool demeanor. His body was keenly aware of hers whenever they were close. He'd noticed it the first time he saw her, on the porch. It was almost as if he knew how her soft curves would feel beneath his hands and against his chest, and how her mouth would taste....

Angry at himself for his dangerous thoughts, Sky brought up the subject that interested him most—or, at least, that was *supposed* to interest him most. "Why did your brother decide to buy a haunted house?"

Cheri nibbled at the last of her chicken. "He liked the place, and the price was right. Jeff didn't believe in ghosts, any more than I do." But she didn't sound quite as certain as she had last Monday.

"Do I detect a slight wavering? Was it my persuasive powers, or has something happened?" Sky felt a twinge of worry. As he'd told Tad, sometimes he ran across a poltergeist phenomenon that defied conventional explanations. And the results could be unpredictable, even risky.

"Oh, I—dreamed about Allie Granger last night." Cheri poked with her straw at an ice cube melting in her paper cup. "I imagined I was someone named Nora, her hired companion."

"Do you remember anything Allie said?"

Cheri bit her lip in concentration. "Oh, just something about this man she was in love with, someone named Jeremiah."

"Did you feel as if she was threatening you?"

A shake of the head. "Not at all. Really, I don't know why I mentioned it. It was just a dream."

"Don't be too sure." Sky could almost taste how much he wanted to go through that house with Vinnie. Above and beyond the boost it could give his career, the place fascinated him. The question of whether ghosts really existed wasn't just an academic one to him.

The research he'd done into the beliefs of other cultures had raised a lot of questions in Sky's mind. Touring the Granger house might not prove anything definitively, but it would be one more piece to drop into the jigsaw puzzle. Maybe it was a spiritual journey rather than a scientific one, but he'd been drawn to the house since the first time it was pointed out to him.

And of course, Sky couldn't deny that taping Cheri Louette's house could be the break he'd been waiting for. Miles Appleby, the syndicate executive he'd been talking to in New York, was concerned that the subject of Sky's show might not be of broad enough interest. Well, no one could deny that a haunted house with a well-known actress like Cheri living in it was of broad interest.

But the more he got to know her, the less he liked the idea of opening up her private life to a TV audience. She was still reeling from her brother's death, and maybe from that actor jerk she'd been going with, who'd dumped her with all the fanfare and publicity he could muster.

"Sky." Cheri leaned toward him, her expression serious. "I do *not* believe in ghosts. And I do *not* want Tad getting any more spooked than he is already. Pun intended."

She was right, of course. At least, Sky hoped she was. A house was just a house, and Cheri and Tad were perfectly safe. *The hard part is keeping them safe from me.* "All right. But if you ever feel threatened, even if it seems irrational, give me a call, will you?"

"Are you speaking as a friend or as a TV host?" Cheri asked.

"As a friend." Sky hoped it was true. Because although he couldn't deny the driving need to make a name for himself, he still wondered whether a little less selfishness might have saved his marriage. If he ever did get close to Cheri Louette, he didn't want to make the same mistakes again.

"You aren't by any chance talking about the Granger house?" Kate inquired, swooping down on them. "There, now I've brought up the subject—well, I suppose it's rather presumptuous of me, Cheri, but I was meaning to call you anyway and introduce myself—and ask the most tremendous favor."

There was something disarming about her bluntness, and Cheri found to her surprise that she didn't feel cornered or intruded on by Kate's statement. "What's that?"

"I'll bet I can guess. The charity league." Sky grinned at his sister, and Cheri felt an aching envy at the obvious closeness between them. That was how she and Jeff had been.

"I'm president of the Family Charity League of Orange," Kate explained. "Every year we have a big fundraiser in the autumn to collect money for Christmas baskets for the poor. This year, I've suggested a haunted house."

It took Cheri a moment to absorb what Kate meant. "You mean—a *real* haunted house?"

"Well, no." Sky's sister glanced up to check on her boys, who were showing Tad how to do wheelies on a skateboard, and then returned to the subject. "I meant one of those places where you take the people up to the attic and hang skeletons and black lights about. But think how much more fun it would be if people imagined there really might be ghosts!"

It certainly was an intriguing idea, but Cheri wasn't so sure it would be wise. "I think it might be too frightening for the children."

"I agree with you." Kate wasn't fazed in the least. "What I had in mind was a costume affair for adults. It would give them a chance to let down their hair and act like kids, with their own haunted house. They'll be paying one hundred fifty dollars a couple—we'd handle all the catering and cleanup, so it wouldn't be any work for you."

"I'll certainly think about it, but I can't make any promises." Cheri didn't like to sound standoffish—after all, the cause was a worthy one—but suppose there really was a spirit in the house? Or suppose something went wrong and a guest fell and injured him or herself? "It's just that I don't like promoting the idea that the house is haunted. Tad has an overactive imagination, as it is."

"If it's privacy you're worried about, I don't blame you, but I think we could get around that," Kate said. "Not many people realize who lives in the Granger house. But it's up to you, of course. Just let me or Sky know."

Joey was calling for his mother to come look at a scrape on his knee, so Kate excused herself.

"You haven't said much." Cheri glanced over at Sky, who was watching her intently.

"I'm surprised you'd even consider it," he admitted. "Knowing your desire for privacy."

"Well, I haven't made up my mind." Cheri looked around, making sure Tad was okay. "Let's take a walk."

"This way." Sky guided her across the lawn and around the house, out of sight of the others. The yard was larger than she'd realized and, as Sky pointed out, the gardening skillfully blended an English sensibility with Southern California free-for-all. Gradually Cheri put aside the subject of the charity event as she quizzed Sky on the names of the flowers.

"Herman," he said, pointing to a purple primrose. "And that one's Mabel."

"You have a weird sense of humor."

"It's one of my many unique qualities." Unexpectedly he lifted his thumbs to trace her cheekbones. Cheri's heart fluttered like a hummingbird debating whether to sip at unfamiliar nectar or dart for safety. "Damn it, why couldn't you be a typical egocentric, boring actress?" Sky's fingers massaged her temples, brushing back the light brown hair that curled loosely about her face. He bent and brushed a dandelion-light kiss across Cheri's mouth, starting a tingle that spread down her neck and arms.

She found herself wanting to feel Sky's lips on hers again, wanting to explore the mystery of him. Without any conscious expression of will, her hands rose to touch his shoulders and her face tilted upward like a morning glory toward the sun.

Strong hands clasped her waist, and when he kissed her again she could taste barbecued chicken and sunshine. The muscles of Sky's back flexed beneath her stroking. She wanted him, with a flare of passion she'd never believed she could feel again. It was too dangerous; if she let herself go, the pain would be more than she could bear when it ended. Cheri took a step backward.

"What's the matter?" Sky was breathing deeply, as if he'd been running.

"I'm sorry." She still couldn't look directly at him. "Sky, I'm not ready for this."

"I know. But Cheri—" Whatever he had been about to say was cut off as a little girl toddled around the corner in pursuit of a rubber ball. Sky scooped it up and tossed it to her.

"We'd better go back," Cheri said.

"In a minute." He was standing close to her, not quite touching. "I've been meaning to tell you about my plans. For syndicating the series. Well, at this point they're more hopes than plans, but I've been dealing with an exec named Miles Appleby in New York...." He went on to describe their discussions. "I knew it would come up sometime, and I didn't want you to think I'd been holding something back."

"I'm not surprised." Cheri had known from the moment she saw his program that Sky was destined for more than merely hosting a local show. "An episode on my house would help, wouldn't it?"

"It might." He shrugged. "It's not necessary, though. I'm going to make it, one way or another."

"I know," she said.

They spent the rest of the afternoon sitting with the other grown-ups. Cheri listened idly to the conversation and watched Tad as he trounced Joey and Malcolm in a game of Uno. Later, when he drove them home, Sky made no further move to renew their momentary intimacy, and Cheri wasn't sure whether to be pleased or disappointed.

That night, Tad filled her ears with plans to get together with his new friends, who turned out to live only three blocks away. For the first time, Cheri began to feel deep inside that she and Tad might really be able to make a home together, a place where he could grow and develop and feel secure.

But she mustn't expect too much too soon, she warned herself as she tucked him into bed and read aloud from one of his Doctor Dolittle books. It would take time. A lot of things would take time. But it was going to be worth it.

She tried not to think about Sky, and about her feelings for him. She'd known him less than a week, after all. Maybe she was just vulnerable because she'd been avoiding men since Terence, and because she'd lost the big brother who had been her closest confidante since childhood.

Sitting alone in her room, trying to concentrate on a novel, Cheri thought about Kate's request to hold the fundraiser here. The fact was, it sounded like fun. The picnic had reminded Cheri how much she missed the company of other people. If she were going to make a new life here, as she planned, she needed to come out of her shell sometime, even if it meant giving up a little of her privacy. She would enjoy having Kate as a friend, too; it would be nice to have someone close by, someone who also had children and could share information and advice.

I'll call her tomorrow, Cheri decided. *Why not? We just might give the Granger ghosts a Halloween to remember.*

Chapter Five

"There she is," Elaine whispered conspiratorially across the restaurant table. "Ingrid Bjorg. Doesn't she remind you of Elsie the cow?"

"Meow." Cheri smiled and finished another bite of her watercress and chicken salad. Actually Ingrid—the Swedish actress that Terence Omara had taken up with, then dumped a few months later just as he'd dumped Cheri—didn't look like a cow at all. She had a slender, athletic build and lots of honey-blond hair, but, Cheri had to admit, the eyes were vacant and the smile bland. Like a cow. Or like an actress who was trying to figure out how to please everyone and offend no one.

It was Elaine who'd suggested they have lunch at the Ivy, a French country-style café on the edge of Beverly Hills that was so trendy it didn't even have a sign in front. They'd chosen a table inside, which provided privacy along with a clear view of the cheek-kissing Hollywood folk sunning themselves at the outdoor tables.

"Now admit it, don't you miss this?" Elaine speared a chunk of crab cake. "All the excitement, all the gossip?"

"A little," Cheri admitted. "But Elaine, it's so—superficial."

"That's okay, as long as you don't take it seriously." Elaine lived at the beach in Santa Monica with her husband, two teenagers, a parrot and three guinea pigs. Real life with sand, she called it.

"Anyway, I loved the script." Cheri handed it over the table, careful to avoid the pewter teapot filled with fresh roses. "The part of Belle is especially well written."

"Not tempted? Not even a little?" Elaine took a sip from a coffee cup so large that it resembled a soup bowl.

"Maybe a little," Cheri admitted. "Isn't that Jamie Jorgenson?" She pointed to a handsome youth who had stopped to sign an autograph on the way to his table. The receipts from his latest film, a teenage adventure romance, were making headlines in *Variety*.

"The very same." Elaine signaled the waiter for more coffee. "You're as star-struck as a tourist. I find it delightful."

"Naive, you mean." Cheri had never lost her awe of meeting people whose faces were already familiar from TV and movie screens, even though her common sense told her they were no different from anyone else. Or from her, for that matter.

"Come back." Elaine was serious now. "You've had months to nurse your wounds. There's no point in shutting yourself away forever. You can well afford a housekeeper, or sell the damn place and move up here."

"I can't." Cheri hesitated. Was it only because of Jeff and Donna that she felt a tie to the Granger house? She couldn't just abandon it, turn it over to a real estate agent as if it were some tract home. *And what would Allie Granger do without her Nora?*

"Must be a man in the picture." Elaine winked knowingly. "Come on, Cheri, 'fess up."

"No." But wasn't there? "The only man I've met in Orange is—get this—a TV show host. Local show on the occult, and he wants to do a segment on my house. Which is exactly what I don't need."

"Sexy?" Elaine always got right to the point.

"I suppose." There was no point in fudging. "If you like tall, blond and self-assured."

"I'm not dead yet," Elaine said. "And neither are you." Before Cheri could respond, she pushed on. "You know, people haven't forgotten you. They're even beginning to say that you've been underestimated, that you ought to get a script that's worthy of you."

"Oh?" Cheri wasn't that gullible. "Who's saying that? You?"

Elaine chuckled. "Among others."

"Elaine, I'll help you in any way I can as a consultant, but that's all." Cheri wished she felt as certain as she sounded. Darn it, the house was awfully quiet while Tad was in school. She enjoyed cooking and puttering around the garden, but it wasn't the same as the mental and physical stimulation that came from performing.

On the other hand, she hadn't forgotten all the political maneuvering that went with being an actress. She wasn't ready for the jabs of critics, the nosiness of the tabloids or the heartless cruelty of so many Hollywood power brokers.

Elaine didn't miss the determination that tightened Cheri's mouth. "Okay, okay. Can't blame a girl for asking. But I will continue to call on your consulting expertise, if that's all right."

"I'd love it."

On the hour-long drive home, it struck Cheri that Hollywood was a nice place to visit, but she didn't want to live there anymore.

Already her thoughts were running ahead to Tuesday afternoon, when she and Kate would begin planning the Halloween party. Kate had been thrilled by Cheri's call, and had immediately offered to put up Tad over Halloween at her house, where her husband—who hated society events—would lead the boys through an orgy of apple bobbing and marshmallow roasting.

It all sounds so normal. Which was exactly what Cheri wanted for Tad.

And she liked Kate, liked her a lot. There was no pretense about her. How had she ever ended up with a brother in show business? Except that Sky was hardly an actor. A documentary filmmaker when he'd started out; it had a scholarly ring to it.

Cheri swung from the Santa Monica Freeway onto the Santa Ana, edging left through the lanes until she arrived at one that wouldn't disappear in the next few miles. Then at last she could give her thoughts free rein again.

As they'd done often since Saturday, they returned at once to Sky.

He was fun to be with, and Tad liked him. But he'd made it quite clear that his career took first place in his life right now.

Ironically, Cheri had to concede that she'd probably be bored by a man who worked at some prosaic job and didn't try to get ahead. Oh, it might be okay for a while, but she'd miss that edge of excitement, the exhilaration of risktaking, the uncertainty she'd grown up with. At the same time, she knew she couldn't handle too much of that. Not in herself and not in a man.

In a funny way it reminded her of Allie Granger, falling in love with a man who was obviously dangerous. At least, it was obvious to Cheri, but Allie was less experienced.

It must have been hard for a spirited woman like Allie, living in an era when most careers were still closed to women, particularly to those of good family. She would have been expected to stay close to home, to marry quietly and raise a family. And yet, like Cheri, she'd felt an attraction to the very kind of man who could hurt her most.

And what about the curse?

Cheri didn't really believe in such things, although the Granger house had certainly seen more than its share of tragedy. Still, it was hardly something out of a Stephen

Kiing novel—no bloody visions in the bathtub, no ravening beasts prowling the garden at night.

As she switched freeways again, she deliberately reached down and turned on the radio. There was nothing like rock music interspersed with traffic reports to drive nonsense out of your head.

It *was* nonsense, this whole business about ghosts. And maybe about Sky, as well. As soon as he hit the big time, he'd be gone, and Cheri didn't intend to be left holding the bag again.

She remembered Ingrid Bjorg, keeping her shoulders straight and her chin up as she strode through the restaurant, only her eyes revealing a hint of fear. Trying to project confidence but not arrogance, wondering who among this field of faces might give her the right opportunity, and who was likely to use and discard her. Terrified that in the end she'd be left with nothing, no career, no family, not even a sense of self.

A wave of pity washed over Cheri, mingled with relief. Her own life had a center now, and a stability she'd never known before. Never again would she be so young and so vulnerable. The last of the bitterness she'd once felt toward Ingrid vanished forever into the sunshine of the day.

CHERI STARED HOPEFULLY into the refrigerator. She seemed to recall saving enough ham for another meal—*no,* that had gone into Tad's lunch sandwiches this week.

There was some ground beef in the freezer, but they'd had hamburgers last night. Tomorrow, on Thursday, she planned to hit the supermarket, but tonight she had to figure out something to cook.

Spaghetti? She'd made that on Tuesday, a quick meal rustled up after Kate left. Cheri flipped through some recipes, but she was out of most of the ingredients.

Well, there was always take-out fried chicken. But wasn't part of being a mother preparing fresh, nutritious meals?

Still undecided, Cheri stopped to listen to Tad's cheers as he scored high on a new computer game. Except for one visit with Joey and Malcolm, he'd spent most of his afternoons this week hiding out in his room or in the house's library. Cheri had suggested tossing a ball around or playing Uno, but he wasn't interested.

I wish I knew him better. I wish I could get inside his head. And his heart.

Time, she reminded herself. It would take time. Meanwhile, what was she going to cook for dinner?

The chime of the doorbell startled her. Not another door-to-door salesman, she prayed as she headed into the hall, unless he was selling pork chops or fresh fish.

She peered through the glass panes. Sky Welton was standing on her porch, holding a pizza box.

Cheri's hands flew to her hair, which could have used brushing; she wished she'd revived her makeup after lunch. But she could hardly run off and fix her face now.

"Hi." She swung the door open. "How did you know I was stuck on what to fix for dinner?"

"Lucky guess." His eyes were warm. "Hope you like pizza. I figured Tad would."

They both looked up at the sound of quick footsteps. "Pizza?" Tad asked. "I hope you got pepperoni. I hate green pepper and that fish stuff."

"No anchovies." Sky led the way into the kitchen. "And yes, there's pepperoni, and mushrooms."

"Tad, help me fix the salad." Cheri began removing lettuce, tomatoes and ranch dressing from the refrigerator. To her surprise, her nephew didn't even protest.

They ate off paper plates, chattering about what they'd been up to this week. Tad rattled away with rare enthusiasm about his teacher and the new family of guinea pigs in his classroom. In between, Cheri learned that Sky was planning a special series of programs on psychics aiding police throughout California.

"I'll have to be away most of October." He frowned. "The timing's not great—" Cheri gathered that he meant because of her and Tad "—but you've probably seen on the news about that case that just broke in San Francisco, so I want to get right on it."

The case involved a psychic who'd led police to a house where a man was holding a kidnapped girl. "But how can you build a series around one case?" Cheri gave in to temptation and took a third slice of pizza.

"There are a number of other, less spectacular cases— I've been thinking about doing such a series, but it needed a focus." Sky crunched up the now-empty pizza box and tucked it into the wastebasket.

"What's for dessert?" Tad asked.

"We've got fruit." He made a face. "Well, I suppose this *is* something of a special occasion." Cheri went to the freezer and pulled out a box of pastries. A quick trip to the microwave oven and they were ready. Tad didn't bother to thank her, but his enthusiasm as he tucked into the dessert was testament enough.

Afterward, Sky accepted an invitation to play video games with Tad. As she cleaned up the kitchen, Cheri could hear them laughing together, Sky's deep voice counterpointing Tad's boyish soprano.

We need someone like him. Both of us do. Not just someone like him, she amended, *but him. Sky.*

Except that soon he'd be going away. Oh, he'd come back, but then he'd go away again. Sky was a man on the way up, and when he got there, things just wouldn't be the same.

The same as what? she chastised herself as she made coffee. *We've only seen each other a couple of times.*

At least she didn't feel quite so much as if Sky's only interest was in persuading her to go on the air. His thoughtful attentiveness to Tad was genuine, and he really seemed to enjoy being here.

Cheri poured two cups of coffee and went to join the men. It was fun watching them, and somewhat reluctantly she let Sky show her how to kill the space invaders. It got to be nine o'clock before she knew it.

"Oops." Cheri rechecked her watch disbelievingly. "Tad, I'm afraid it's time for bed. You've got school tomorrow."

"That's dumb. I'm not tired."

Debating whether to risk antagonizing him with a reprimand, she was relieved when Sky said quietly, "Tad, that wasn't very polite, was it?"

"No," he admitted. "I didn't mean you were dumb, Aunt Cheri, just— Oh, okay. I'll go get ready."

They both tucked him in. Cheri hadn't realized before how helpful it was to have a man around the house, particularly when it came to raising a boy. Lots of women raised children alone, but it was nice to have his support, at least for tonight.

"I don't quite know how to handle Tad," she admitted when they were downstairs again, drinking coffee on the porch. It felt natural and easy, sitting side by side in the old swing, listening to the metallic scrape of the chain as they moved rhythmically to and fro. "I don't want to come down hard on him, but his hostility hurts me."

"You might try telling him that it's okay to feel angry or sad, but it isn't okay to be rude," Sky pointed out.

Cheri thought about the suggestion. "You think that would work?"

"He's probably not aware of how his actions affect you. Remember, he's just a kid. And he really does love you, Cheri."

How could Sky be so sure when she wasn't herself? "I hope so." She leaned her head back. The sky was very clear tonight, the stars crisp and bright. But there was something cold about them, too. With a shiver, Cheri moved closer to Sky.

He wrapped one arm around her shoulders. "You've taken on an enormous task. I'm surprised you haven't hired a housekeeper and gone on with your career."

"I don't want a career." Cheri told him about her lunch with Elaine on Monday and her mixed feelings about the Hollywood scene. "I'm not sure I ever really belonged there, even when I was on top. In some ways, I'm only beginning to find out who Cheryl Lewiston really is."

"If you need any help, just ask." Sky's tenderness took the teasing edge off his words. "I have lots of appropriate adjectives. Like—honest. Loyal. Sensitive."

"Thank goodness for sensitive. I was beginning to sound like a dog."

He nipped lightly at her ear. "Let a guy pay you a compliment, would you?"

"Oh, I suppose—" Cheri turned toward him and stopped speaking as she found her mouth only inches from his. Her lips parted before she could think, and Sky's arms tightened around her as he drew her into a kiss.

He was gentle at first, almost hesitant, and then the kiss deepened into something both intimate and fierce, a quest for closeness that alarmed her, even while she found herself snuggling against him.

She felt safe here in his arms. And free, free to stroke the powerful muscles of his shoulders, to run her cheek across his jawline.

Sky cupped Cheri's face in his hands. "I want a lot more than this. I want to explore you and love you all the way, but not now, not when I'm about to leave."

His words disturbed and tantalized her at the same time. Cheri had never expected them to respond to each other so strongly, not this soon.

Thoughtful, she drew away. "Even if you weren't going out of town, Sky, I'm—I'm just not ready for this kind of involvement."

"You're stronger than you realize." He made no move to embrace her again. "But the last thing I want is to rush you into anything. I'm not even sure—" He paused to weigh his words. "I told you about my marriage. I'm an ambitious man, and I think one of these days you'll discover you're ambitious, too. Neither of us needs to feel like a drag on the other."

Cheri turned her head away to hide the disappointment. As she'd told him, she had no desire at all to go back to acting, and fortunately no financial need to pursue a career. It was obviously Sky who didn't want to be held back. She didn't exactly blame him, but she didn't have to like it, either.

"Cheri, I didn't plan to meet someone like you just now." He laid one hand gently over hers. "Although I'm certainly not sorry. But we're going to have to play this by ear."

She forced herself to smile, and found it wasn't as difficult as she'd expected. "We're on very different tracks. Sky, thanks for helping me with Tad tonight, getting him to be more polite without coming down hard. I don't know much about being a parent yet, but I'm doing my best. That's the challenge I have to confront the next few months, and I suppose I don't have a lot of energy left for other things."

"How neat and tidy," he grumbled, half amused and half serious, as they stood up. "We're both being so damn civilized, Cheri, when what I really want is to carry you up those stairs and—well, okay, not with Tad in the next room—carry you into the living room and make mad, passionate love to you on the sofa."

Cheri turned her head away to keep him from seeing the longing that had to be mirrored on her face. "Oh, Sky, I really do hope your special series is a success. Maybe it'll bring you some national attention."

"Who knows?" He brushed a strand of hair off her forehead. "I'll call you. And I'll see you when I get back."

"Yes," she said, and watched from the porch until his car disappeared down the street.

Now what, she wondered as she went into the house, would Allie Granger have thought of all this?

"HE CAN'T TREAT YOU like this. Not my daughter."

The angry male voice rang through the night. Tad woke up with a start and pulled Buster close, wondering why Aunt Cheri didn't come running. But then he remembered that she couldn't hear the ghosts.

Why did they keep showing up in his room, as if they wanted him to hear them? Maybe they had a special message, just for Tad. Only it was hard to think straight in the middle of the night.

Already the male voice was fading. What had he said? Could it be Dad, trying to reach Tad somehow? It didn't exactly make sense, but maybe that was the way ghosts worked.

Now a young woman was speaking, the one he'd heard before, who sounded a little like Mom. "I love him. We just have to be apart for a little while, until his brother comes around."

"A little while? You're a fool if you believe that. I've heard he's courting that rich widow on Glassell Street."

"No." The woman's voice dropped to a whisper. "Charlie wouldn't do that to me."

"You're darn right he won't." Who was Charlie? Why was the man so angry? Tad felt as if he'd turned on a TV program in the middle. "I'll make sure of that. I'm going to write to that brother of his right now."

"Papa, don't! Please! It'll just make things worse...."

The voices faded, as if the ghosts had walked away. Where did they go? Tad wondered.

He lay awake, staring at the moonlight that filtered through the branches of the cypress tree outside his window. It washed out the colors of the balloons on his wall-paper, turning everything gray and white.

It was hard to figure out what the ghosts had been talking about. Maybe they were acting out a movie script, like Aunt Cheri used to do. Tad had visited the set of a film once. Mostly it was boring, people waiting around for the lights to get ready, then saying the same thing over and over. But it wasn't boring when Aunt Cheri had come on, shouting at someone. She hadn't seemed like Aunt Cheri at all; her hair was a different color, her voice was lower, her skin had kind of a faky look to it, and she didn't act sweet and gentle like she usually did.

Maybe the ghosts were like that, playacting. They didn't want him to know they were really Mom and Dad, come to make sure he was all right.

Tad rolled over onto his stomach, still hugging Buster the bear. It had been fun tonight, playing video games with Sky. And the pizza was good, too. Aunt Cheri cooked okay stuff, but not as good as fast-food hamburgers and pizza. Somebody ought to tell her that real mothers took their kids to McDonald's at least once a week.

His thoughts wandering to ice-cream sundaes and chocolate doughnuts, Tad drifted off to sleep.

Chapter Six

Vinnie Dumont flew back from San Jose a day ahead of the rest of the cast and crew. She had an uneasy feeling, maybe because of the crimes they'd been dealing with on the series, or maybe because it was getting close to Halloween. This time of year, when the days shortened and the nights turned cold, an ominous sense of peril lay over her dreams.

She'd only gone along with Sky as a consultant; she hadn't expected to get caught up in the case. San Jose had been their last stop, to interview a woman who'd helped the Highway Patrol locate a missing truck, which turned out to have gone into a ravine. Unfortunately, the driver had been killed on impact.

As they were stringing up their lights in her overstuffed living room, another call came in, from the mother of a missing teenage boy. While their hostess was still on the phone, a boy's face had flashed into Vinnie's mind, a young, defiant face. He was in Los Angeles, she knew that at once, in a run-down apartment with a bunch of drug users. She could see the room clearly, bleak and curtainless, a neon sign flashing across the street.

She'd passed her insight along to their hostess, but Vinnie wasn't sure what good it would do. How could you find a boy in a big city with such vague information? And what guarantees were there that he wouldn't just run away again?

As she collected her luggage at John Wayne Airport and set off for the drive to her apartment in Santa Ana, Vinnie felt a surge of anger at the unknown forces that had endowed her with these special powers. She'd never wanted to be a psychic. Why couldn't she have been born with the artistic talent she'd always longed for? To her critical eye, her best efforts were merely passable landscapes and seascapes, ordinary and uninspired. Her psi powers, on the other hand, were powerful and original, but also disturbing and sometimes frightening. She didn't like sharing the dark shadows of other people's lives. There were enough in her own, after all.

When she got home, Vinnie flung open the windows, airing out the stuffy apartment. It was a small place she'd moved into four years ago, after Vick died. The walls were covered with paintings she'd made of their travels, of Venice and Paris. In the living room, books and maps and magazines jammed the bookcases. The apartment was really too small, and she'd had her eye on a neighborhood a few miles away, one where the streets were lined with picturesque old California bungalows. Well, maybe one of these days she'd think about buying a house.

The phone rang while Vinnie was still unpacking. It was Sky.

"I thought you'd like to know they found the boy," he said. "He was in pretty bad shape, some kind of drug overdose, but they got him to the hospital in time."

"I didn't give them much to go on," Vinnie said.

"Remember the sign outside the window? Apparently it rang a bell with the police."

"Well." Vinnie felt relieved. "I'm glad. I just hope he gets some counseling, or he'll be right back in trouble again."

"I wonder how many lives you've saved over the years," Sky said.

"Not many."

"Down in the dumps again? You always are when we finish a project."

Vinnie had to chuckle. Sky was too perceptive by half. "Just thinking about life. Wishing we'd had kids."

"But you couldn't."

He must have a million things to do, getting ready to close up shop and come home, but from his tone you'd have thought his only concern was shooting the breeze with Vinnie. *Darn,* but she loved that man.

"There's no point in stewing over what's beyond anyone's control."

"We could have adopted." Vinnie swallowed hard. "At the time, not being able to have kids seemed like a bad omen. I was afraid if I adopted, something would happen to the child. I couldn't take the risk. Now I wish I had."

There was a brief pause on the other end of the line. "I wonder if someday I'll be looking back, wishing I'd had the courage to take certain risks."

He didn't have to spell it out. The one time Vinnie had met Cheri Louette, at the party, the attraction between the couple had been obvious. "It was kind of you to let me know about the boy. I won't keep you; I know how busy you must be. Have you told Cheri you're coming home tomorrow?"

"I'll call her when I get there," Sky said. "In case I get delayed; I wouldn't want to disappoint her. Take care."

"You, too," Vinnie said, and hung up wishing she'd had a son like Sky.

She puttered around warming up a frozen dinner and opening a bottle of diet cola. Somewhere in the middle of eating, the uneasy feeling came back.

Now that she was home, it was easy to pinpoint it. A disturbance at the Granger house.

Now, why should I pick that up? Who asked me to meddle in their affairs, anyway?

But the alertness had come unbidden, for whatever reasons of its own. The spirits were disturbed; not angry, exactly, but fretful.

Vinnie remembered Sky telling her that the house would be used for a Halloween party. That was only a couple of nights away. Probably someone had begun cleaning up the attic, perhaps opening a few trunks. It wasn't a good idea, this party, although Vinnie didn't sense a tragedy in the making. Sky had pointed out that it was for a charitable cause, and that Cheri didn't believe in ghosts, anyway.

But it doesn't matter what any of us believe. What's there is there.

She half wished that she'd bought a ticket to the party. It was sold out now; but of course, Sky could probably arrange to get her in.

No. Vinnie spooned up the last of her brown Betty. If she were called on to do a show on the Granger house, she would, but other than that she was going to stay away.

Something in that house had the power to stir up her deepest anxieties. People said that you had to confront your problems in order to get rid of them, but Vinnie had no intention of doing that. Not if she could help it.

Chapter Seven

"What we really need up here is a vacuum cleaner, but I don't see an outlet." Kate dusted off her hands against her jeans. In the far reaches of the attic, the boys whooped as they chased each other around. "Oh, dear, we'll need some way to string up our spooky lights."

"The outlets are down along the baseboard; there's plenty of them. Jeff and Donna had the place rewired, thank goodness." Still panting, Cheri leaned against one of the trunks they'd just cleared from the center of the floor. The room looked bigger than it had, partly because there was now a broad open area and partly because workmen had cleaned the windows yesterday.

Kate had offered to bring a crew over to move the trunks as well, but somehow Cheri didn't like the idea of a bunch of strangers handling Allie Granger's possessions. Besides, she didn't want people hanging around today. Not now that she had the keys and could actually begin exploring the trunks.

It was only this morning that the bank had been empowered to release the contents of Jeff and Donna's safe deposit box. Along with some bonds and a few items of jewelry, Cheri had found an old embossed leather cigarette case, its faded surface still showing traces of Italian-style gilding.

Inside, wrapped in a faded handkerchief, lay three trunk keys. For whatever reasons, her brother and sister-in-law hadn't been ready to use them. But Cheri was.

Only not yet, not until she was alone. It might be foolish, but she felt as if Allie would object to anyone else seeing the contents. And she certainly didn't want to give Tad any ideas; he had enough kooky notions of his own.

"Actually, I'm too pooped to do any more work right now," she admitted, coughing a little from the dust they'd raised. "A person could choke in here. Do you suppose your friends could bring some cleaning gear when they come over to decorate on Saturday?"

"Sure. As a matter of fact, I think they were planning on it." Kate snared Malcolm as he dashed by. "Come on, boys, let's go downstairs."

There was some half-hearted grumbling until Cheri reminded them she'd baked chocolate chip cookies earlier, and then the boys nearly knocked each other over heading for the steps.

"You know," Kate said as the two women headed down at a more leisurely pace, "I don't know if I've ever thanked you properly. Getting the use of this house has been a tremendous attraction, and we've absolutely sold out all the tickets. It's the best fund-raiser we've ever had."

"It's my pleasure," Cheri said. "Really, it's such a big house for just two people, I'm glad it can be put to good use."

Just two people. She remembered again how comfortable and right Sky had looked sitting in the kitchen, drinking coffee. No, she didn't want to think about what it might be like if the three of them lived here together. Because it wasn't going to happen.

Sky had been gone for two weeks now. He'd phoned a couple of times, but the conversations had been rushed and impersonal, mostly about the program he was taping and, on her part, about how Tad was barely limping along with his schoolwork.

Cheri turned to close the attic door behind them. As she did, Kate said, "You know, I had the strangest feeling we were being watched today."

"Must be the ghosts." Cheri winked.

"I do hope we're not being foolish, holding a Halloween party up there." Kate led the way down past the second floor. "I know my brother makes a career out of these things, but I'm not terribly happy about the chance of running into a blob of quivering protoplasm."

Cheri's answering laughter died away quickly. After all, if she was sure ghosts didn't exist, why was she being so protective of Allie's trunks?

The phone was ringing in the kitchen as they reached the ground floor. Cheri snatched it up, hoping against her own good sense that it was Sky. "Hello?"

Elaine's New York-accented soprano vibrated over the line. "I've got a favor to ask."

"Ask away."

"I've just heard about an actress named Marianne Weaver who might be right for the part of Belle. Assuming, of course, you haven't changed your mind."

"I haven't."

"Well, she's in a comedy at South Coast Repertory, which is down your way, and it's closing tonight, and I've got dinner with a *very* rich man who's thinking of dabbling in movies, and we just can't afford to risk losing him. So would you be a darling—?"

"I suppose..."

"Good. I've already paid for two tickets in your name. They're holding them at the box office. Talk to you tomorrow." Elaine rang off.

Cheri hung up and explained the situation to Kate. "Would you like to go? Assuming we can find a sitter, that is?"

"Oh, dear, I've promised the boys we're going bowling tonight. But of course we'd love to have Tad come with us." Kate thought for a moment. "Now, Sky did say he was trying to get back by today—do you have his number?"

Cheri nodded. "Yes, but I don't want to seem pushy. If he'd wanted me to know that he was coming back . . ."

"Let's have no false modesty." Kate kept one eye on the boys, who were rummaging through the refrigerator for soft drinks. "My brother's very taken with you. I'm sure he didn't want you to be disappointed if he had to stay another day or so. At any rate, we'll count on Tad coming over about six-thirty, all right? I'm sure you can find someone to go with you."

"Thanks."

"Aunt Cheri!" Tad flipped open a can of root beer. "Can't Joey stay a while and play video games?"

"Fine with me." Cheri checked her watch and saw it was almost four o'clock. "Kate, I'll feed them both and then bring them over tonight, if that's okay."

"Lovely." They double-checked their calendars—decorating crew on Saturday, caterer arriving next Tuesday afternoon for Halloween—and parted, a reluctant Malcolm grumbling along behind his mother.

As soon as the boys were out of earshot in the library, Cheri dialed Sky's number.

He answered at once, his voice slightly hoarse, as if from too little sleep and too much work. Cheri was surprised how much she wanted to rush over there and ply him with hot tea and muffins. And feel those strong arms around her, and see those sharp gray eyes of his soften as he gazed at her.

"I was wondering—" Why did she feel so awkward? "Well, Kate said you might be willing—" Cheri stopped. "Oh, darn, I'm calling to ask you out. There's this play I have to see tonight at South Coast Rep. To evaluate an actress. Can I tempt you with free tickets?"

Sky laughed. "Best offer I've had in weeks. What time shall I pick you up?"

They agreed on seven.

"I hope I don't fall asleep in the middle," Sky said. "Frankly, I'm a bit tired or I'd have called you this morning when I got in. But how can I resist such an invitation? Besides, I haven't been to the theater in months."

"Did you accomplish what you hoped on your trip?"

"I'm really excited about it. I'll tell you more tonight."

It was strange the way a new relationship could make her feel as clumsy-eager-uncertain as a teenager. But then, for a woman of twenty-seven, she hadn't had much experience with male-female relationships.

Cheri checked on the boys and found them noisily battling dragons on the computer. Reassured, she went upstairs and got the keys from her bureau drawer.

The house felt strangely still, as if frozen in time, as she mounted to the attic. She'd only come up here alone once or twice, and had left quickly. As Kate said, someone seemed to be watching.

It's just the power of suggestion. But would that account for her strangely vivid dream about Allie?

Cheri stopped in front of the trunks. Two of them had a solid, housewifely air that hinted of blankets and old sheets within. The third was more ornate, covered with faded stickers from Paris and Rome. Had Allie made the Grand Tour in her youth, or had the trunk been handed down by someone else?

On her second try, Cheri fitted a key into the lock. It creaked in protest and then opened slowly.

Dust and the smell of mothballs billowed faintly into the air, making Cheri sneeze. The linen cloth on top had a double set of crease marks, and she gathered that a previous owner must have opened it some years ago.

Setting aside the cloth, Cheri lifted out a dress. It was made of white satin in the short, sleek style of the 1920s. A pair of silk stockings, a cloche hat and a cigarette holder had been tucked alongside. The fabric looked a bit fragile but still serviceable.

Laying it on the linen cloth, Cheri carefully removed several bangles, an aged and obviously cherished teddy bear, and a framed photograph of three men and two women clowning on the hood of a Model T.

She recognized one of the men from her dream as Jeremiah, and the woman with a large mouth and merry eyes as Allie Granger. But how could she have known what they looked like, when she'd never seen them before?

No, surely she'd seen a picture somewhere. Maybe Donna had shown it to her and she'd forgotten.

The other woman, she realized with a start, must be Allie's companion. She appeared to have light brown hair, like Cheri's, but there was no way to judge the rest of her coloring through the sepia tone of the print, and her cheekbones were much broader. Her nose was longer and slightly crooked, and her hair was cut short—shingled, didn't they use to call it? She didn't really look much like Cheri, except for a certain knowing expression in the eyes that critics had commented on in their reviews of *Young and Eager*.

Cheri laid those items atop the clothing and lifted out a thick volume with a padded velvet cover. Carefully opening the clasp, she read on the title page: "Being the most secret diary of Alice Granger. Keep out!" The handwriting was rounded and irregular like a child's, but Cheri guessed that the volume had served Allie well into adulthood.

The pages were fragile with age, but well preserved. Regardless of whether some previous owner had read this diary, Cheri didn't intend to. It would be wrong to intrude on Allie's private thoughts.

Although, she reflected, she might take a peek one of these days, if she got the feeling Allie wouldn't mind.

Underneath lay bundles of letters, none of which appeared to have been disturbed since they were originally laid here. Some were dated as late as the 1930s, others were from the 1890s and by several hands, she discovered as she flipped through them. Apparently the Granger family had a penchant for saving its correspondence.

One letter was sticking out slightly from the oldest pile. Cheri pulled it out, careful of the brittle paper, and opened it gingerly.

It was dated Feb. 10, 1892, and signed by Perry Dotson. *The pharmacist!*

It was addressed, quite formally, to Mackenzie Granger. Mack, she remembered, had been Allie's father.

In its entirety the letter read:

Am in receipt of your letter of Feb. 5. Your threat to harm my business was most unnecessary. My daughter Jane is well quit of your brother's company, and my inquiry to you was rendered as a courtesy to her finer feelings.

Beneath the polite phrasing, Cheri thought she could sense the outrage of a father over his wronged daughter. Still, there was nothing here that would cause the father to lay a curse on the Grangers. Something else must have happened later on. If indeed there had been a curse at all.

She glanced down at the packets of letters, wondering what secrets they held. As she read through a handful, however, she found that most had to do with routine business matters, or contained gossip about people who meant nothing to Cheri. The only one of particular interest had been written by Mack to his brother Charlie in March 1892, while Mack was in San Francisco on business. The letter read:

I am pleased at your decision to cease these idle flirtations, which were occasioning so much comment. I am particularly gratified to hear that you are keeping company with Mrs. Marcella Cray, as I understand her late husband left her quite comfortably fixed, and she is well regarded in the community.

The rest of the letter contained instructions on how to handle various business accounts.

Cheri settled back against one of the trunks. It was surprising how intrigued she found herself by the dealings of these people so long dead. They were not historically significant, and yet they mattered a great deal to the house that she and Tad now shared.

And I keep feeling as if... As if what? As if somehow she and Allie Granger had more in common than she wanted to admit.

Cheri shook her head, and the motion reminded her that she needed to wash and curl her hair, fix supper for the boys and get dressed for the theater.

Carefully she tucked most of the items back into the trunk, but carried the diary, some more letters and the white satin dress down to her room. She might want to examine them more closely later, and she certainly didn't care for the idea of rummaging through the attic again.

After checking on the boys once more, Cheri went to clean up, glad to be back in the safety of the present.

"SHE'S A GOOD ACTRESS, but not as good as you are."

Sky and Cheri were drinking coffee at the Upstart Crow, a bookstore-café in South Coast Village, not far from the theater.

He was wearing a fisherman-style turtleneck sweater that had a rich masculine texture. Cheri could still feel the warmth that had rushed through her when she opened the door this evening and saw Sky standing on the step.

She'd felt completely at ease with him as they drove to Costa Mesa, chatting about Tad and Kate and her boys. They'd watched the play in companionable silence, making appropriately analytical remarks during intermission as if they'd known each other for a long time. As if they shared a vast subtext of opinions and experiences.

"Well?" Sky leaned across the table. "What did you think of her?"

"Marianne Weaver?" Cheri stared through the windows at the cafe's outdoor patio, which was empty in the late-night coolness. "Well, she was good in the part, but she didn't have the light touch I'm looking for. Belle needs to be sophisticated but vulnerable, a bit deadpan at times, even a touch outrageous."

"Sounds like you've got a good feeling for her," Sky said.

She turned to meet his gaze straight on. "You think I'm going to end up playing the part."

"I can't imagine that you won't."

"I'll admit it's tempting." Cheri searched her heart carefully as she spoke. Sky would know if she was trying to fool him, or herself. "I love acting; if it were just a question of playing the part, I probably couldn't resist."

"But?"

"But it isn't that simple." She inhaled the scent of her spiced tea. "There's so much else bound up with it. The Hollywood scene, publicity, being away from Tad, the critics—it's a life I don't want anymore."

He didn't answer right away. Cheri waited until he said, "I'm sorry. I'm kind of distracted tonight, aren't I?"

"Tired, I imagine." *And tense,* she wanted to add, but that might sound like prying.

Still, she was glad when he didn't beat around the bush. "Cheri, this series of programs I've been working on, well, it might be the key to syndicating my show. I've got to impress them or move on. There are other syndicators, of course, but Miles Appleby has showed more interest than anyone else. Which means right now, I can't afford to do less than an outstanding job. There's still a lot of editing and writing to complete. I guess I'm impatient to be done with it."

Impatient to be done with it, and with his quiet life here in Orange County? That wasn't really fair; a local program could hardly contain a man as dynamic as Sky for long. But she didn't like to think about what it would mean if his show were a big hit nationally. A lot of traveling, the attention of the press...

"You're very quiet." Sky's hand closed around hers on top of the table. "What's going on, Cheri?"

"Just—thinking about what it will mean when you hit the celebrity circuit." She tried to make it sound like a joke, but he wasn't smiling. "It's a rat race, Sky. There won't be much time for sitting on porch swings and playing video games."

"Maybe you got a skewed view of things." He waited as a couple in their late forties swung by, arguing cheerfully about the merits of a poet whose name was only vaguely familiar. "Fame was thrust on you; you didn't ask for it, and you didn't have much control over it."

"I'm not sure anybody has much control over it."

Sky tapped a finger against his coffee cup. "You might be right. After all, you've been there and I haven't. But Cheri, it's something I have to do. I don't know why. Being rich has never been important to me; neither has seeing my face in the papers. I just want to be the best at what I do, and in television, that means making a name for yourself."

"Tell me about the last few weeks." She knew she was changing the subject, but there was no point in speculating further. It was impossible to predict what would happen to him, or to the feelings taking root between them, if he achieved his goals. Or, for that matter, if he failed.

Sky relaxed at once. "It was terrific! Cheri, we got some incidents on tape that I didn't expect. And the police were very frank. Usually they don't want to talk about using psychics because it brings the nuts out of the woodwork, but they've had a couple of striking cases recently and they wanted to give credit where it's due."

He told her about Vinnie Dumont's insight and the boy who had been located. "Apparently he's okay, physically, and he seemed glad to be found. Sometimes kids need outside help to get a rein on themselves."

"I hope nothing like that ever happens to Tad." Cheri shivered. "How do parents ever know if they're really doing the job right? Especially when they're stepping into it halfway through."

"You never really know, I suppose." Sky was watching her intently. "You love him a lot, don't you?"

"Yes, but I'm not sure he knows it."

"He does. He just may not be ready to accept it yet." It surprised her how perceptive Sky could be, when he wasn't even a parent himself.

"You like kids, too," she said.

"I'm crazy about them. I'd like to have two or three, one of these days." His mouth tightened. "If that's possible, in my line of business. I suppose I'll need the kind of wife who's willing to stay home and hold down the fort, but—I seem to be attracted to stimulating women with lives of their own."

"I'll take that as a compliment." She smiled, and was glad to see his expression soften.

"Yes, you are stimulating, Cheri, and that's why I don't think you'll be content hiding out in the Granger house for long," Sky said.

She made a face. "I'm not hiding out. I'm making a home."

"Do you suppose that's what Allie Granger thought she was doing?"

They had finished their snack, and Cheri picked up her purse. "I don't see that there's any comparison. She didn't have a child, for one thing, and she never had a career, either."

"Has Tad heard any more bumps in the night?" Sky asked as they paid and strolled through the outdoor plaza to the parking lot.

"Well, he hasn't said anything. But he sometimes seems restless at night. Do you think I'm doing the wrong thing, discouraging him from talking about it? I don't want to give his imagination any more to feed on."

Sky didn't answer, and Cheri remembered that, after all, he would love to go through the Granger house with Vinnie. That wouldn't hurt his chances of getting syndicated, either. But she didn't want to expose Tad to that kind of publicity, and she wasn't sure she wanted to put Allie Granger through it, either.

Put Allie Granger through it? They must have spiked that tea.

"Anything I say on this subject would be distinctly self-serving." Sky held open the door of his BMW.

Cheri waited until he slid in beside her to ask, "Are you coming to the party on Tuesday?"

"I wouldn't miss it." He brushed his thumb lightly over her earlobe, an unexpected gesture that brought a sparkle of heat to her cheek. "Someone's got to be there to protect you from all those spooks."

As they stopped outside Kate's house, it felt natural and right for Sky to take her into his arms and for his lips to find hers. His cheek was slightly rough, and he smelled of coffee and English Leather. Cheri closed her eyes and burrowed against him, wanting to nestle there forever.

But she wasn't a single girl anymore; she was a mother, even if a substitute one. "School night," she murmured reluctantly.

"Think the boys are still up?"

A shout from the house followed by giggles provided the answer. "Guess so."

They walked in together to take Tad home.

IT MIGHT HAVE BEEN the tree branches scraping against the window that woke Cheri, or the way the full moon was peering boldly through her window. She awoke feeling confused; it was too bright to be the middle of the night, and yet her clock said it was 4:00 a.m.

Something rustled downstairs. A squirrel outside in the bushes, perhaps, or the refrigerator clunking through its ice-making cycle. Or the echo of the wind, sounding like a dry old voice.

Cheri pulled on her robe and went to check on Tad. He was sleeping quietly. If ghosts were walking tonight, at least they weren't troubling his dreams.

She could tell she wasn't going to be able to fall right back to sleep. A cup of hot milk might help.

The steps creaked a couple of times beneath her slippered feet on the way downstairs. It felt good to switch on the track lights in the kitchen and let their cheerful clarity flood away the shadows.

By the time she'd finished heating the milk in the microwave and had sipped it slowly, she was beginning to feel sleepy again. Grateful, Cheri turned off the lights and went back upstairs.

A shaft of moonlight fell across the bed and touched the surface of her bureau. About to walk by and pull down the seldom-used shade, Cheri stopped abruptly.

Someone had opened the diary.

She tried to remember if she'd fastened the latch when she closed it this afternoon. She was almost certain she had. How could it have come open by itself?

She turned on the lamp, and saw the entry was dated September 15, 1929. Without even thinking about it, Cheri began to read.

I will cherish tonight always in my memory. Tonight, as we sat in the porch swing and talked and laughed, Jeremiah Hunt asked me to marry him. I agreed at once, of course. I don't believe in that old-fashioned idea that a lady ought to say no at least once. And we're to be married in two months' time!

So far I've told no one, not even Nora. She won't approve, I know she claims that he's a fortune hunter. I loathe the prospect of arguing with her yet again, so for tonight I'm selfishly clutching this wonderful news to my bosom.

The future stretches ahead, so lovely and assured. Was there ever a better time to fall in love? The war is long past, life is merry and gay, and if one wishes to speak of money—which Nora certainly will—I must confess that I'm terribly rich just now. I've more than doubled the money Papa left me, just these last few months on the stock market. And what's wrong with money, after all? It does smooth the path so.

I'm so glad we can afford to have the wedding I've always dreamed of, a big church filled with flowers, all my friends dressed in their Sunday best. It will be a scene from a fairy tale!

I have never been so happy in my life.

A shiver ran up Cheri's spine. What had Sky said, something about Allie suffering a disappointment in love? She could see it so clearly, the pain and misery that lay ahead, and yet there seemed to be no way to stop it. Was this how Nora had felt?

Nora. Cheri stared down at the name written so clearly in Allie's curlicued handwriting. *That really was her name, just like in my dream. How could I have known that?*

Surely Jeff or Donna had mentioned her. It made sense that, after Allie died, Nora might have inherited the house and lived on here. Her name would be listed somewhere as a former owner.

There was a rational explanation for everything, if you thought about it hard enough, Cheri told herself firmly, and went back to bed.

Chapter Eight

Cheri stood in the kitchen doorway, wondering at the transformation of her quiet home.

Lights were blazing; the music of *The Sorcerer's Apprentice* soared from the stereo in the living room; and here in her culinary domain, a dozen caterer's assistants were scurrying to and fro preparing a buffet dinner. Only an hour left until the guests arrived.

There were no dark corners tonight, except up in the attic, and outside where the rising wind presaged a storm. Well, the forecasters had been wrong before. Maybe the squall would get stuck out at sea, or blow itself inland.

It was almost six, and Cheri reluctantly left her observation post to go upstairs and dress. She'd had her hair done earlier, and had applied her makeup as carefully as if she were going before the cameras. This was, in a way, her debut in Orange County society, and she wanted to look her best.

Upstairs in the bedroom, she pulled the dry cleaner's bags carefully from the three dresses she'd had laundered. Among them was Allie Granger's gown, which Cheri had decided at the last minute to include. She wasn't sure exactly what she planned to do with it, but, irrationally, she wanted Allie's clothes to look their best if Kate or someone else should see them.

Now, what to wear? Cheri debated silently between a cherry silk off-the-shoulder dress and her black two-piece with its white-appliquéd sleeves. Neither really appealed to her tonight, but they were the most appropriate things in her wardrobe.

Allie's white dress seemed to be biding its time, watching her indecisiveness. As if it knew that, sooner or later, she would come around to it.

What nonsense! Cheri thought, hanging the old gown away in the closet. She wasn't about to wear antique clothing that didn't even belong to her.

But it did, of course. The house was hers now—well, Tad's, really, but she was the lady of the house.

She wondered suddenly why this dress had been laid in the trunk. Had it been intended as a wedding gown? Or had Allie been wearing it the night Jeremiah proposed?

It had been saved for some reason. Almost without willing it, Cheri found herself pulling the dress out of the closet again. She might as well try it on. It probably wouldn't fit, and then she could forget about temptation.

But although it was loose around the hips and a tiny bit snug across the bust, the dress did fit.

Cheri studied her reflection in the mirror. White had never been one of her best colors, but the satin had a softening sheen. Rummaging through a drawer, she found an emerald and silver necklace and matching earrings that had been a birthday present from her mother. Set in place, they brought out the green of her eyes and removed any harsh contrast with the white fabric.

She added a pair of silver shoes, then stepped in front of the mirror to assess herself again.

The woman who looked back at Cheri came from another era, with her luminous, defiant eyes and her delicate cheekbones. *It's me, but it isn't me, too.*

She shook herself to dispel the sense of being some other person. Well, she hadn't intended to wear a Halloween costume, but the Twenties style *was* right in line with what the guests might expect.

Retouching her lipstick and adding a spritz of perfume, Cheri stepped out of the room just as Kate, coming from the attic, swished by in a voluminous antebellum-style gown.

"One of the skeletons just wouldn't rattle properly, but we got it fixed," Kate informed her. "My, you look stunning. Where did you get that?"

"It belongs to the house," Cheri said.

Her friend smiled. "I ought to take a picture so Tad can see how you look." He'd left for Joey's house just before supper.

"Let's take pictures of everything!" Cheri fetched her camera from the bedroom. By the time she'd covered the attic and the kitchen, and she and Kate had snapped shots of each other, it was time for the guests to arrive.

Sky was among the last; he explained apologetically that the cleaners had gotten lint all over his tux and he'd had to have it redone at the last minute.

People were swirling around them in the living room, sampling hors d'oeuvres and clinking their cocktail glasses, but Cheri hardly noticed.

The formal black and white suit gave Sky a classic, sophisticated look that suddenly carried Cheri back to her dream, to that party of Allie's. *It could have been us that night, wearing these very clothes.*

"Something wrong?" His face was close to hers, his eyes searching.

"No, I—" Cheri gestured around her. "All these people. Didn't Allie Granger use to give big parties?"

"So they say." He wasn't paying any attention to the others, only to Cheri, as he reached down and touched her waist. An unexpected excitement flashed through her and she realized his breathing had quickened, too. "You look beautiful tonight." His tone was low. "I wish there were an orchestra. We ought to be dancing."

Yes, I want you to hold me in your arms. The thought was thrilling—and a bit frightening. Cheri drew back. "I—I'm forgetting my duties. I haven't greeted everyone yet."

"I don't like sharing you," Sky admitted. "That's strange, isn't it? I never thought of myself as the possessive type. I'd suggest we tell all these people to go home, but my sister would have my head."

The wry reference to Kate broke the tension that had held Cheri motionless. "Yes, what would people think?"

"Who gives a damn?" But he accompanied her without complaint as she made the rounds, thanking everyone for their patronage, making sure the caterer was refilling plates and glasses promptly.

"You certainly picked your weather," boomed a matronly woman costumed as an owl.

"Is it raining?" Sky asked. "It wasn't a few minutes ago."

The woman shook her stubby owl wings. "No, but the wind's enough to ruffle my feathers."

Cheri smiled. "I hope you have a good time."

"How could I help it? Halloween in the Granger house!"

The mood was jovial, and Cheri was pleased to find how easily she fitted in with her guests. This was nothing like the Hollywood parties where people were only interested in trying to butter up anyone who could advance their careers.

Here, everyone seemed quite comfortable with each other. If she sensed an undercurrent of nervousness, she attributed it to the "haunted attic" they all knew awaited after dinner, and perhaps to the natural uneasiness that preceded a storm.

The buffet dinner turned out to be artfully prepared, with heaps of grilled shrimp and light-as-air potato puffs. Even the usually garish black and orange Halloween colors managed to look reasonably elegant tonight.

After the last slice of pumpkin pie had been consumed and the coffee served, Kate turned off the music on the stereo. The effect was probably eerier than she'd intended: the silence was invaded by a sudden shriek of wind, and the house shuddered.

"I knew you had influence, Kate, but how did you manage to conjure up this storm?" someone called. There was a scattering of laughter, but it sounded thin to Cheri.

"More coffee, anyone?" Kate asked. "We'll be going upstairs in a minute, and the caterers are just leaving, so don't be shy."

No one seemed interested in the coffee. "Bring on the ghosts!" someone exclaimed, and a man cheered.

"All right, everyone." Kate gestured to them. "Follow me. Stay close, now. We wouldn't want anyone getting lost."

The lights had been turned off in the second-floor hallway except for the electric wall sconces that Cheri hardly ever used. As she emerged from the staircase into the dim corridor, her arm tucked through Sky's, she had the sense of stepping into an earlier century. Was it possible for multiple eras to exist at the same time and in the same place? Fed by the eeriness of the setting, her imagination scanned the possibilities—that the Granger house was some kind of way station between worlds, that science fiction stories weren't wild inventions at all....

Without warning, lightning jagged its way in through the bedroom windows. A blast of thunder followed. Someone shrieked, and others responded with chuckles.

"All part of the show," Kate called from up ahead.

"I'm glad Tad isn't here." Cheri took a firm grip on Sky's arm. "This really is kind of scary."

"Are you feeling all right?" He sounded worried, although she couldn't see his expression clearly. "We could sit this one out."

"No, I—need to be there." Cheri glanced up, and whatever explanation she might have given stuck in her throat. In the uneven light, Sky's profile took on a hawklike ferocity, a remoteness that made her wonder if he'd been transported from another reality. She had the sense they might be walking through an English country house centuries ago, far from civilization, with only farmland around for miles, and ghosts stirring in the stormy night....

A board creaked overhead.

"Is somebody up there?" the woman behind Cheri asked nervously.

"The people who're running the show," she assured the guest. Several of Kate's charity co-workers were already in place, serving as puppeteers and special effects manipulators.

Two at a time, the guests trooped up the attic steps. The last sound Cheri heard as she left the hallway was the rattle of windows as another gust of wind struck.

The attic produced noises of its own, mostly from a tape Kate had bought: rattling bones, whispers, distant laughter. Over it all came the patter of rain against the roof and the recurrent swell of the wind.

"I wish Vinnie were here," Sky muttered as they stepped aside to let others enter.

"Why?" Cheri moved closer to him in the dark. Lights danced around them like glowworms, one of Kate's clever effects. "There's nothing really psychic about all this." She hoped that was true.

"I just wish the storm weren't so appropriately timed." This edginess was unlike Sky, but then, Cheri reminded herself, he'd investigated a number of paranormal phenomena. No doubt he'd developed a healthy respect for the unknown.

"Allie wouldn't hurt us," she said.

"How do you know she's the only one here?"

Before Cheri could think of a reply, a clammy hand grasped her wrist and led her forward. Only a faint glow from an unseen source kept her from stumbling. "Sky?" she asked, but apparently he'd been led away, too.

"Through here," hissed the possessor of the clammy hand.

Cheri moved cautiously in the direction indicated. This must be the tunnel that Kate's friends had constructed. Furry things brushed her neck and arms; something reptilian slithered over her foot.

Then she turned a corner and a glow-in-the-dark skeleton leaped at her, laughing viciously. Before she could stop herself, Cheri uttered a little shriek.

She felt embarrassed until she realized that all around her the attic was full of the cries, giggles and gasps of the other guests. Kate had done a terrific job of filling the attic with rubber spiders, dancing lights and slimy surprises. Cheri, of all people, appreciated the skill it took to create the illusion of reality. That was what show business was all about. Thank goodness, it was only make-believe.

Then the whole attic glared with a ghostly whiteness and the house shook with the roar of thunder. The faint ambient light and the ghostly sparkles vanished, and they were left in darkness.

"Hello?" came Kate's voice. "Is everybody all right?"

"What a rotten time for a blackout," someone grumbled. "It'll probably take the electric company hours to get it fixed."

"I think I'd like to go downstairs," a woman added shakily.

"Where's the flashlight?" Kate called. "Andrea?"

"It scared me so much I dropped it," came the disgruntled answer. "I'm groping around down here on the floor, but it seems to have rolled away."

A man flicked on his cigarette lighter, but was quickly cautioned to put it out. "This is an old house and the wood's dry," Kate said. "The last thing we need is a fire."

It was Sky who spoke next. "Everyone stay where you are. It's too dangerous to have a group of people stumbling around in the dark. Just sit down if you're uncomfortable; Cheri and I will go downstairs for a flashlight."

It was comforting to realize he wasn't more than a dozen feet away; she just wished she were better prepared for such an emergency. "I'm afraid my batteries went dead, but there's quite a stock of candles in the pantry," Cheri said.

It seemed to take hours to find the door, moving carefully so she wouldn't trip or knock someone down. Finally a strong hand caught her shoulder and Sky murmured, "Here. I'll go first."

"No, let me." The staircase was pitch-black. Cheri had played a blind woman once in a TV movie, and had spent hours rehearsing with a black cloth tied over her eyes. The heightened awareness of space and sound came back to her now; she could feel the faint vibration of her body heat reflecting off the walls and hear the scuffle of Sky's breathing behind her. She set each foot squarely in place before trusting it with her weight.

It would be so easy to slip, to tumble head over heels down the long flight, crashing into the door below. All it would take was the slightest nudge, the mischievous prank of some hostile spirit....

Cheri's hand touched the door and, with a profound sense of relief, she opened it.

There was some light in the second-floor hallway from the windows, but not much. Outside, rain spattered against the glass, and only the occasional spurt of lightning enabled them to hasten their progress.

"I'm glad nobody had a heart attack." Sky came alongside her. "I'm surprised Kate didn't make better provisions for an emergency."

"She positioned someone right by the light switch, I think," Cheri protested. "Nobody was expecting a blackout."

From the attic behind them came the sound of Kate belting out "Row, Row, Row Your Boat." Other voices quickly joined in the round.

"Good." Sky kept a tight grip on Cheri's hand as they descended to the first floor. "I'd hate for anyone to panic."

There was a bit more light downstairs because of the many windows, but the house was a large one, and it took them several more minutes to stumble their way into the pantry.

"Right here." Cheri felt along one of the shelves until she came to the row of tapers. Thank goodness, Donna had loved candlelight dinners.

"Got a match?"

"Over here somewhere." Her groping hand met something firm and cloth-covered. Sky's chest. "Hi," she said softly.

"Hi."

He drew her hands up to his mouth and lightly kissed her fingertips. In the darkness she could feel his breath sigh across her skin with an almost unbearable intimacy. Without thinking, she lifted her mouth to his.

Sky pulled her to him, his hands exploring the curves of her back and waist. Cheri leaned close, wanting to drink in his spicy scent, the slight roughness of his jaw, the firm demand of his mouth.

They clung together with growing hunger. Cheri's body, so long silent, was making urgent demands. Sky tasted so good, and his gentle stroking was turning her skin to flame.

Sky stiffened, and then Cheri heard it, too. A rustling noise, coming from the library.

"Do you suppose the others got downstairs somehow?" she whispered.

"They'd call out if they did." Sky exhaled deeply before releasing her and stepping to the pantry door. "The matches."

"Oh. Right." Cheri found them quickly and lit two of the tapers. They flickered but cast a circular glow bright enough to guide her steps. Remembering the others upstairs, she tucked a dozen tapers into a small basket and looped it over her arm.

"Maybe you should stay here," Sky muttered.

"Not on your life!"

"All right. But keep back."

What could be making the now quite audible thrashings in the library? Some wild animal, driven inside by the storm? Or...

Or nothing, Cheri told herself firmly, following Sky quietly through the hall. She positioned a candle in front of her to keep the wax from dripping onto her arm, squinting a little to see in the flickering faintness. How odd to think that a few centuries ago this was all people had had to fight back the invasion of night.

From up ahead came a thump, and then silence.

"Is someone there?" Sky called. "Hello?" When no one answered, he pressed forward, and Cheri followed him into the library. Nothing moved, even in the combined light of both their candles.

There was no other way out except through the tall windows, which appeared to be firmly shut. "Whatever it was, it would have had to go by us in the hall, or else it's still in here." Sky prowled through the room, inspecting the dark corners without results.

"Is there any damage?" It was hard to tell much by candlelight. The guests had left their coats and purses in here, and Cheri didn't think they'd been in such a jumble. "It looks like some of these got knocked to the floor."

"Damn." Sky stared around them in frustration. "What the hell was it?"

"I don't think I like your choice of words," Cheri said.

"I didn't mean that literally." He lifted his candle higher so its shadows danced around the room. "I wonder if..."

"There." Cheri pointed. The latch on one of the windows was loose. "Someone could have gotten in and out that way. I hope nothing was taken."

Sky ran his hand across the sill. "It isn't wet. I don't think this window's been opened, but you'd better have that latch fixed. Well, I suggest we go rescue our stranded guests. I'm sure they're getting tired of 'Row, Row, Row Your Boat' by now."

Neither of them mentioned the moment of passion that had been interrupted by the noises. It had been wildly foolish, Cheri could see now. She didn't often lose control like that, and she hoped she wouldn't again.

Growing accustomed to the darkness, they made their way fairly rapidly back up to the attic. "Sorry for the delay," Sky said as the others greeted them. "We heard some rustlings in the library and went to check it out, but we didn't find anything."

"Must be the ghosts," someone called cheerfully.

"I've had enough ghosts for one night," a woman grumbled in reply.

Cheri began lighting the tapers and handing them around. "Be careful, now. I wouldn't want anyone to get burned."

"At last!" From one corner, a woman who must be Andrea issued a triumphant cry as she flicked on the flashlight. "The darn thing rolled between two trunks."

The beam had an artificial brightness that seemed out of place after the last half hour. Cheri almost wished it had stayed lost.

"This way." Kate was guiding everyone carefully down the steps. "Walk slowly, now."

With the help of Andrea's flashlight, they reached the ground floor without incident. Then, just as Kate was trying to decide what to do next, the electric lights popped on again, almost blinding in their intensity. Several people whistled and clapped.

"Wouldn't you know it?" Andrea said. "They had to wait until we didn't need them anymore."

Sky didn't appear to share in the general good humor. "I think we'd better have a closer look at the library."

A minute later, Cheri stood looking in, aghast. Coats had been strewn around, contents of purses dumped out and books thrown to the floor.

"Oh, my." Kate frowned at the mess. "I do hope nothing's missing."

The guests set about recovering their belongings. After a few minutes' confusion and the return of several wallets from the wrong pockets and purses, it was determined that nothing had actually been removed.

No one, fortunately, accused Sky or Cheri of the mischief; it was obviously not the sort of thing a responsible adult would do. Which made her think of the boys.

She and Kate exchanged looks. Obviously Joey's mother was thinking along the same lines.

Yet how could the youngsters have escaped undetected? As far as Cheri could see, there weren't even any wet marks on the floor.

Fortunately no one seemed unduly distressed. Soon they were all downing final cups of coffee and pastries and then everyone was on their way, declaring themselves quite satisfied by their scary Halloween experience.

"That was a bit more excitement than I'd counted on," Kate said when only her crew was left. "Cheri, would it be all right if we came back to clean up tomorrow afternoon? It is getting rather late."

"By all means." Cheri waved them away. "Besides, you might get stuck up there in another blackout."

"Thanks so much. What a success! People will be talking about this party for years." Kate kissed Cheri and Sky on the cheek and went out with her friends amid a flurry of waves and farewells.

"Whew." Cheri sank onto a wooden swivel chair. "What a night."

"I'll put the candles away." Sky disappeared for a few minutes. When he came back, he said, "All the doors seem to be locked and I can't find any broken windows."

"Tad has a key."

"Tad also has my brother-in-law watching over him." Sky held out his hands and pulled her up from the chair. "It's cold in here. What do you say we light a fire?"

Cheri refrained from commenting on the symbolism. "There's some wood on the back porch. I hope it's not too wet."

Expertly Sky laid a fire in the hearth and soon had it blazing. Now that the wind had died away, the crackle and hiss of old logs was the only sound.

"Something to drink?" When he agreed, Cheri brought in small tumblers of Amaretto from the kitchen. "It's so cozy in here."

Sky was sitting on the floor, his head resting against the sofa. Although his eyes were closed, there was an alertness about his face as if he were listening carefully. Or trying to sense something.

After a moment Cheri said, "Are you a little bit psychic yourself?"

Sky's gray eyes opened slowly. "Not really. But I've learned what to listen for."

"You don't really believe..."

"In ghosts? I'm not sure. But something made that mess in the library tonight." He reached out to touch the soft satin of her sleeve.

Allie's dress. She'd almost forgotten she was wearing it. For some reason she felt wilder than usual in this slim gown, more aware of being a woman, of needing to be touched. Or was that just because of Sky's nearness?

"I can't let you stay here alone tonight," he said quietly. "Especially since we don't know who or what was in the library."

"There's no need—" Cheri stopped herself. She hadn't given much thought to the fact that, with Tad away, she would be here alone for the first time. Not that a young boy was much protection; on the other hand, she'd never felt this intimidated by the house before. She wanted Sky to stay, even if his presence might prove dangerous in its own way. "All right. Thank you. The couch makes over into a bed."

He tilted his head in what appeared to be a gesture of agreement. "Tell me about Allie."

"What about her?"

"You seem to feel some kind of affinity for her."

There was no reason to keep secrets from him. "I found some old family letters and her diary. I wasn't going to read it, but one night last week it just sort of fell open by itself."

"What did it say?" Sky sipped his liqueur without taking his eyes from her face.

"She's gotten engaged to a man named Jeremiah Hunt," Cheri said. "I think he's a fortune hunter."

"You talk about her in the present tense." The firelight played across his strong cheekbones, reminding Cheri of the image she'd had earlier tonight of him as a remote English lord. Someone she hardly knew, and yet felt urgently drawn to.

Realizing he was waiting for an answer, she said, "Their story may have happened a long time ago, but it's new to me."

"And you feel as if she's reliving it, right now." It was a statement, not a question.

"In a sense." Cheri hadn't wanted to confront her own feelings about Allie. She *didn't* believe in ghosts. "Don't forget I'm an actress. Characters become real to me after a while."

"Ah, so the Granger house is sort of a theater, with you as central player?"

Cheri tapped his arm lightly. "Don't go making a big deal out of this. I'm not the type who overdramatizes everything that happens to me."

His thumb traced the rim of the now-empty glass. "Not at all. But you're very vivid. Larger than life sometimes, Cheri." He set the glass aside. "You feel it too, don't you?"

The air between them radiated with desire. Yes, she felt it. She ought to say no, to turn away, to busy herself making up the couch for the night.

To hell with good sense.

"Yes," she said. "Of course I feel it."

His hand brushed the shoulders of her dress, of Allie Granger's dress. Fire throbbed through her body, but Cheri couldn't move.

It had been different with Terence. He had, she could see now, choreographed every move with practiced and probably indifferent expertise. Young and naive, she'd mistaken her own long-suppressed sexual response for real passion.

But the longing rising in her now was something else entirely, not merely physical but a deep hunger for fulfillment. She wanted Sky in every way, in her arms, in her bed, in her heart, with a need that seared away all hope of resistance.

Her momentary paralysis vanishing, she wound her arms tightly around him. Fiercely her mouth found his. They were almost one already, almost merging....

"Cheri." He cupped her face in his hands, pushing her slightly away. "Slowly, honey. Slowly."

"But..." Bewildered, she pulled back a little. Was he rejecting her? Didn't he really want her, after all?

There was no mistaking the desire in Sky's face, in his flushed skin and parted lips. "Let me show you, Cheri."

He leaned down, his breath caressing her neck and shoulders. With great care, he kissed the pulse of her throat and then, with agonizing slowness, moved lower. His hands circled her breasts and passed on to her waist.

Her body responded with an instinct she hadn't known she possessed, moving sinuously to an unheard rhythm. It was a dance, this love they were making, a silent tango with its own melody and its own gradual unfolding.

Carefully he slid the dress down her shoulders, along with her bra straps. An inch at a time, his lips explored her tightening breasts, teasing her, enflaming her, drawing her deeper and deeper into the dance.

Sky knew just where to touch her, how to draw back for a minute, when to intensify his movements and when to let her lead. He was an expert at this tango, yet there was nothing premeditated about his moves. He was caught in it just as she was, discovering for the first time the subtleties of a primeval measure.

She wasn't even sure how the dress came to slip over her head, or at what moment they lay unclothed together, skin against skin, fire feeding fire. These sensations were new to her, and yet as ancient as the earth, fundamental to life. How had she lived so long without knowing this?

Sky's body was hard and strong, perfectly controlled. Again and again he savored her, nipping, tasting, tantalizing, until Cheri felt as if she would burst. Only then did he join them, with a primitive beat that melted into rivers of fire and then hardened again, carrying her away into the music of the senses, into a dance that lifted her among the stars and spun her into the night and then brought her ever so gently back to herself again.

"Oh." It seemed so small a sound, this hoarse whisper from her throat. Yet how could she hope to find words to tell him what she'd experienced?

"Did that seem—like—nothing that's happened to you before?" His tone was puzzled, the voice uncharacteristically halting. "Cheri?"

"You, too?"

"Me, too." His arms encircled her and pulled her cheek to rest against his shoulder. The rich scent of their bodies mingled with the tang of smoke to form a smell so alluring that Cheri knew at once it was what the perfumers had sought through the centuries and never quite caught.

A few minutes later, Sky moved away and then came back, bringing the thick comforter that had lain on the couch. He spread it over them and there, before the dimming fire, they fell asleep together.

Chapter Nine

When Cheri awoke, the fire had died and yellow dawn light was seeping weakly through the curtains. There was no more sound of rain or wind, but the small patch of sky she could glimpse was leaden and threatening.

She rolled over beneath the comforter, feeling the early-morning chill brush through the crochet work. Sky lay on his side, his face relaxed like a child's, his breathing even. He looked so young that she felt like protecting him, watching over him as she did with Tad. But it wasn't he who needed protection.

What on earth had she done? At the realization of the step she'd taken, Cheri's chest constricted in fear.

She couldn't regret last night; the experience had been too profound, too self-revealing. But she didn't know if she could face what lay ahead.

Moving quietly so as not to wake Sky, Cheri picked up her clothes and went upstairs. A few minutes later, clad in jeans and a sweatshirt and carrying an old bathrobe of Jeff's, she tiptoed back down. After leaving the robe near Sky, she went into the kitchen and made coffee.

Sitting at the table and sipping the hot brew helped her gather her thoughts. Well, what was done was done. There was no denying the link that she and Sky had forged between them, but it was still a fragile thing.

His career came first right now. She didn't blame him; she knew how that felt. At one time, making her feature film had seemed the most important thing in her life. She wasn't sure, in all honesty, that she wouldn't eventually have given up Terence if he'd stood in her way, although that would have been different from the callous way he'd first used, then discarded her.

There was nothing like that about Sky. His responses to her had been genuine. But, trying to be brutally honest with herself, she had to concede that his feelings probably weren't enough to sustain the kind of relationship she needed.

The coffee was beginning to taste bitter. Suddenly irritable, Cheri poured it out and mixed some orange juice. Then, needing an outlet for her restless energy, she began whipping up a bowl of pancake batter.

I don't need a man to make me complete. I wasn't looking for a love affair, but I found one. Now we've both got to act like grown-ups about this. Not get all emotional about it and make unreasonable demands.

Her mind might be sensible, but Cheri could tell, as she measured butter into a skillet and turned on the burner, that her feelings weren't about to fall in line without a struggle.

Bringing up a child wasn't going to be easy to do alone. Neither was coping with this house: getting the latch fixed was a small matter, but Cheri knew things broke a lot in old homes. The plumbing was at least twenty years old, and wasn't the garden starting to look like a tangle?

She caught herself sharply. Already she wanted to lean on Sky the way she'd leaned on her mother and her agent. Not again. Not ever again. Especially with a man whose work was likely to pull him away.

But he could be so tender; she needed to be cherished sometimes. And what she'd felt last night had opened new spaces in her heart. Spaces that demanded to be filled.

"That smells terrific." She hadn't heard Sky's approach, and his appearance in the doorway caught Cheri off guard. The gray velour robe was tantalizingly skimpy, revealing the furred strength of his chest and legs. His eyes were still sleepy, his mouth curving into an inviting smile.

"I—just felt like cooking." She almost wished Tad were coming home this morning, instead of going straight to school from Kate's house. Anything to give her a break, so she could think things through and come to some rational course of action.

"Can I help? I'm terrific at microwaving bacon."

"Sure." She gestured toward the refrigerator, and Sky set to work. From time to time he gave her a puzzled glance, as if sensing her remoteness and unable to understand it, but he didn't say anything until they'd cooked and eaten most of the food.

"Okay." Sky rested his elbows on the table. "Out with it. Having second thoughts?"

"Not exactly, but—the timing is all wrong." She didn't want to make demands on him, not when everything was so tentative and new between them. "We both have a lot of things to sort out." Cheri took a deep breath. "Sky, I think we should stop seeing each other for a while."

"Don't be ridiculous." He speared another slice of bacon with his fork. "What did you expect, that we'd instantly know each other as if we'd been dating for years? Of course it takes time to sort things out. That doesn't mean we can't be together."

"Yes, but your job will involve a lot of traveling...."

"We're not syndicated yet." His hand closed over hers. "Cheri, what's going on with you?"

"I'm out of my depth, Sky. I've had too many things happen in the past few months; I'm not ready to take on a relationship now." The words tumbled out too quickly.

"Sounds like you're panicking."

"Maybe." Cheri pulled away and began clearing the dishes. "Humor me, will you? I need time to think things over, Sky. It's happened too fast."

"We're both adults. And it hasn't happened that fast." He was maddeningly calm. "I'm not going to let you shut yourself away in this house like Allie Granger. I'll come over tomorrow night and take you and Tad out for dinner."

"No!" Darn it, that *was* panic surging through her. Already he had the power to hurt her. The more she saw him, the worse it would get.

It isn't going to work out. Sooner or later, irresistible force will meet immovable object. And I'm not sure I'll be able to bear it.

Nothing she was feeling was rational. Maybe he was right; maybe the stories about Allie Granger *were* having an effect on Cheri. After all, the previous mistress of this house had thrown everything away for love, and where had it got her?

"Sky, please go. I need to think."

He looked as if he wanted to argue, then reconsidered. "All right. But have you thought how it's going to look when I walk out of here in a tuxedo at this hour of the morning?"

"Oh." Well, there was more where that robe came from. "I've kept some of my brother's clothes. I kind of thought Tad might like to have them someday." She gave him directions and, after he disappeared upstairs, she found a cleaner's bag for the tuxedo.

Jeff's sweater had to stretch to fit across Sky's chest, she saw when he came back down again, but the jeans lay neatly over his slim hips, and he'd found a comfortable pair of loafers. For an instant, she wondered what it would be like if he lived here, if he came downstairs like this every morning and kissed her lightly and went off to work—except that he wouldn't be here every morning. Maybe not for weeks or months at a time.

"You're the strangest woman I've ever known." Sky lifted the cleaning bag out of her hands. "Last night you were passionate and free, and today it's as if you'd drawn a curtain between us."

"Please try to understand," she said. "I can't see you for a while."

His eyes searched hers. "I'll give you a couple of days. More than that I won't promise." With his free arm, he caught Cheri's waist and held her tightly for the length of a kiss. "You'll change your mind."

"It isn't my mind I'm worried about."

Sky hesitated as if he wanted to reassure her, but couldn't. Because, she thought, he knows what lies ahead, too.

"It won't be easy," he said softly. "But it will be possible."

She walked to the door and stood there for a moment as he passed across the porch into the weak daylight. Part of her heart went with him.

Unwilling to stand there while he drove away, Cheri forced herself back into the house. After cleaning up what was left of the breakfast dishes, she went upstairs to get the mystery novel she'd been reading.

Allie Granger's diary and the letters from the trunk were still lying on her bureau. Cheri hadn't disturbed them since the night when she'd read about the engagement. Maybe it would help if she pieced this story together. She was probably making too much of the parallels, anyway, and the more she read, the more she was likely to distance herself from the events that had unfolded in this house some sixty years ago.

With that rationale, she began sorting through the letters until she came to one in an unfamiliar feminine handwriting. Taking a seat on the bed, Cheri glanced down and saw that it was signed by Nora Leeds.

I wrote this letter.

Nonsense. She wasn't Nora; that had been a dream. Still, intrigued, Cheri began to read.

It was dated November 3, 1929. Under the date was written:

San Francisco.

My dearest Allie,

What rubbish! I can't believe you would even consider that I might refuse to come back to you!

I was deeply troubled to hear of your losses on the stock market. You will recall that I warned you some months ago not to invest so heavily, but it's true, as you said, that I've always been extremely cautious. I'm sad to learn that this time I was right.

At least you still have the house and a small annuity, which will be enough to sustain you. With my secretarial training, we should be able to live well enough together. I have never been merely a companion but a friend, and as such I require no salary.

As for Jeremiah, I wonder that you are going ahead with such elaborate wedding plans. Surely he would be just as content with a small ceremony at home, and it would save you the expense of inviting so many guests. But this must be as you wish.

My aunt is making a fine recovery from her influenza, and she understands my wish to return home next week to help with the wedding plans.

All my love,

Nora

Thoughtful, Cheri stared down at the letter, wondering if Allie had appreciated how lucky she was to have such a devoted friend.

It was so clear, to Cheri and evidently to Nora as well, that Allie's primary attraction for Jeremiah had been her fortune. Surely now he would call the wedding off. It was a painful prospect, but she couldn't imagine someone as vital as Allie shutting herself away because of it.

She was tempted to read more in the diary. But it had been opened for her as an invitation; now it was closed.

Outside, a car pulled into the driveway, and she realized Kate's cleaning crew must have arrived. With a sense of relief for the distraction, Cheri went downstairs to let them in.

ON THURSDAY NIGHT, the first episode of the subseries aired on *Sky's the Limit*. It provided an overview and history of cooperation between psychics and police, including snippets of many of the interviews that would be featured at length in later episodes.

The station had arranged for heavy publicity, and dozens of phone calls came in afterward from people seeking help in locating missing persons. Sky's staff had provided the station's operators with a list of available help, including psychics along with conventional private detectives. Even if the show didn't lead to syndication, Sky hoped it might help reunite some desperate families.

As he sat at his desk Friday reviewing plans for a followup, he knew that he ought to be thrilled with the program's success. It looked as if the station were going to have its highest ever ratings over the next few weeks, and that was sure to boost Sky's career one way or another.

But he couldn't stop thinking about Cheri.

He didn't like to admit it, but in a way she was right. The timing *was* lousy. He was finally at the point he'd worked toward for years, on the verge of gaining a national reputation. In this business, that would mean eighteen-hour days, extensive traveling, and a single-minded focus on promoting his career.

Right now he wasn't sure that was what he wanted, after all.

He'd seen from the beginning that Cheri was a naturally sensuous woman, but he'd been surprised by the intensity of his own response to her. It had gone far beyond the merely physical into something almost spiritual.

Sky smiled. That was an odd term for someone in his line of work to use.

Besides, he was concerned about Cheri and Tad. *Something* had rearranged the coats and purses in the library, and he really didn't see how the boys could have sneaked out on such a stormy night without leaving some trace or having their absence noted.

He wished Cheri would let Vinnie go through the house. But he didn't want to appear to be using their newfound relationship to boost his program. Maybe if Vinnie did it unofficially...but she'd said something once, something about having odd feelings toward the Granger house. Was it possible she might stir something up rather than lay it to rest?

Actually Sky had never much believed in ghosts, but he did believe there were phenomena that scientists still couldn't explain. Some of those phenomena could be helpful, others even amusing, but some could be downright dangerous.

His phone rang twice before he snapped out of his reverie. Sky picked it up.

"Welton? Appleby here." The connection to New York crackled with intermittent static, but he could hear well enough.

"Did you get the tapes?" He'd sent copies of the complete subseries to the syndicator, but hadn't really expected them to have been reviewed yet. Appleby was a busy man, and he hadn't seemed in any haste to take on *Sky's the Limit*.

"Been through them. Great stuff." Appleby, whom Sky recalled as a rotund man with an impressively large nose and an ever-present cigar that he rarely lighted, was a man of few words. "Think you've got something here. Maybe we could expand this. Must be psychics in all the major cities—great for ratings. I'll need your help, of course. Romancing the station owners, that sort of thing."

"You're saying you want to go ahead with it?" Now that it was happening, the break he'd been waiting for so long, Sky was surprised to feel uncertain rather than elated.

Couldn't he have waited a few more months? I need time to get close to Cheri, to win her trust.

"Yep. We could get into action in time for the February sweeps. Really make a splash. Can you fly out tomorrow? We'll do some planning over the weekend and then send you on the road with our best salesman, see what we can line up."

It was on the tip of Sky's tongue to protest that he had work to do right here in Orange County, but of course, that wasn't entirely true. The subseries needed only a bit more minor editing, which his staff could handle, and it would run until well past Thanksgiving.

There was no good reason to delay. Not even Cheri; putting things off a few days, even a week or two, wouldn't really give them enough time to work things out.

"Fine," Sky heard himself say.

He had his secretary make the travel arrangements. The rest of the day was taken up with preparing for his absence, making sure the staff knew what needed to be done.

When he called Kate to tell her, she let out a long cheer. "I knew you could do it!"

In the background he heard boys' voices. "Is Tad over there?"

"Yes." She caught the implication at once. "Cheri mentioned wanting to do some gardening."

"Thanks, Sis."

Fifteen minutes later, Sky pulled up in front of the Granger house. Tuesday night's storm had left the air crisp and clean all week, and the house looked peaceful in the late-afternoon sunlight. A small chill laced the mild air, warning of a cool autumn night ahead.

When there was no answer at the door, he walked around the house, swinging open an unlocked gate that led into the garden.

The large old-fashioned backyard was a maze of overgrown bushes and disappearing pathways. Climbing roses ran amok over a decrepit trellis, while ferns vined their way up the side of a potting shed. The air smelled of old roses and honeyed alyssum.

"Cheri?"

In answer, some bushes trembled and a quizzical face appeared. With a blue-and-red bandanna wrapped around her hair, and dressed in a baggy sweat suit with dirt on the knees, Cheri looked more like a tomboy than a movie star.

Sky wasn't sure what sort of greeting to expect, but she looked pleased to see him. "I wasn't expecting company, but..." She shrugged unself-consciously and dusted off a crumbling stone bench. "Have a seat."

In the fading light, the garden took on an enchanted quality that suited Cheri perfectly. What classical features she had, and those big, gamine eyes. He was reminded of Audrey Hepburn in *Green Mansions*.

"I got the call from New York today," he said, still standing. "I have to fly back East tomorrow."

"For how long?"

"A few weeks. I'm going to insist on being home by Thanksgiving. It's a big Welton family affair."

"Do you know," she said suddenly, "that there are buds all over the camellias already? And that poinsettias grow as big as trees? I'm learning so many things."

"Cheri?"

"I'm going to miss you." She moved toward him and then stopped. "Oh, I don't want to get your suit dirty."

"To hell with—!"

"Let's go inside." She tossed her clippers and canvas gloves into the potting shed and led him to the house. "I'll be back in a minute."

He had coffee ready by the time she came down again, her hair now held back by a clip, her face bright from scrubbing and enlivened by a dash of makeup, and her slender body shown to advantage in silk slacks and a sweater.

Producing a jar of cookies and curling up in a kitchen chair, she said, "Now tell me about New York."

He didn't want to discuss business right now. He wanted to lean across the table, cup her chin in his hand and kiss her mouth thoroughly. He wanted to loosen that hair from its saucy clip and watch it curl through his fingers.

Instead, he told her about Appleby.

"So it's definite?"

"Apparently so. If we can win over enough stations. As you know, syndication's the big thing these days. Not only the independents but some of the network affiliates are picking and choosing." He stopped. "Cheri, this isn't a good time for this to happen. I wanted to give you a few days to cool off, and then I was hoping we could be together for a while."

To his surprise she said, "We will." Seeing his confusion, she added, "I've been wanting to apologize. For overreacting. I got scared. But I've been thinking it over, and well, life doesn't come with guarantees. We just have to take things one step at a time."

He didn't want to take things one step at a time; he wanted to make a big leap, in spite of all the warnings his experience and his common sense were issuing. But if he pressed too hard, he might scare her off. "I'd like for you and Tad to plan on spending Thanksgiving with me, at my parents' house. I promise to back by then."

"Okay." Cheri held out the cookie jar. "Go on, stuff yourself. It'll give you something to remember me by."

"I'll take you to dinner," he said.

"Don't you need to pack?"

"Well, yes..." And to give Kate a key to his condo so she could water the plants, and to pick up some clothes at the cleaners, and to take care of a hundred other details. *Damn it.* "We could grab a quick bite."

She shook her head. "I've got to pick up Tad. And he notices things. I don't want him getting the idea we're involved, and then having you disappear for so long. He needs stability right now."

He didn't want her to be right, but she was. "I'll keep in touch."

"You'd better." She grinned.

"Walk me to the car. I've got something to return to you."

At the sidewalk he lifted out a cleaning bag with her brother's clothes inside. "I figured you'd be wanting these."

Cheri looped the bag over her arm. "Sky, I don't want to hold you back. Don't worry about me while you're working. I'll be fine."

"Do you have to be so reasonable?" he growled in pretended annoyance. "Whatever happened to old-fashioned hysteria?"

She laughed. "You'd hate it."

Their kiss didn't last nearly long enough. Sky had to fight the desire to linger, to make conversation about anything and everything, to keep Cheri by his side a little while longer.

Instead, he slid into the car and drove away with a wave. In the rearview mirror Cheri looked small but determined.

Sky couldn't wait until he came back again.

THAT NIGHT after Tad was in bed, Cheri took Allie's diary downstairs and sat in the library, holding it on her lap. She wasn't sure whether it was curiosity or something else that made her want to find out what had happened to Jeremiah. Maybe, she realized, she was waiting for a sign to tell her it was all right to read on.

Jeff and Donna had repainted the room, providing a modern pinewood desk and game table along with practical tan-gray carpeting. The pine emitted a fresh wintry smell, intensifying the masculine feel of the room. This had been Jeff's hideaway as now, so often, it was Tad's.

The floor-to-ceiling bookshelves contained an odd mixture of volumes, from leather-bound children's classics to the latest paperback best-sellers, along with a dog-eared section of scripts. A set of encyclopedias filled one shelf, while another sported Donna's collection of bells from every city she'd ever visited. *She would have brought one back from Rome.*

Cheri shivered, knowing her melancholy thoughts were the result of Sky's departure. It didn't help to recall that he was still here in Orange tonight. His heart and mind were gone already.

The diary still felt heavy in her lap, as if it wanted to remain shut.

"Well, Allie," Cheri said aloud. "I guess I'll lock this away somewhere nice and safe, where I won't be tempted to pry."

For some reason, though, her body didn't want to move. She was probably just tired; her muscles ached from bending and stooping in the garden.

There did seem to be something odd about that particular section of bookcase directly in front of her. Maybe it was the thin outline of cracks that ran around one section. They didn't look like ordinary cracks; they were too regular and even.

Slowly she stood up and set the diary aside. Walking across the room, Cheri ran her finger along the cracks with a growing sense of excitement mixed with apprehension.

Donna and Jeff painted this room. If there was anything strange here, they would have noticed it. On the other hand, Cheri wasn't sure she would have noticed anything either, if she hadn't been sitting here alone at night, letting her thoughts wander.

And if I weren't still puzzled by the way those purses and coats got scrambled on Halloween.

Feeling a bit foolish, she began pulling out books, checking behind them. Nothing, just solid wall—until she got down near the floor.

There, behind the lowest shelf, she spotted a small rectangular area outlined by cracks. Cheri stood back a little and pressed the panel with her foot.

The bookshelf swung out almost noiselessly.

A breath of cold air wheezed over Cheri as she stared into the secret passageway. It was pitch-dark in there, but she'd bought new batteries and an extra flashlight this week in case of another blackout, so she retrieved it now from the desk.

The light barely dented the blackness of the passage, just enough to show that there was nothing really mysterious. She climbed inside, carefully straightened, and walked cautiously along the narrow walkway as it snaked behind the pantry, until it ended abruptly near the back of the house.

After checking all around with the flashlight beam, she kneeled and tugged at a small knob underfoot. She found herself lifting a section of the floor and smelled the damp mustiness of the crawl space beneath the house.

Cheri shivered, realizing that an intruder could have come in this way. On the other hand, who would go creeping around under a house on the off chance of finding a loose panel in the floor?

On her knees, she shone the beam down into the crawl space. A thick spiderweb trembled ghostlike and on the ground an insect skittered away. Then the light reflected off something blue, a small round object. A china shooting marble.

It was the one Tad had found in the attic. He'd been looking for it on Wednesday, grumbling that it must have fallen out of his pocket.

The pounding of Cheri's heart slowed as she began to smile. Apparently Jeff and Donna had found the passageway after all, and had passed that information on to Tad. The mystery of the mixed-up coats was solved.

She reached down and plucked the marble from its nest of old leaves, then replaced the floor panel. Tad would understand where she'd found the marble, without her saying anything. Meanwhile, Cheri decided, she'd leave the passageway as it had stood for nearly a century. No one but a restless child was likely to come this way.

Back in the library, she swung the bookcase into place and dusted off her hands. Vaguely she recalled reading somewhere that people often used to build secret passageways in old houses, although it seemed to her that had been in foreign countries, where invaders were always a threat and a family's life might depend on having such an escape route. But, she supposed, if she had planned to build a house like this, she would have wanted to include such a romantic touch herself.

Oddly, Allie's diary felt lighter when she picked it up to go upstairs. *As if I'd gone back in time, and the weight of all those years had been lifted away.*

Maybe this was the sign she'd been waiting for. At any rate, she no longer felt like an intruder in her own home. With a philosophic shrug, Cheri sat down and paged through the diary until she found the entry dated November 16, 1929.

Today was to have been my wedding day, and tonight my wedding night. I have such a jumble of thoughts, dear diary, that I must put them down willy-nilly. You, my old friend, will forgive the tears of a foolish girl, I know, and perhaps those of the equally foolish woman I have suddenly become.

Cheri's chest tightened. When had she come to care about Allie Granger so much?

Nora was worried, I know, but I had no such qualms. The church today was filled with flowers, and the pews with guests, old friends of my family and gay companions from Los Angeles. If their faces were a bit strained from the events of this autumn, and their pockets as much lightened as my own, there was no sign of it today.

Never one to adhere too closely to tradition, I had chosen not a traditional wedding dress but the white gown I wore the night Jeremiah first kissed me, the night our breathing mingled and became one. There were flowers in my hair instead of a veil, because I had nothing to hide.

The hour grew later and later, and still he did not come. We were all in place, the players on the stage, without our leading man. The curtain could not rise, and the audience became uneasy.

I made excuses to myself, to others. But the time ticked past, and finally Nora went in and told the guests the groom had been unavoidably detained. How kind she is, and how brave to face all those people.

I was determined not to weep and make a pitiable object of myself. Nora and I came home together and began to unpack the valises I was to have taken on our honeymoon to Catalina.

In the evening, an acquaintance of mine called to say she has heard the most amazing rumor that Jeremiah was secretly married all the time to Deirdre Reilly, that red-haired tart who used to work here as a maid until she was fired for stealing. It seems she was going to let him go through with the wedding, then the two of them would run off with my money, but of course, now I haven't got any.

What a complete and utter fool I am. If I had any self-respect I would take poison, as that poor girl Jane Dotson did on Uncle Charlie's wedding day. And the saddest part of that was that he never really loved Aunt Marcella, and then Jane's father went crazy and put some kind of curse on our family. It's nonsense, but I think Aunt Marcella always believed it was why my cousins died.

So here I am, cursed not by old Mr. Dotson but by my own blind stupidity. I am determined to live very quietly here and to protect myself from my own weakness by having nothing more to do with men, so I can never make such a mistake again. Nora says I will change my mind someday, but I never will. As long as she stays with me, I am content.

Cheri closed the book with a deep sense of loss. There had been nothing dramatic in Allie's decision, merely a deep sense of resignation and a mistrust of her own judgment.

Just as I began to doubt myself after all my failures.

Was she hiding here just like Allie? But Cheri had made no resolution to stay here forever. This was temporary, while she and Tad worked things out and recovered from their grief. Then, well, maybe she would find some kind of work, perhaps even try acting again.

And Sky? She would just have to bide her time until Thanksgiving and see how they both felt.

Cheri laid the diary on one of the bookshelves, beside some old volumes of fiction by now-forgotten authors of a half century ago. She had an idea Allie would feel at home there.

Chapter Ten

The blue marble was still sitting on the kitchen counter a week later, Cheri noticed one morning as she set scrambled eggs and bowls of cereal on the table. She'd given it to Tad right after she found it, but he hadn't seemed interested.

"Tad! Breakfast's ready!"

He didn't answer, which wasn't unusual. Tad often ignored her, or pretended to. At other times he would cling tightly, then suddenly push away.

Mixed emotions. Well, she knew about those. She kept looking forward to Sky's next call, and then feeling let down afterward.

"You'll be late for school!" She didn't want to nag. Tad was usually good about getting his homework done on time and cleaning up his room. But it was frustrating sometimes, working so hard to please him and getting so little response.

Cheri remembered what Sky had said about explaining her feelings to Tad. Maybe today would be a good time to try it.

Sneakers squeaked on the floorboards and Tad trudged into the kitchen. "How come you keep fixing eggs?" he said as he sat down. "I don't want them."

"You ate them yesterday," she reminded him. "You asked for more, remember?"

He made a face and didn't reply.

Cheri took a deep breath. Why was it so hard to say simple things about her feelings? Maybe, she realized, because she'd never learned how as a child, so it didn't come naturally.

"Look," she said, "I know things are tough for you. I hear you tossing and turning at night, and I know you miss your parents a lot. I miss them, too. But Tad, it hurts my feelings when you're rude to me."

"Was I rude?" He stopped with his spoon in midair.

She nodded. "I went to all the trouble of scrambling eggs today because I thought you liked them, and now you won't eat them. How would you feel if you did something nice for me and I didn't appreciate it?"

Tad squirmed. "Yeah, but you're a grown-up."

"So?"

"Grown-ups do stuff like that. Fixing eggs that kids don't eat. I mean, it's part of the job."

Cheri was startled into a laugh at his honesty. "That's what you think. I'd much rather be reading the paper than cooking, believe me."

"Oh." Tad mulled the idea while he drank his milk. "Okay, I'll eat my eggs tomorrow. But I don't want to be late for the bus." Grabbing his lunch box off the table, he hopped down onto the floor.

"Tad!"

He stopped in the doorway. "What?"

"Aren't you even curious about the marble?" Cheri held it out to him. "Don't you want to know where I found it?"

He shrugged. "In the passageway, I guess. Joey has a whole bunch of marbles that are prettier than that one. You can keep it."

Then he was off, and Cheri heard the bus pulling up. *Darn it!* She felt like tossing the marble into the wastebasket, but instead she tucked it into a drawer. It was a part of this house, after all.

Part of this house. Like the nightmares Tad had been having? He refused to discuss them, but she'd heard him talking in his sleep many nights, even crying out. When she went in to comfort him, he'd clutch that teddy bear and turn his face away.

It was hard to know whether to bring up the ghosts again. What if he picked up on the fact that, although she had stayed away from Allie's diary ever since reading about the disastrous wedding, Cheri, too, sensed a presence in this house?

She knew it was just in her imagination that people in fiction could become real, and so could those from the past. But Tad wasn't old enough to make that kind of distinction. She might inadvertently intensity his dreams instead of banishing them.

The phone rang. Cheri jumped and then, annoyed at her nervousness, picked up the receiver.

It was Sky. "Greetings from Nashville."

"Nashville? I thought you were going to Atlanta."

"That was yesterday." He groaned. "My internal clock's a mess, but we've signed up quite a few stations."

They chatted for a while about his program's syndication. Then Cheri said, "I'm worried about Tad, Sky. He's brooding and I think he's having those dreams again."

"Have you talked to Kate?"

"Yes, but she hasn't had any experience with this kind of thing. Her boys never went through a trauma like Tad has."

"I wish I were there." His voice tightened. "Damn, I feel like some kind of traveling salesman. Cheri, I miss you. I miss the way you smell, I miss the way your hair feels against my skin."

A soft answering prickle ran through her body, a swelling bud of desire. "When are you coming home?"

"By Thanksgiving." That was still two weeks away. "Not much before, I'm afraid."

She tried to swallow the dark disappointment. "I know you don't want to be there." *But this is the way it goes, isn't it, when your career is taking off? Always busy, always on the run, always wishing you had a few more hours in the day and a few more days in the week, so you could rediscover what life is about.*

"I'm going to make a point of sticking around in Orange County through Christmas," he said. "Miles would like to have me jump every time he calls, but I'm standing firm. Two more weeks and then back home for a while."

Thanksgiving. Christmas. Cheri could smell the pies baking at her grandmother's house. Had that really been twenty years ago? She ached for those smells, the heady mix of potpourri, pumpkin pie, chestnuts and roasting turkey. The scent of home.

"I miss you," she said before she could stop the words. "I'm sorry. I don't mean to be a drag on you."

"I want you to miss me." Sky's voice was full of a yearning that matched her own. "I want you to think of me every time you eat a chocolate chip cookie, every time you lie down to sleep, every time you slip into the shower and let the water flow over that golden skin of yours...."

"Sky." How did he have the power to arouse her long-distance? It wasn't fair. "This conversation should be censored."

"I'd like to see somebody try." Another male voice was speaking now in the background. "Damn. I've got to go. I'll call you soon, Cheri."

And then he was gone.

Her skin tingling, she went into the living room to study the revised script of the movie now entitled *Beverly Hills Belle*. It was a derivative title and Cheri didn't like it, but it was better than the screenwriter's original choice, *For Whom the Belle Toils*. Ugh.

The production money was trickling in and Elaine had begun scouting locations, but the leading role remained to be cast. Cheri resolutely refused to think about it. Tad needed her now more than ever. Sky's absence reminded her all the more of what it was like to be working in one place while your heart was in another. She wouldn't do that to herself, or to her nephew.

She began to make notes on the script.

SKY GLANCED at his watch. An hour or so till lunchtime. He didn't have an appointment until three, which meant that theoretically he had a choice between going sight-seeing, reading something educational, or taking a nap.

The nap won hands down—except that Sky had never been good at dozing off in the middle of the day. He picked up a copy of the *Nashville Tennessean*. There was nothing like a bunch of newspaper stories about unfamiliar people and issues to put you into a soporific state.

He stretched out on the bed, a comfortable oversize model in a comfortable oversize hotel room that looked like all the others he'd been staying in. He wanted the next few weeks to be over. He wanted to get back to Cheri....

She missed him. The recollection of her words glowed through his weary muscles and dimly penetrated his foggy brain. She missed him, maybe almost as much as he missed her. Living people couldn't have ghosts, but some shadow of Cheri had dogged every step of his trip, whispering hidden desires into his ear at night, making wry comments about the fellow passengers on airplanes, laughing at his unspoken jests. An image of her had constructed itself inside him, a whole personality from the soft jasmine smell of her to the momentary hesitations that gave her voice a soft, almost Southern intonation.

This wasn't helping him fall asleep. If anything, it was waking him up again. Reluctantly, Sky rattled the newspaper open and scanned the first few pages.

He didn't much care what the Tennessee legislature was up to, or what the weather would be like for the rest of the week. By then, he'd have inherited somebody else's thunderstorms or early winter chills.

His eyes were getting ever so slightly heavier. He'd just flip through the rest of the paper and then . . .

The name jumped out at him, even though it was in small body print, virtually indistinguishable from thousands of other words. Arlene Bronofsky . . .

He didn't know Arlene had taken back her maiden name. But it figured.

Blinking his eyes into focus, Sky scanned the short article. Dr. Arlene Bronofsky of Stanford University, attending a conference here at Vanderbilt, would be speaking to the scientific community tonight on the latest developments in gene splicing as applied to cancer research.

Arlene was in town. He hadn't seen her or talked to her in half a dozen years. They'd tried to stay in touch after the divorce, to maintain the illusion of friendship, but it had become more trouble than it was worth. The passing years had revealed how little they really had in common.

The picture of her that emerged in Sky's mind was more a blurred old photograph than a sharp image. And it wasn't Arlene as she'd been during the last years of their marriage. It was Arlene at the University of Southern California, where they'd met in the mid-seventies. She'd worn her hair long and straight then. He recalled vaguely that she'd cut it later into something chic and practical. It was her expression he saw most clearly, the determined set of her jaw, the excitement in her eyes. Her youth and untempered enthusiasm.

Without any more thought, he rolled over and flipped through the phone book until he found a number for Vanderbilt information. Three phone calls later, he reached a professor who had just seen Arlene headed out with some other conferees for a restaurant called the Cockeyed Camel

Pub. Sky jotted down the name, thanked the professor, and called a cab.

The restaurant turned out to be noisy and informal, its guests flushed with heat after the frostiness of the November day, people crowding around its wooden tables and bar. On the far wall, a painted camel eyed him insolently.

It took Sky a minute to identify Arlene, sitting with three men at one of the tables. Somewhere along the line she'd given up her contact lenses for designer glasses, and her hair was now short and frosted. She looked confident and attractive, but he didn't feel anything for her except a trace of nostalgia.

Maybe it hadn't been a very bright idea, barreling in here uninvited. Hell, he only had a couple of hours before he had to meet the sales rep for yet another courting call on a station manager. Arlene was probably looking forward to hashing over DNA and RNA with her companions, anyway.

He was about to swing around and leave when she spotted him. "Sky?" Arlene stood up and waved. "I don't believe it!"

With her usual efficiency, she took less than five minutes to make explanations to her friends, commandeer another table and find out what Sky was doing in Nashville. He sketched in the process of syndicating his show.

"I'm pleased for you." She glanced up at an approaching waitress and barked out an order for peel 'n' eat shrimp. Sky, who barely had time to glance at his menu, asked for a corned beef sandwich. He'd forgotten how impatient Arlene was with the little niceties of life, the need to deal with waitresses and auto mechanics and anything else that didn't involve a test tube. "But ESP, Sky? That's all a bunch of mumbo jumbo."

"Let's just call it manifestations of natural laws we haven't discovered yet," Sky said.

The smile she gave him was alight with memories. "You always did know how to put me in my place. I miss that."

"You do tend to take things rather seriously, but I suppose that's part of your profession. You've done well, Arlene. I expect to hear your name every time the Nobels are announced."

He'd meant it as banter, but she took him seriously. "We're close to some breakthroughs, Sky. My name's been proposed once, or so I hear via the grapevine, but I need something really big."

"Learning Swedish already for your acceptance speech?" He cocked an eyebrow.

This time she caught the joke. "You rascal. And I suppose you don't heave little sighs of disappointment each time the Emmies pass you by?"

He had to admit it was true. "Okay, so we're both ambitious. Ever wish we'd done things differently?"

Platters overflowing with food were set in front of them. Arlene began peeling a shrimp as if she expected to discover something momentous inside. After a moment, Sky realized her intensity was due to her focused introspection, something Arlene had never been good at. "Well," she said at last, "every now and then I get a twinge about not having children. But I just can't see them fitting in, even if I were married."

"You don't miss having someone to talk over the events of the day with?" Sky wasn't sure what devil prompted him to keep probing.

Arlene looked up at him in surprise. "Why, no. I'm in the lab until ten o'clock most nights, sometimes later. When I get home, I'm too tired to talk to anybody."

He knew the feeling. On the trip to Northern California, meeting with police and psychics, planning out the next day's schedule, reviewing his notes and script, he'd often worked until midnight, adrenaline pumping through him.

He loved that feeling, the electric tingle that ran through his brain. Sometimes it was almost like a sexual thrill.

"How about you?" Arlene took a sip of diet soda. She'd certainly kept her figure, although he suspected she didn't eat very healthy foods. As he recalled, her specialty was meals from vending machines.

"I need more balance," Sky said, unsure how much he wanted to tell her about Cheri.

Arlene knew him well enough to read between the lines. "So you're dating someone. I always expected it. In a way, I'm glad I'm not like you, Sky. You were torn between wanting to get ahead and wanting to have a home."

"And you're not." It was a summation, not a question. He'd wondered for a long time if Arlene was beginning to regret her choices, especially now that the watershed age of thirty-five was looming close ahead of them both. Now the answer was obvious.

Arlene rested her elbows on the table. "No, I'm not. Sometimes I wonder about myself. Aren't people supposed to yearn for someone to grow old with? But I don't care if I grow old, as long as my health is good."

Sky wasn't entirely convinced. If she was content alone, why did Arlene take such care with her appearance? *So she'll look good when she picks up her Nobel Prize in Stockholm, of course.*

She'd been right, though, about how he felt at Emmy time. Not that he'd done anything worthy of an award since his early, documentary days. But his best work lay ahead of him.

Other diners were starting to leave, and Sky realized it was time for him to get back to work. "I'm glad we had a chance to see each other. Ironic, isn't it? We live five hundred miles apart and we have to come two thousand miles to get together."

"It isn't distance that matters, it's time," Arlene said. "Neither of us had to go much out of our way."

Which was about as good a summary of their relationship as he could have come up with.

In another cab, on his way back to the hotel, Sky wondered if he and Cheri would ever sit across a table from each other, talking calmly, even lightly, about why their love affair had fallen apart. He couldn't imagine it. For both of them, the hurt would be too deep ever to heal completely.

Chapter Eleven

Turkey. Stuffing. Cranberries and sweet potatoes, mashed potatoes and gravy. Pie. How could Cheri have forgotten the stretched, strained feeling in her stomach after she'd stuffed it this way?

Conversation had died when the food was laid on the long dining-room table at the Weltons'. Even Tad had set to without hesitation, loading up his plate with the tantalizing food and wolfing it down.

Leaning back in her chair with a groan, Cheri surveyed the company of people who had begun the day so merrily and now looked as if they were candidates for suspended animation. Only Sky's mother was still moving, sluggishly pouring herself another cup of coffee. His father, his sister and her family and Sky himself were nodding in their seats, halfway into unaccustomed midday naps. Even Malcolm, Joey and Tad looked on the verge of falling asleep.

Cheri's gaze came to Vinnie Dumont directly across from her.

The psychic was still sitting straight in her chair. Although her eyes had a faraway look, her expression was alert. Was she slipping into some kind of trance?

"Vinnie?" Cheri spoke softly, so as not to disturb the others.

The woman turned and blinked. "Oh, I'm sorry. I was just thinking about Vick—my late husband. He preferred apple pie to pumpkin, and I was thinking I should have made one today. In case anyone else feels that way, too."

So much for psychic trances! Cheri reflected ruefully. "You must miss him a lot."

"Terribly." Vinnie studied her for a moment. "Have you ever had any odd feelings, any bits of insight that might be considered psychic? Especially since you've been in that house?"

"Not really." Cheri thought about her dream of meeting Allie, but she didn't think that was what Vinnie meant. "I'm afraid not."

"Be thankful," the psychic said.

Around them people began to stir. "I think I ate too much," Sky muttered.

"Go take a nap." His mother laid her spoon on her saucer and lifted the cup of coffee.

"Isn't that supposed to be bad for your heart?" Sky looked over at Tad. "How about if we go for a walk, Tad? You and me and your Aunt Cheri."

"How about just you and me?" Tad said.

To Sky's questioning look, Cheri said, "Go ahead. It's okay. I can hardly move, anyway." Maybe Tad would open up to Sky when they were alone.

Gradually the company dispersed. Sky and Tad put on their jackets and went out together.

"He's still nursing his grief, isn't he?" Vinnie asked as, after helping clear away the dishes, she and Cheri settled into overstuffed chairs in the living room.

For some reason, Cheri felt very comfortable with Vinnie. "Yes. I think he resents me for trying to take his parents' place. I guess I just have to let time do its work."

The other woman's eyes were sad. "I wish I could advise you, but I don't know much about children." There was a world of regret in her voice.

"Neither do I," Cheri admitted. "This is called learn-as-you-go."

Vinnie hesitated, as if there was something she wanted to say but wasn't sure about.

"What?" Cheri said.

The older woman looked startled. "Oh, nothing. Well, nothing that concerns you, anyway."

"Try me." She felt as if she knew Vinnie on many levels, as if they'd been casual acquaintances for years and were now becoming friends. It was something about the way they seemed to understand each other instinctively, almost as if they were related.

"I sense something going on in the Granger house." Vinnie looked as if she might like to recall the words, but realized it was too late.

"Going on?"

"Some kind of—energy—rising. I hate to say a disturbance, because that may be putting it too strongly. Have you felt anything?"

Cheri was glad they weren't having this conversation in her house. Here at the Weltons' she felt free to speak openly. "I had a very vivid dream that I was Allie Granger's friend Nora, her companion. And—I've read several passages in her diary. I felt as if somehow she were inviting me to."

"How about the boy? Has he mentioned seeing anything?"

Slowly, Cheri said, "No, but—I'm afraid I've discouraged him from talking about it. He's been very restless at night."

Vinnie picked up a foil-wrapped candy from a dish in front of her and turned it over and over in her hand. "You ought to find out what's there. Without the boy knowing, if necessary. But—"

"Would you—?" Cheri was surprised to hear herself ask. But what could it hurt to learn Vinnie's impressions, as long as it was done privately?

The psychic's grip tightened on the hapless bit of candy. "Cheri, I don't know. I'll have to think about it. You see, I've had strange feelings about that house for a long time. As if whatever's going on there has some personal meaning for me. And I'm not sure I'm ready to face whatever it is."

Watching Vinnie's thoughtful face crease with tension, Cheri realized that the other woman was deadly serious. "Couldn't it—whatever Tad is feeling—couldn't it just fade away as he comes to terms with his grief?"

"It's quite possible," Vinnie said. But she didn't sound convinced.

The front door opened and Tad and Sky stomped in, accompanied by a blast of cool air. "It's downright frosty out there," Sky grumbled as he shrugged off his jacket. "Isn't this supposed to be Southern California?"

"There's a warming trend predicted for tomorrow," said Kate as she emerged from the kitchen, and suddenly the room filled with people and movement, the boys running and whooping, Mrs. Welton carrying in a tray of coffee and after-dinner mints. Everything felt normal and safe again.

Sky settled next to Cheri. "I hope you don't mind—I promised to take Tad roller-skating on Saturday, just the two of us."

"Thank you." Cheri rested her head against his shoulder, not caring how much the intimate gesture might reveal to the others. "You're good for him."

"Tomorrow, however, he's going to Disneyland with my sister." Sky lifted her hand and lightly massaged her fingers. "We're going to relax, you and I. How does that sound?"

"Lovely." Cheri closed her eyes. They'd hardly had time to exchange pleasantries this morning when he arrived to pick her up, having just gotten back into town on Wednesday. She ached for time alone with him; her skin needed his touch, her soul needed the sound of his voice close to her ear.

Looking up, she caught a pleased but faintly envious look in Vinnie's eyes. *She's lonely.* The realization touched her deeply. It might take time, but somehow, Cheri vowed silently, she would find a way to get closer to Vinnie.

"ALL THOSE STAIRS?" Cheri stopped inside the door of Sky's condominium, holding the sack of Chinese food in front of her. "You have to walk up all those steps to get to your living room?"

"Up!" he commanded from behind, paper rustling in his hands. "I'm afraid this soup is going to spill."

Cheri mounted the steps quickly. "What's through that door downstairs, anyway?"

"My bedroom and an office." He moved around her through the living room and set his package on the dining-room table. "They built this place upside down."

From where she was standing, Cheri had a clear view of the ultramodern kitchen and, through an oversize window, of the rest of the gray clapboard condo complex, its New England-style elegance looking oddly out of place among the palm trees. "It's charming."

"I don't spend much time here." That explained the meticulous neatness of the thick cream rug and Indian-print sofa.

Cheri turned to watch Sky as he set out the Chinese food, produced plastic dishes from the cupboard and began brewing tea. There was a buoyant energy about him that she'd noticed all day. Part of it, she knew, had to do with her. But not all.

"You haven't said much about your program." She lifted napkins and little packets of soy sauce out of a paper bag. "Except that you'd signed more than a dozen stations."

He looked up from the stove and grinned, a lock of dark blond hair falling boyishly over his forehead. "The first episode will air in January. We're starting with the police subseries, to build up some momentum for the February sweeps."

"Sounds good." But it didn't explain why he looked like a cat who'd caught a chocolate-covered canary.

"How do you like your tea? Weak or strong?"

"Medium." She waited while he poured two cups, and they began dividing the fragrant contents of the little white cartons. Mu shoo pork, sweet and sour shrimp, spicy beef, sizzling rice soup—maybe they'd overdone it, but Cheri didn't mind stuffing herself two days in a row. It was Thanksgiving weekend, after all.

Sky downed most of a burrito-like pancake filled with pork before he went on. "Right after New Year's, I'll be doing some additional programs, expanding the subseries to include half a dozen major cities where we'll be syndicated. And then—" he stopped to sample the other delicacies on his plate.

"Well?" Cheri wasn't sure whether to laugh or cry at his obvious enthusiasm for whatever came next. *I want him to enjoy his work, but not more than he enjoys being with me.*

"Appleby's been working on some contacts in the State Department and he thinks we can get permission to tape in the Soviet Union, maybe as soon as March."

The excitement radiating from Sky's face was irresistible. Cheri could feel how thrilling it would be for him to have this rare opportunity to talk to Soviet scientists about their renowned psychic research.

"That's—fantastic." And it was. Delving into rarely explored territory, uncovering new and fascinating information, visiting exotic places—that was exactly the kind of challenge that a man like Sky needed. It would be terrific for his program, too, and probably bring a lot of publicity and recognition.

It's really happening. He's going to be a big star.

"Not just to Moscow," Sky pressed on. "A lot of facilities are being opened up to the foreign press now for the first time. We'll be there at least a month, maybe longer. I'll have to stock up on earmuffs."

"It'll be spring by then." Cheri hoped he didn't catch the wistful note in her voice. Her roses would be in their first, most beautiful bloom. And he wouldn't be here to share it with her.

"Cheri—" he reached across the table for her hand. "I know it will be hard, being apart so much, but you have to understand."

She looked at his glowing face. "I do. And I'm glad you're so happy, Sky."

He chatted on about the places he would visit and the researchers he wanted to talk to, as the mounds of Chinese food rapidly disappeared. Cheri tried to listen intently, although her mind kept playing back the afternoon, which they'd spent down at Newport Harbor, wandering through quaint little shops, eating fresh fish, walking on the beach. The day had taken on a timeless quality, and she didn't want it to end.

After the cartons were thrown away and the dishes rinsed, they sat on the sofa together, listening to progressive jazz. With a lazy inevitability, their lips and bodies found each other.

The laziness dissolved like a calm night sky bursting into fireworks. Sky nipped lightly at Cheri's throat, and she leaned her head back, her hands barely touching his shoulders as he tasted her. Blood soared and sang through her, flushing her cheeks, tightening her breasts, softening her inner core.

A hot golden light seemed to envelop them both as he lowered her onto the sofa, his own being shuddering with the intensifying strokes of her hands against his hips. This time he didn't try to hold back, to slow down the showers of sensation as their clothing fell away and they touched each other length to length.

Cheri was barely aware when he paused to slip on some protection, and then with firm command he united them. Sparks of yellow and violet danced across her eyes as she matched him thrust for thrust, hunger for hunger. They clawed and flew together, splattering the sky with brilliance, until at last they settled into a soft green pasture.

"More," he whispered.

She laughed, then realized from his movements that he meant it. The second time was more deliberate, tracings of white light that slowly coalesced into a great hot flame. It lasted so long that she lost track of time, of reason; at last the fireball burst into a final soft pattering of fiery rain.

"I don't want you to go away," she murmured without thinking.

He tensed slightly and then relaxed. "I'll be here until New Year's," he said.

Cheri closed her eyes and held him tight. There were other things she wanted to say, questions to ask, reassurances to seek, but she knew this wasn't the time for them. Maybe there never would be a time for them.

At least she had this moment, right now.

"NO!" THE MAN'S VOICE cut through Tad's dream and he woke with a start to the painfully familiar blackness. He scrabbled under the covers but couldn't find Buster.

"No!" The cry rose to a shriek. Tad pulled the quilt up to his chin and waited for Aunt Cheri to come racing in, but apparently she couldn't hear it.

Where was the ghost lady's voice? He wished she'd answer, so the man would stop that hoarse sobbing. Nobody on TV cried that way. The only time Tad had heard anybody sob like that was Aunt Cheri, after she found out that Daddy and Mommy weren't ever coming home.

"She's dead! Oh, God, why?"

Tad's fingers found the fuzzy paw of his teddy bear and he pulled it against him. Buster felt smaller than usual. What was the man talking about? Was it Mommy? Had she come back for a little while and then gone away again? If it was Daddy talking, why didn't he come and sit next to Tad and tell him stories, instead of making those awful weepy noises?

"I'll get them for this. Both of those damn Grangers."

"Go away!" Tad was surprised to realize he'd spoken out loud. He'd never tried to talk to the ghosts before. "This is my room! You get out!"

The man didn't say anything. The room felt empty. From down the hall, Tad could hear Aunt Cheri snoring softly.

"It's okay, Buster," he said to reassure the quivering bear. "They can't hurt you. I'm here. And if anything were really wrong, Uncle Sky would come."

He wasn't sure when he'd started to think of Sky as his uncle, but he liked it. Uncle Sky was coming tomorrow morning to take him skating. Maybe he'd ask Uncle Sky about moving into one of the spare bedrooms. Then he'd always be here to protect them.

Just thinking about tomorrow made Tad feel better. He liked the roller rink with all the noisy kids running around and the wheels going *ka-thump, ka-thump* on the wooden floor, and the rock music blasting. And you could get pizza at the snack bar, and ice-cream bars afterward. Uncle Sky would hold onto him so he wouldn't fall, and it would be almost like having Daddy back again.

Tad closed his eyes and held tight to Buster, in case the bear got scared again.

Chapter Twelve

Cheri was stumbling around in the kitchen Saturday morning, still half-asleep as she made coffee, when Sky telephoned.

"I'm afraid I'm going to have to postpone my date with Tad." From the echoing announcements in the background, she realized he must be calling from an airport. "I've got a flight to New York in half an hour. It seems the Soviet foreign minister is giving a speech to the United Nations and he can spare us a few minutes tonight. It could mean the difference between getting permission to tape in Russia or winding up with egg on our faces."

"Oh, Sky." Cheri sat down on one of the chairs. "I guess there's not much you can do about it, but Tad was so excited about today."

"Is he awake?"

"Not yet." She listened, but there were no sounds from overhead. "He was restless last night, and I hate to get him up."

"I'll be flying back on Monday. Tell him I'll call as soon as I get in and we'll set another date. I'm really sorry about this. I tried to get a flight out this afternoon, but with the time difference I'd be too late."

"He'll just have to understand. Disappointments are part of everybody's life." What else could she say? Cheri thought grimly.

"Take care of yourself. I've got to run." With a hurried goodbye he rang off.

Well, what did you expect, Cheryl Lewiston? she demanded silently as she switched the coffee maker to Low and poured herself a cup. *That's life in the fast lane for you.*

She baked blueberry muffins, Tad's favorite, as a peace offering, but she didn't feel very optimistic twenty minutes later as she heard him pad down the stairs in his Bert and Ernie slippers. The little face that poked through the door had dark circles under the eyes.

"What time is Uncle Sky coming?" he asked.

"He just called a little while ago." Cheri lifted the muffins out of the oven. "Look what we're having for breakfast!"

"What time is he coming?" the boy repeated as he slipped into his chair.

"I'm afraid there's been a change of plans." Cheri lifted the muffins out of their cups with a spatula. "He has to fly to New York to meet with the Soviet foreign minister. He'll be back on Monday and he promised to call you right away."

"He isn't coming?" Tad stared at her in disbelief.

"Not today. But we could go skating, you and I." Her voice sounded falsely cheerful in her own ears. "Oh, Tad, I know you're disappointed, but he'll take you skating next week."

Tad picked at the muffin she set in front of him. "It's too hot."

"Let me get some margarine. By the time it melts, it'll be perfect."

His small mouth settled into a pout. "Don't want any muffins."

"How about some cereal? And then we'll get dressed and go skating, okay?"

"No," Tad said. "I hate skating." He pushed away from the table, snatched the muffin as an afterthought and went thumping up the stairs. Cheri's stomach felt hollow as she watched him go.

When it came, the spurt of anger was directed at Sky. Why did he have to come into their lives right now? She was an adult; despite her old wounds, she could handle the letdown when Sky breezed past on his way to stardom. But Tad didn't need any more broken promises.

The boy slouched downstairs a while later, dressed in his grubbiest jeans, and closeted himself in the library. He ignored her suggestion of inviting Joey over and refused to come out for lunch, although she noticed that the blueberry muffins kept disappearing when she wasn't looking.

The weather didn't help any, either. After a sunny Friday, it had turned gloomy, with wisps of fog lingering past noon. Putting on a heavy sweater, Cheri forced herself to go outside and tend to her gardening. There was no point in both of them brooding in the house all day.

The garden looked different in the fog, she noticed as she knelt to dig weeds out of what had once been a flower bed. The climbing roses took on a dusty, ancient appearance, robbed of color and scent. Figures seemed to move through the overgrown bushes, a man and a woman, heads bent together, voices whispering like the chilly breeze that rustled through the waxy camellia leaves.

Cheri shivered. It didn't help to remember what Vinnie had said on Thursday about some kind of energy gathering at the house.

I don't believe in ghosts. This is ridiculous. But Sky himself had conceded that there were things science couldn't explain yet.

The chill of the day was penetrating even her thick sweater, and Cheri decided that gardening was a lost cause.

Standing up, she brushed the dirt off her jeans, put away her spade and went back into the house, grateful for the thick warm air that greeted her as soon as she entered. Thank goodness Jeff and Donna hadn't wasted any time getting the heating system updated.

A check of the library showed Tad fast asleep on a love seat, a comforter pulled around his shoulders. Maybe he'd just been tired this morning, Cheri told herself. He'd feel better after his nap.

Stopping briefly for another cup of coffee and the last muffin, she curled up on the living room sofa with the Calendar section from last Sunday's paper, which she'd put off reading. The articles on show business stirred up too many painful memories, but she and Elaine would be meeting to discuss plans and review tapes of actors Monday. In a business as trendy as the movies, you had to keep up to date.

Plodding through an article about the trials and tribulations of the latest massively over-budget film, Cheri felt her own eyelids begin to close. Sagging against the cushions, she let herself be carried into a dream.

It was a warm spring day in the garden. Bright red roses heavy with fragrance curled around a trellis, still damp with dew. From down the street came the rumble of a milk truck.

A man was sitting on the stone bench, staring into the distance. He had a stocky build and heavy glasses masked his eyes, but there was a sweetness to his expression that touched Cheri at once.

Then he saw her. Standing up, the man held out his hands. "Nora!"

She crossed the grass slowly. "I'm sorry I'm late. I was trying to be so quiet, not to wake Allie."

His arms enfolded her in a gentle but undemanding hug. "You're so good," the man whispered. "Nora, you must know why I asked you to meet me here today. I can't be satisfied any longer with seeing you once a week at choir. I know I don't earn much at the store, but at least I have a job, and they say two can live as cheaply as one.''

Nora held up her hand to stop him. ''Hank, I—I've given it a lot of thought. I love you, but I can't leave Allie. I'm all she has.''

''You could still see her every day. . . .''

''No.'' Nora smoothed her hands nervously over her narrow skirt. ''She'd wither away, turn in on herself, Hank. Those long nights, alone here at the house. She couldn't bear it. And I can't bear the thought of it. I promised her long ago that I'd never leave, and I can't go back on my word.''

There was infinite sadness in his eyes, blurred and over-large behind the thick lenses. ''You'll change your mind, my sweet Nora.''

''No.'' Her throat felt thick, ''I—I can't.''

His shoulders drooped, and in that moment he seemed to age right in front of her. ''I'll wait, Nora.''

''You deserve more than this.'' She was having trouble getting the words out. ''A wife, children. Bessie Brownlie has been in love with you for years, Hank. Maybe you . . .'' She couldn't finish.

''There'll never be anyone else for me,'' he said. ''I've got to go now. Mr. Jarvis hates for us to be late.''

As he walked away, her heart ached for them both. But mostly for herself. Because, Nora knew. Hank would marry. He might not love Bessie, but he would love their children.

A woman's voice floated out through the fresh air. ''Nora? Where are you?''

She turned heavily to go back into the house.

Cheri awakened with a start, as if she'd heard some noise, but there was nothing.

Was that real? she wondered as the dream came back to her. Did Nora really turn down the chance to marry out of loyalty?

Sitting up and stretching, Cheri tried to tell herself it was just her own imagining. A reflection of her own low spirits about Sky's unexpected departure.

Well, there was no sense in dwelling on it. A check of her watch showed it was past noon. Time to fix lunch, whether Tad wanted to eat it or not.

She had a feeling this weekend was going to pass very, very slowly.

"NOT BAD." Elaine rewound the videotape of the young actress. "What did you think?"

"For the younger daughter? Yes, I'd like to call her in for an audition." Cheri watched as her friend reached for another tape. "My mind is beginning to glaze over."

They'd been watching tapes of actors for the past three hours, weeding through the casting director's suggestions. It felt strange to be on the other side of moviemaking for a change, watching actors instead of waiting nervously to find out if she'd be offered a part.

Not that Cheri had had to audition very often. She'd been successful enough to be handed quite a few roles, usually by TV producers who knew she was popular with viewers. It had left her feeling like a well-known brand of cereal.

"It's hard to tell about the chemistry. I'll have her read with some of the others," Elaine said. "I'll call you when we've set it up."

Cheri hesitated. "You're not planning to lure me into co-producing, are you?"

"Of course I am."

"Elaine, you know I don't want to get that involved." Cheri cut off the flow of words; no point in going over old ground again. "And I think you should go ahead and cast Belle without my approval. I can't seem to be objective about it."

They'd reviewed a dozen actresses and rejected all of them. Guiltily, Cheri wondered if they were being fair.

"Hold on." Turning up the lights, Elaine plunked her feet on her desk and took a bite out of a Twinkie. The lean, modern office with its view over Century City had amassed a cluttered look as the day progressed. Half-filled paper coffee cups, the remains of a deli lunch brought in by Elaine's secretary, and ragged stacks of résumés and composite photographs littered every available surface.

"Let's not go into this, okay?"

Elaine tossed the plastic Twinkie package toward the wastebasket and missed, which didn't seem to bother her. "It's only been five months since your brother died, Cheri. *Bonjour, Bel Air*—" that was the film's latest title "—doesn't go before the cameras until May. Did it ever occur to you that you might change your mind between now and then?"

"You sound like Sky." Why did everyone else think they knew Cheri better than she knew herself? she wondered irritably. "Oh, no, is that rain?"

Elaine swung around to stare out the window. "That does look like more than a twenty percent chance of showers," she grunted, acknowledging temporary defeat. "All right. You'd better head home; the freeways will be a mess."

"Bye." Cheri brushed a kiss against her friend's cheek and headed for the elevator.

It didn't help, as she retrieved her car from the parking garage and headed into the downpour, to remind herself that Sky would be coming home today. The gray weekend had cast what felt like a permanent pall over Cheri's spirits. Tad's moodiness had abated only by degrees, and the house still echoed with Nora's broken heart.

The one thing she hadn't expected from ghosts, if they really did exist, was a lot of emotional baggage.

IT WAS FOUR-THIRTY when she got home, and the house was dark. Even before she turned on the light and called Tad's name, Cheri knew he wasn't there.

But the house didn't feel empty.

As she walked from room to room, calling and looking for signs that at least he'd dropped by after school, Cheri felt as if she were pushing through invisible spectators, hearing voices mutter around her as the rain thrust against the windows.

Tad's lunch box lay on the kitchen table. Well, that was a good sign, anyway. He must be over at Kate's.

But it felt so cold in here. Cheri went into the hall to check the thermostat, but it was set at a solid seventy-two degrees.

Someone's walking on my grave.

Now where had she heard that phrase before? Probably in an old movie, Cheri told herself firmly as she went upstairs to change out of her suit into something more comfortable.

She stopped in the doorway of her room.

Allie Granger's white dress lay crumpled in one corner, although Cheri had left it hanging neatly in the closet. The letters were scattered around the floor, and Allie's diary hung precariously over the edge of Cheri's dressing table. The thin half-light filtering through the window gave the scene an eerie, threatening air.

She reached for the light switch. Nothing happened. *Not another blackout.* But, turning, Cheri saw that the lights were still on downstairs.

Unwilling to acknowledge the thudding tightness in her chest, she strode over to the dressing table and turned on the makeup lights.

They didn't work, either.

Was it possible for part of the house's electricity to go out? She supposed it could be a blown fuse. But, that wouldn't account for the mess in her room.

A flash of lightning, followed by a sharp clap of thunder, made her jump. Still, Cheri had no intention of racing out of here in a panic the way she had the day she met Sky.

There really is something funny about this house.

She heard something creak upstairs in the attic. Like the lid of a chest opening slowly.

Maybe there was someone else in the house. Or could it be Tad, playing a grisly joke on her?

Cheri picked up the new flashlight from her dresser drawer and walked down the hall. It seemed longer than she remembered, and very dark by now, a darkness the beam of light barely penetrated.

At the steps to the attic, she called Tad's name again, but didn't really expect an answer.

I must be crazy, going up here. But it's my house and I'm not going to cower downstairs.

The lights didn't work in the attic, either. Cheri crisscrossed the open space with the flashlight beam, unable to force herself to step past the head of the stairs.

One of the trunks was open. She was almost certain she'd left it locked, although it was always possible Tad had found the key in her bedroom. At least the contents appeared to be undisturbed.

Suddenly the beam hit something shiny, a cloud that swayed in a draft. Cheri couldn't move, until she realized it must be one of the fake spiderwebs Kate's crew had created up here. Training the light on it, she let her breath out with a whoosh of relief. Nothing but a Halloween trick.

Something ice-cold blew over the back of her neck.

She'd never believed it when she'd read of people's hair standing on end, but now every inch of her skin prickled, every hair follicle tensed. *Someone's up here with me. But not someone living and breathing.*

With all her strength, she forced herself to turn and examine the area behind and above her. Nothing, and no one.

No crevices in the wall, no cracks in the ceiling. No fan rigged up by a mischievous seven-year-old.

The wind intensified outside, making the house creak like old bones. Tree branches tapped against the roof like ancient voices. *Go away. Go away. Go away.*

Swallowing hard, Cheri backed down a couple of steps, then turned and fled all the way down to the kitchen.

Its bright lights made her feel a little better, and the smell of this morning's pancakes lingered in the air. Trying without success to smile at her panic of a few minutes ago, Cheri dialed Kate's number.

"Hi," she said when her friend answered. "Is Tad over there?"

"Why, no," Kate said. "Isn't he with you?"

"I was later getting home than I expected." Cheri was beginning to get angry with herself for letting the meeting with Elaine go on so long. She had responsibilities, and Tad was too young to be left alone, even in the middle of the afternoon. This once, she had let her adult interests come first, and look what had happened....

"Do you suppose he's at the library?" she said.

"I'll check." Kate, as usual, wasted no time on wild speculation. "Why don't you call Magic Arcade and see if he's there? Maybe he went with some other kids from school."

"Okay. You're probably right."

But a hurried round of phone calls failed to turn up any sightings of a boy matching her nephew's description.

Tad was gone. Cheri leaned against the counter and fought back the tears. She couldn't give in to emotion now. Somehow she had to find him.

Chapter Thirteen

A few minutes ago in the attic Cheri had thought she knew what fear was, but it was nothing compared to what she felt now. Images flashed through her mind of Tad lying injured in the street, being kidnapped by a shadowy figure, or running away to the grimy back streets of Hollywood.

She shook her head angrily. This was no time to panic. She had to form a plan.

The first step was to call the police. Before, she'd been afraid of publicity; now it no longer seemed to matter.

Her call was forwarded to a detective in Juveniles. "How long has he been missing?" he asked.

Cheri looked at the clock. It was almost five, and Tad got out of school about three. "Two hours," she said.

"Has he ever run away before?"

"No, of course not!" she snapped. "I'm sorry. I know you're just doing your job, but I'm so worried."

The detective questioned her further about Tad's habits and about any signs of foul play, then said, "I'll let our officers know about this so they can keep an eye out for him, but I'd suggest you wait until later tonight to file a missing person report. He'll probably turn up."

"Yes, I'm sure you're right," Cheri said before ringing off.

She had no intention of sitting here and waiting meekly. Clearly, Tad had come home on the bus after school and then gone out again. She would just have to make a list of possible destinations and start checking.

The sound of a car stopping outside made Cheri's heart leap into her throat. She raced for the door, hoping against hope to see Tad's small figure ambling up the walkway.

Sky was getting out of his BMW. Alone. "Kate called," he said as he started toward her. "Any word yet?"

She shook her head mutely, so glad to see Sky that she was momentarily at a loss for words. Tad's disappearance no longer felt quite so overwhelming. With his London Fog overcoat and sturdy black umbrella, Sky looked as if he could solve any problem.

Inside the hallway, they reviewed her actions so far, and then he said, "Any place nearby that he might have gone?"

"Not that I can think of." Cheri stared glumly out at the rain. "There's a bus stop two blocks away. He could have gone anywhere."

Sky frowned, staring toward the bus stop. "He could have headed for The City shopping center or the Mall of Orange. I'll check The City, you check the mall, and let's meet back here in an hour."

She would have felt better if they could search together, but Sky's plan made sense. "I'll leave him a note, in case he comes back before we do."

The next hour passed in a nightmarish blur. The sky was eerily dark, the rain gusty and uneven. Even the usually cheerful mall felt depressed and almost empty, the few shoppers wet and silent. Cheri checked out the restaurants and the toy departments, even got permission to look through the movie theaters, but there was no sign of him.

He wouldn't really have run away, would he? And where could he have gone? Tad might have saved some money out of his allowance, but it wouldn't last long. On the other hand, a seven-year-old probably wouldn't think of that.

She got home before Sky. After snapping on two switches she found in the wrong position in the fuse box, she went up to check Tad's room. It was a small comfort, at least, to see that none of his clothes were missing and that Buster was perched atop the bed, as usual.

There was hot coffee waiting by the time Sky arrived. "Sorry I'm late," he muttered wearily as he snapped his umbrella shut, and Cheri remembered that he must have had a long flight from New York today. "I forgot about Main Place. I went by there, but no luck. Any other ideas?"

The only message on the phone machine had been from Kate, asking if Tad had turned up yet, and Cheri's mind was blunted with anxiety. "He hasn't mentioned any favorite places he used to go with his parents except the pizza parlor, and I swung by there on my way back," she said.

"Tell me what's been going on since I left. What might have made him run away? Was he that upset about my canceling our plans?" Sky poured out a cup of coffee and then, without waiting for an answer, he blurted, "The skating rink!"

A minute later, the coffee left untouched on the counter, they were on their way in the BMW.

Cheri had never been there before, but Sky easily found his way to the Holiday Skate Center, just a block off the freeway. It was a one-story cement building with a red tile roof and a two-thirds-filled parking lot. Apparently a lot of people were looking for a way to have fun and stay dry.

"We're looking for my nephew," Cheri told the ticket seller, and he waved them inside. She blinked in the dim light, momentarily disoriented by the booming rock music and the shouts of children racing back and forth, lacing up skates, demanding food, challenging each other to races.

A check of the large, wooden-floored rink showed no one who resembled Tad. Cheri checked out the low benches around her.

"There." Sky's voice was heavy with relief.

A small, thin figure huddled on a bench near the snack bar. Tad seemed lost inside his jacket, his eyes fixed on the youngsters scooting their way around the rink.

"Tad!" She hurried toward him, dodging kids and piles of shoes and raincoats. "Oh, God, I've been so worried!"

A forlorn face turned toward her. Tad's arms came up to catch her, and he burst into tears as Cheri hugged him close. "I'm sorry." His voice cracked. "I didn't mean to make you worry."

Sky's arms encircled them both. "Thank goodness you're safe."

"I just—I got scared." Drawing back a little, Tad peered up at Cheri. "The house—I mean, it didn't feel safe."

Sky squatted down to face him. "It's a big house, and gloomy in the rain, is that it?"

"Well..." Tad checked Cheri's reaction. "I mean, I've been hearing...well..."

Guilt flushed through her. She'd been trying so hard to help him overcome his fears, and all the time she'd been going about it the wrong way. He needed to talk about his feelings, not pretend they didn't exist. "It's all right, Tad. Was it the ghosts?"

He nodded gratefully. "I kept hearing them at night, Aunt Cheri. And then today, they didn't want me there. They told me to go away."

She could still hear the wind hissing angrily at her this afternoon. "I think I know what you mean. Tad, did you go into my room?"

Pinpricks of pink showed in his cheeks, feverish against the pale skin. "I'm sorry, Aunt Cheri. They made me. Those ghosts, they—forced me."

"It's okay," she said softly. It was probably healthy for Tad to vent his anger against her for taking his parents' place. Even the mess in her room was better than the silent withdrawal of this past weekend.

"Hungry?" Sky asked.

"I had half a hamburger. This little girl didn't want it," Tad said. "Can we go skating?"

"Sure. Cheri?"

"I'll watch." She smiled for the first time in hours. "I'm a terrible klutz on wheels."

Sky went out and paid for another ticket, then came in and picked out two pairs of skates. He helped Tad into his, and they went onto the floor together.

Cheri called to notify the police that Tad had been found. Her body still felt tight, her heartrate accelerated. Gradually the realization seeped through her that Tad was safe. The tension faded from her muscles, leaving her weak but contented.

When she sat down to watch them, the tall man and the delicate boy were whizzing in a circle, Tad's legs pumping to keep up with Sky. They shouted at each other and laughed as the music and the other skaters swirled around them.

If it weren't for Sky, would I ever have thought of coming here? Cheri shuddered. She supposed eventually Tad would have called home, but she didn't like to think about waiting alone all evening in that house.

For the first time, she considered what it would be like to go back there tonight. For all its history and peculiarities, the Granger house had never really frightened her before. She supposed it was partly because of the weather, and also because of Tad's absence. But what if there was more to it than that?

Maybe it was irrelevant, the question of whether the house really was haunted. On the other hand, as long as Tad thought it was, he would continue to have nightmares. They couldn't go on living in a house full of ghosts, even if the ghosts were the distorted memories of Jeff and Donna.

Half an hour later, Sky and Tad clumped back toward her, both of them breathing heavily, their eyes shining.

"Why don't we go out for pizza?" Cheri said.

"Really?" Tad plopped down on the floor and began pulling off his skates. "Honest, Aunt Cheri? You mean we get to eat junk food like real people?"

At Sky's quizzical look, she admitted, "I guess I've overdone the dedicated mother bit. I've always felt like I should cook nutritious meals and... Oh, heck, yes, let's act like real people, Tad."

She waited until their pizza had been ordered and they were seated at a booth before she said, "Tad, would you like us to have Vinnie go through the house and find out if there are any ghosts?"

The look of sheer relief on his face twisted her heart. "Oh, Aunt Cheri, could we?"

Cheri looked at Sky. "I suppose we might as well tape it, if we're going to do it at all."

"It's not necessary." His gray eyes were solemn. "Not that the showman in me wouldn't love it, but Tad's well-being is the most important thing."

"Those ghosts would really be scared off if we had cameras, right?" Tad demanded.

"I'm sure they would." Cheri clenched her hands together in her lap, trying to picture the bright lights and camera crew tramping through her house. Instead of alarming her, the image was strangely comforting. Until she remembered something else. "Sky, Vinnie said she felt some reluctance to visit the house, as if there was something in it that concerned her personally."

The counter clerk called their number. "I'd prefer to work with her—she's the best there is. But if not, there are other psychics I've used in the past," Sky said, and went to get the pizza.

Not until they were safely home, the house brightly lighted and a fire laid in the fireplace, did Sky take the time to call Vinnie.

He came back a minute later. "I had to leave a message on her machine. I told her to call here. I'm sleeping on the sofa, Tad. So if you have any bad dreams, you just call Aunt Cheri and me and we'll come running."

"We'll teach those ghosts a lesson," Tad said with all the confidence of a child putting his trust in a superhero, and then dragged Sky off to battle the dragons in his computer.

VINNIE PULLED into her carport and gathered the blank forms from the meeting. She still wasn't sure why she'd gone.

The rain had eased off, and she dashed into the apartment without opening her umbrella. The wind left her hair rumpled, but at least the forms hadn't gotten wet. Of course, she didn't intend to fill them out, so it wasn't as if it mattered.

As she turned on the lights, Vinnie noticed that there was a message on her machine. Well, she'd get to it in a minute.

In the bedroom, taking off her coat, she paused to study the half-finished painting she'd left on an easel by the window. It was an attempt to render her own impressionistic version of a photograph that had caught her eye in the *Los Angeles Times*, a portrait of a small girl digging on the beach.

The child in her painting looked out of focus, not impressionistic but merely blurry. *I can't really see her. I can hardly see children at all*.

Which was why it was absurd even to consider applying to become a foster parent.

Vinnie had read the article in the newspaper last week, about the desperate shortage of foster parents. What had particularly caught her eye was that single parents were quite acceptable; in fact, that some young girls who'd been abused might feel safest in a household headed by a woman.

It didn't seem fair that she'd been unable to have the children she desperately wanted, and that other people produced them carelessly and then neglected or hurt them. *But whoever said life was fair?*

Comfortably changed into a quilted housedress, she walked over to the phone machine and played the message.

Hi, Vinnie, it's Sky. I won't go into the details, but for Tad's sake, Cheri feels we ought to do a show on the Granger house. I'd like to set it up as soon as it's convenient. I'll be at Cheri's tonight.

He had left the number.

Oh, no. I'm not ready for this.

Vinnie folded herself onto the sofa and messaged her temples. She'd been trying not to think about the Granger house these past few days since Thanksgiving, about Cheri's invitation to visit. But now she was going to have to reach a decision.

She'd never turned Sky down before, except once when her aunt was hospitalized. What would he think if she leveled with him? And did she really want to go on running away from whatever it was about the house that frightened her?

Frightened? Vinnie had never put it quite that bluntly to herself before. Was it possible she was physically afraid, or was it something else she felt?

Closing her eyes, Vinnie visualized the front of the house as it had looked when she drove past it a few days before. She'd noticed immediately that the bushes had been trimmed and smoke was coming out of the chimney, giving it a cozy air.

But that house had never truly been cozy.

Vinnie had been aware of the place all her life. Driving by with her parents when she was about ten, she remembered seeing a woman carrying groceries in through the front door. At the time, the woman had seemed quite old to Vinnie, but now she realized the shopper—Allie's companion, it must have been—had probably been in her mid-forties, half a dozen years younger than Vinnie was now.

But she's not the one who scares me.

Who, then? Allie herself? Vinnie didn't think so. *No.* There were other presences in that house. Perhaps the legendary Jane Dotson? Or—who?

There was only one way to find out.

All these years, Vinnie had felt as if her unwanted psychic insights were leading her along a hidden path, to a destination she couldn't foresee. Now she was about to turn a corner; what lay beyond, she had no idea.

One thing was clear: she had to keep on traveling, or be stuck on this wild and uncharted path, forever retracing her footsteps.

With a deep, quavering breath, Vinnie went to dial the number at the Granger house.

Chapter Fourteen

Hard to believe it was going to be Christmas in a few weeks, Sky reflected as he turned a corner a few blocks from Cheri's house.

The colored lights on several homes had been left on to prick the morning's gloom. Instead of providing cheer, however, they seemed to intensify the glowering storminess of the morning.

Dark winter days were relatively rare in Southern California, but when they descended, they were somehow bleaker than back in England or in New York, where they might be softened by rain or snow. Under lowering clouds, the palm trees took on a ragged, forlorn air and pedestrians, unaccustomed to cold weather, huddled grumpily inside their ill-fitting coats.

It was less than a week since Tad had run away to the skating rink. Once Vinnie agreed to do the taping, Sky had geared up his staff, making sure they had extra cameras. This was one show that couldn't be reshot if anything fouled up.

He'd spent most evenings with Cheri and slept on the sofa for the first few nights, until it became clear that Tad was doing fine. It was inconvenient, having to rush home in the mornings to get ready for work, and Sky didn't want to suggest moving in, because Tad might get the wrong idea.

He wasn't even sure Cheri would want him to.

Not that she hadn't been grateful for his help with Tad, and responsive when they'd made love after Tad was asleep. But there was a part of her that she kept in reserve, and he couldn't blame her.

Cheri was a complex woman. Right now, she was coping well with the knowledge that soon he would be gone for an extended period. But she was neither naive nor self-confident enough to love him freely, knowing that circumstances and their own inner drives might destroy the relationship that was building between them.

Sky almost hoped he was wrong about the inevitability of Cheri's returning to movies. It would make life a lot easier if she were free to adjust her schedule to his, even to move to another city if necessary. But he couldn't picture her tagging docilely along in his life forever.

Arriving in front of Cheri's house, Sky was half annoyed and half relieved to see that the equipment truck was already there and that his staff was busy setting up. He'd hoped to beat them by at least a few minutes, to have the time alone with Cheri.

Entering through the wide-open front door, he found her in the kitchen. The air smelled of fresh coffee, and a double-dozen box of doughnuts already showed gaps in its ranks.

"Everything okay?" he asked.

Cheri nodded. "Just fine. Tad's really excited. He's running back and forth like a maniac."

"Is Vinnie here?" He'd sensed a reluctance in the psychic's voice when she called to confirm, but she hadn't been willing to discuss it. Vinnie was a private person in many ways.

"No," Cheri said. "She called to say she's on her way."

"Sky? Miss Louette's needed for makeup." It was the assistant director, clipboard in hand. Cheri and Tad were whisked away and Sky went in to watch the crew installing light and sound equipment in the living room.

Vinnie arrived just in time to have her own makeup applied. Her eyes showed traces of red, as if she hadn't slept well, but her manner was as crisply efficient as ever.

Sky wished he'd spent more time this week probing into her concerns. Like most psychics he'd met, Vinnie lived close to volcanic emotions, yet she was remarkably stable. Maybe he took it too much for granted that she could cope with anything. Still, why should the Granger house be different for her than any other place they'd visited?

At last the lights were adjusted and the cameras positioned. Furniture had been shifted and dirt tracked into the hallway, but he'd arranged for a cleaning crew to take care of that later. What disturbed him was that the atmosphere of the place had changed. The high-tech equipment seemed to dominate the living room; he was used to that effect when taping his show, but not in the Granger house.

What did you expect? That everything would be different with this show, simply because this house and the people in it mean so much to you?

He ought to feel elated. Appleby had been overjoyed at the prospect of a program featuring Cheri Louette. It was, after all, the reason Sky had come to this house in the first place.

But it wasn't the reason he was here now. He almost wished he'd refused to tape today's events, except that Vinnie might not have agreed to participate otherwise. Tad had loved the idea, and even Cheri seemed resigned to it.

Uneasy, Sky reviewed the notes he'd prepared. Later, when the light was better, the crew would shoot the exterior, and he could narrate his introduction then. But even though the script couldn't be finalized yet, having notes gave him a sense of being in control. Right now he needed that.

The director, Shannon Brewer, signaled that she was ready. Cheri and Tad sat on the sofa; Sky took a chair nearby. Vinnie remained off camera, watching with her eyes half-closed, already isolating herself.

"Cheri, Tad, welcome to *Sky's the Limit*." He felt oddly out of sync as the taping began. There was no time on television for the pauses, offhand remarks, irrelevancies that studded normal conversation. "Cheri, would you describe for us some of the things that have happened since you moved into the Granger house?"

"Tad's the one who has the strongest feelings about it." He could see that Cheri knew out of long habit how to turn toward the camera, how to position herself to advantage, and yet she had a preoccupied air as if her thoughts were far away. "I've had some strange dreams and heard odd noises in the night, nothing spectacular."

"Tell us about the voices you thought you heard in the attic last week. And you've felt odd drafts of air several times?"

Gradually warming to the subject, she answered his questions in detail. *Yes,* she said, she'd often felt as if someone were watching her. *And yes,* the diary had fallen open to just the right place, and she'd dreamed about Nora even before she knew that someone by that name had lived here.

He noticed particularly that when she talked about Allie Granger, Cheri sounded protective, almost defensive. Would the viewers pick that up? What would they think of it? He'd never been concerned before about how his subjects came across, as long as it didn't appear that he'd chosen nuts and crazies. Cheri was different. If this program hurt her public image, he'd never forgive himself.

Tad was much more eager to persuade the viewers that what he'd experienced was real. Sky suspected he even em-

broidered a bit as he told about the man and woman arguing in the night, about how he'd been "forced" to sneak
back on Halloween and toss the coats around, and to mess
up his aunt's room the week before.

When he was finished, they took a break. Shannon
wanted Cheri to elaborate on a few points and, as he reviewed what had been said, Sky came up with a few more
questions of his own. By the time they had finished taping
the additional material, it was almost noon.

All the time, Vinnie sat by herself, not visibly reacting to
any of the comments. Sky knew better than to interrupt her
thoughts. It looked to him as if she was picking up some
strong impressions already.

A gofer arrived with sandwiches and soft drinks. Tad
beamed excitedly as they ate, wandering around to ask
questions of the camera operators and the sound and
lighting engineers.

"How do you feel?" Sky asked Cheri as they sat in the
kitchen, a little away from the others.

"Funny. Like I'm not quite myself," she admitted. "Like
I'm reading from a script, only it's about my own life."

"Look, I didn't mean to pressure you into this." Sky
wanted to be sure she understood. "Especially since I'll
probably be out of town when it airs. I'd rather be here in
case you need me to fend off all the reporters, but Miles
wants to run it during the sweeps, and I'll be in Chicago at
the independent station owners' convention."

"And then you'll be going to Russia," she said softly.

He wished all these other people would disappear. There
was so much resignation in Cheri's voice, and he didn't like
it. *I'm going to fight to make this work. You have to believe in us, too.*

He needed to take her into his arms, to kiss her and reassure her. When they were making love, everything else
faded away and time seemed to stretch on forever. Having
his crew around made him feel rushed and awkward.

He wanted to tell her he loved her. But did he have the right to do that yet? He didn't want to strip away all her defenses, all her reserve. So much of the future was still a question mark—how his absences would affect their feelings for each other, when and under what circumstances she would be ready to act again, even how Tad adjusted or failed to adjust to his new life.

If things didn't work out, he couldn't blame her for wanting to minimize her hurt. If such a thing were possible.

She finished her sandwich and stood up. "I'll make some more coffee."

"We have a gofer to do that."

Cheri waved the offer away. "It's still my kitchen."

She felt better, bustling around, having something to do with her hands. It wasn't Sky's fault that she'd felt so uncomfortable on camera. *I chose to do this. But maybe it was a mistake.*

The sequence of events that had made her uncomfortable about this house sounded almost ridiculous when put into words. If she were in the audience, she knew she'd be skeptical about such subjective reactions—feeling as if she were being watched, having realistic dreams, finding the diary "mysteriously" opened to a significant passage.

Some critic is going to say I'm just trying to shore up my career, to boost myself by pretending to believe in a lot of hocus-pocus. I'm going to look like a fool.

Then her eye fell on Tad, earnestly showing the old blue china marble to one of the crew members. He loved every minute of this. It could be a healing experience. If so, it was worth it.

She didn't have to prove to anyone, whether in the media or in her personal life, that her motives were unselfish. Because deep inside, she knew what mattered. *To hell with everything else.*

The corners of Cheri's mouth tugged upward into a smile as she refilled the sugar bowl and creamer. *I'm getting ornery in my old age.*

It was time to tape some more. Cheri was grateful that Tad wouldn't have to be on camera during Vinnie's segment. She and Sky both felt that the boy's reactions should be kept private, particularly if it turned out he really had heard something involving his parents.

A lump formed in Cheri's throat. She hadn't been willing even to think about it before now. But what if Jeff and Donna had come back? What if they, too, resented her?

That was nonsense. She'd loved them, and they'd loved her. But right now anything seemed possible.

As she, Vinnie and Sky took their places in the living room and the crew quieted, Cheri heard the wind pick up outside the house. Branches rustled against an upstairs window, and a soft sighing seemed to drift down the chimney. As if the place itself were waiting tensely.

She focused on Vinnie, steadying herself by concentrating on the woman's strong features. At that moment, all Cheri's skepticism about psychics and ghosts vanished. Maybe later it would come back, but for now she urgently wanted to know what Vinnie was going to say.

"Vinnie?" Sky asked as the taping began. "Are you picking up anything?"

She nodded and lowered her head. Her body swayed almost imperceptibly. "Someone is coming through. I see a young girl, about eighteen. She wants to speak to us."

For a long moment Vinnie continued to rock slowly, her head down. When at last she raised her face, her eyes were teary and her mouth trembled; she looked as if she'd lost thirty years off her age, and the voice was young and desperate. "I'm sorry. I couldn't—I just couldn't bear it. Oh, God, I'm so tired of wandering around here. I want to go home."

"Jane?" Sky asked gently. "Is that Jane Dotson?"

The voice became Vinnie's again. "Yes, she's gone now." After a moment: "There's someone else here. A man. I think it must be Perry...."

Her eyes narrowed abruptly and Jane's father was speaking. "I heard her. Where's my daughter? Damn it, where is she?"

"Papa?" It seemed incredible that Vinnie could switch so quickly and so convincingly from one person to another. Of course, Cheri knew that some performers could do that, but she'd never seen any acting quite like this. "I'm here, Papa. Papa, what have you done?"

Cheri looked at Tad. His face had gone white. Darn it, camera or no camera, she was going to rush over there if he needed her. But no, Tad was signaling to her that he was okay.

He mouthed the words: "It's them."

Jane and Perry Dotson. That was who he'd dreamed of hearing.

"I've cursed them, Jane. The whole stinking lot of them. Their line will end with the next generation. They did this to us and they'll pay for it."

"Oh, Papa, no. It wasn't Charlie's fault; he really loved me. It was his brother who made him turn away from me. Charlie never loved Marcella. He's here now, Papa. Charlie's with me. I love him, Papa. Please forgive us."

"Jane. I just want my baby back." The hoarse voice broke. "Baby, Papa's here."

Tears pricked Cheri's eyes. Looking across the room, she saw that Tad was weeping openly. Oddly, he didn't look sad. Relieved; that was it. He looked as if a burden had been lifted from his small shoulders.

Vinnie spoke again, this time as herself. "You've wandered too long, you restless spirits. Go home now. Go beyond, to where you belong. Your time here on earth is finished."

As if in response, windows rattled sharply throughout the house. Cheri flinched, and she could see that the crew was startled, too. A tight wind howled around the eaves, and from the library she heard books thumping to the floor. When quiet returned, it was an intense silence unbroken even by the usual distant sounds of traffic.

Vinnie's whole body stiffened, but she wasn't looking at anything in the room. Sky reached out in alarm, touching her wrist, but Vinnie pulled away.

"It's all right," she said.

After a minute, the director called for a break.

"What's going on?" Sky moved onto the couch next to Vinnie. "What happened there at the end?"

"There's someone else here," she said.

"Save it!" Shannon called from the hallway. "Somebody get her some coffee."

When they resumed, Vinnie looked more relaxed but still not entirely at ease.

"Vinnie, tell us what happened while you were in your trance," Sky said.

"As legend has it, the Granger family was put under a curse by Perry Dotson." Except for a hint of strain, Vinnie seemed to have recovered her poise. "Perry and his daughter appear to be the voices Tad was hearing, arguing with each other. They're reconciled now, and Charlie's spirit is with Jane. Apparently he never stopped loving her."

"Anything else?" Sky watched her closely.

"There were many spirits in this house, some faint, some strong." Vinnie's hands moved restlessly in her lap. "Most of them were held here by the strong energy surrounding Jane and Perry—Charlie and Mack, and Charlie's two sons who died young."

"They're gone now?"

Vinnie hesitated, as if there was something she didn't want to say publicly.

Or doesn't want Tad to hear?

"I don't think there'll be any more trouble," she said finally.

The crew wasn't done for the day. They shot some tape in other rooms of the house, including the attic and the library, then went outside so Sky could narrate the opening, giving the background on the Granger family.

Tad tagged along at every step. Vinnie remained sitting in the living room.

When everyone else was out front, Cheri perched on an overstuffed chair. "Vinnie? Can you tell me who else is here?"

"Most of it you know." The older woman looked drained from the day's experiences. "Allie can't seem to go on, as if her decision to shut herself away extends even into death. And Nora won't leave her."

"Did Nora ever marry?" Cheri asked.

Vinnie studied her a moment before replying. "From what I've read about this house, and I did quite a bit of research this past week, there's no indication that she did."

"What will it take to set them free?"

"I don't know." Vinnie leaned back, resting her head as if her neck had suddenly grown too weak to support it. "Something needs to be resolved. I think Allie wishes she could go back and live her life again, do things differently. She needs to accept that what's past is past. But she's not a dangerous spirit, Cheri. And I don't think they'll disturb Tad."

"I don't think so, either." One part of Cheri's mind couldn't believe she was talking seriously about ghosts, as if they actually existed. With the other part of her mind, she wholeheartedly believed in them. "Vinnie, is there anyone else?"

The psychic started to shake her head, then shrugged. "Well, I did sense someone who—who strikes a strangely familiar chord with me. A woman about my age, a very unhappy and lonely woman. Not that I'm describing my-self, mind you.''

Aren't you? But it would be impolite to ask, of course. Instead, Cheri said, ''Allie's mother?''

''Oh, no. She was a flighty little thing.'' Vinnie reached for her coffee cup and sipped the last drops. ''I believe it's Marcella. The widow Charlie married and never loved.''

Until now, Cheri hadn't even thought about how that woman must have felt. ''Her sons both died young. And none of this was her fault.''

''It wasn't Allie's or Nora's, either,'' Vinnie pointed out. ''Well, Marcella may mope around a bit, but she won't hurt anyone.''

''I wish I could help her,'' Cheri said. ''But how could we make up to her for all those terrible things?''

''We can't.'' Vinnie stood up with more firmness than she'd shown all day. ''This isn't your problem, Cheri, and it isn't mine. What's done is done. That's the thing restless spirits have to come to terms with, and then they can leave us alone.''

''Thanks.'' Cheri walked her to the door. ''I know it was difficult, what you did today. But you've helped Tad a lot.''

''Good.'' Vinnie shook hands with her. ''It's odd, but I have a feeling that we might have been related in some for-mer life.''

Cheri didn't believe in former lives, but she didn't want to say so. ''It's nice to think we were.''

The crew tramped around some more, and finally the cleaning team came in and put everything to rights. Well, to Cheri's expert eye, a number of items were in the wrong place, and would have to be rearranged in the morning. But she didn't mind that.

''Glad it's over?'' Sky put his arms around her as soon as everyone else was gone.

Cheri pulled back instinctively nodding toward Tad. ''I think so. Tad, what do you think?''

"It was fun!" He hopped up and down. "Can we do that again? Maybe I could make up something about a monster. What do you think, Sky?"

Sky pretended to consider it seriously. "I think it might make people wonder if you'd really told the truth the first time. Maybe we should leave well enough alone."

"Okay." Tad shrugged. "It might juice up your show some. Can we go out for hamburgers?"

"Sure." They'd had fast food twice in the last week, and Cheri was afraid they might be overdoing it, but she certainly didn't feel like cooking tonight.

Tad continued to chatter happily about the day's events until bedtime. Then he pulled the covers up to his nose and listened intently as Cheri read a chapter from *The Shy Stegosaurus of Cricket Creek.*

"Do you think there might be dinosaurs hiding in the backyard?" he asked when she was done. "I mean, some of those bushes have been growing for years."

"What do you think?" Sky asked from the far side of the bed.

"I guess it's just my 'magination," Tad admitted reluctantly. "But I didn't make it up about those ghosts. I really thought they might be Mom and Dad."

"Jeff and Donna are at peace." The words sounded too stiff to Cheri, so she added quickly, "I'm sure they miss you a lot. But they know I'm here to take care of you."

"Yeah." Tad yawned. "Can I have a hug?"

Cheri and Sky both hugged him, then turned out the lights and walked quietly downstairs.

"I think he'll be okay now," Sky said as Cheri poured them small glasses of Amaretto. "He seems—I don't know—more open, more sure of himself."

"It's the first time he's asked me for a hug." She led the way into the living room, glad for the heat of the fire that Sky soon had blazing. Outside, the brief afternoon sunshine had long ago faded into a chilly darkness, but at least the wind had died down, too. "Do you believe what Vinnie experienced was real?"

"Do you?"

"More than I would have expected." She curled up on the sofa, and he sat beside her. "Sky, thank you. You've helped us more than I'd anticipated."

"You don't expect much from me, do you?"

"What?" She turned toward him, surprised at the angry note in his voice.

"You're so busy protecting yourself, from me and from anything else that might hurt you, that you can't see how much you're missing. All right, I can't make any promises of eternal happiness, but that doesn't make me callous like Terence Omara."

"I didn't mean—" But hadn't she, in a way? "Oh, Sky, I'm sorry. This past year has been hard on me, and I just can't seem to let go of it." She fell silent. This was the only time they had, these few weeks before Christmas, and it wasn't going to be enough.

He seemed to sense it, too. "I didn't mean I was giving up on you, Cheri. Let's try to enjoy the moment. I'm not very good at that, either. Always thinking ahead, planning, forgetting about the present. Between now and Christmas is our time. All right?"

"Yes," she said softly, and rested her head against his shoulder. His arms came around her, and tenderly they moved from gentle kisses to fiery lovemaking.

Afterward, lying beside him under the comforter, she thought about their conversation. Neither of them was ready to make promises for the future. Maybe there wouldn't be a future.

But he was right about the present. She intended to enjoy every tiny little bit of it.

Chapter Fifteen

Where the children had come from, Vinnie didn't know. She didn't remember giving birth to them, but there they were, two little boys playing in the attic of the Granger house, and somehow she knew she was their mother.

One of them had a mop of blond hair that kept falling across his eyes; whenever it did, he would push it fiercely away. The younger boy had brown hair and a sweet expression, except when his brother tried to snatch away his favorite blue marble.

This must be a dream. I'm Marcella. But if it's a dream, how come I'm thinking about it?

A man's footsteps passed by in the hall. Perversely she hoped it was her brother-in-law, even though she'd never particularly liked Mack and especially didn't like having to live in such close quarters with him and his wife.

At least Mack was strong. Charlie was so weak. She'd mistaken it for gentleness when she married him; now she knew that he was incapable of strong emotion or decisive action. If he were, he would have done them both a favor and married that poor girl who'd killed herself.

But then she wouldn't have had the children. And without them, Marcella knew, her life wouldn't be worth living.

She didn't regret anything, not the decision to marry Charlie, not even staying with him after she'd realized how little he cared for her. He'd gone out and gotten drunk both times when she was in labor; there'd been no one there to hold her hand except the nurse. But she'd pulled through. She would pull through this whole life, as long as she had her boys.

The dream faded, but when Vinnie awoke the next morning, it remained painfully clear in her memory. She didn't like remembering her dreams; they always upset her. And especially last night's. Marcella had died decades ago. She had no business coming back now and disturbing Vinnie's rest.

Irritable, Vinnie shuffled into the kitchen of her apartment and began to fix breakfast. Why hadn't she noticed before how small this place was? Or maybe the trouble was all the junk she'd been accumulating over the years, the books and paintings, the souvenirs of her trips. One of these days she was going to make a clean sweep.

Her eye fell on the application to become a foster parent. Her instinct was to throw it into the trash, but a more conservative side of her intervened. The form was very thick, and had been printed at some expense by the county. The least she could do was to return it.

Very well. One of these days she'd send it back.

She sat down and sipped her coffee. Instant. It didn't taste nearly as good as the stuff Cheri brewed. Some people seemed to have a knack for domesticity. Vinnie never had.

It wasn't unusual for her to dream about things that had happened the day before, so why was she feeling so uneasy?

Naturally, after that draining session at the Granger house, she'd needed to work out some of her impressions in her sleep. It was a logical explanation, but she wasn't convinced.

Why had the dream focused on the children when they were young and healthy? All she'd seen of Marcella yesterday was a grieving old woman. Not really old, of course; middle-aged, but back then women aged faster than they did now.

Was this what she'd sensed all along, the dangerous link between herself and the Granger house? Somehow she and Marcella were tied together by their mutual bitterness, by the ultimate emptiness of their lives.

Annoyed at her own self-pity, Vinnie stuck a piece of rye bread into the toaster oven. She had a fuller, busier life than many women she knew. Lots of people were widowed before they reached fifty, and plenty of them didn't have children, either.

But there was a difference where Vinnie was concerned, even though she didn't like to face it.

Unfinished business. Unresolved issues left from the past to intrude into the future. That was why spirits hung around after they were supposed to pass beyond. That was why she was still rattling around this apartment that she'd outgrown, daubing futilely at canvases that never looked the way she intended.

There was something she needed to come to terms with. Something related to the goings-on in the Granger house.

A radio in the next apartment began playing Christmas music. Snow and sleigh bells, a lonely birth in a stable, bright stars in the night. All the sharply painful hope of a new world just starting out.

I wish I were young again. I wish I could start over.

Vinnie pulled the toast out before it was done and smeared it impatiently with margarine and jam. Crunch. Sweet and salty. All the flavors were still there, but she was tired of them.

She rested her chin against the palm of her hand and stared out the window at the apartments that faced hers and the palm trees feathering the sky behind them. *Time for a change. But what?*

She'd have to give it some thought.

"HE'LL LOVE THE BIKE," Cheri admitted as Sky hoisted the shiny blue bicycle into the trunk of his car. "I'm glad I let you talk me into it."

"I wish you'd let me pay for it," he grumbled, then smiled. "Oh, hell, I know I'm being selfish. All other gifts will pale before this one."

"Next to a set of antique car models?" As Sky well knew, Tad had become fascinated with the era of the Granger house's early days. But Cheri had to add honestly, "I guess you're right. The thing is, the bike's kind of symbolic. I've been trying to shut him away with me, keep him wrapped up tight like a baby in swaddling. The bike is, well, a little bit of freedom."

"You're one heck of a good mother, you know that?" Sky opened the car door against the crisp December breeze.

"I'm learning." His compliment felt good, and Cheri was pleased to realize that it was true. She no longer felt the need to cater to Tad's whims or put up with his rudeness. At the same time, she understood his moods much better and knew when to tease and when to listen quietly. In turn, he volunteered more of his thoughts and had begun to make more friends at school. Sky's frequent visits had helped boost Tad's confidence tremendously.

Tad was attending Malcolm's birthday party today at the roller rink, which had given Cheri and Sky a chance to buy his Christmas presents unobserved. It should have been a relaxing day, but much of the time Sky had seemed preoccupied.

Well, he had a lot on his mind, Cheri told herself. Although Sky, true to his promise, had stayed in Southern California this past month, he'd been busy taping programs to cover the month of March, when he would be in the Soviet Union, and updating segments for his local station. It needed them to fill in until the syndicate finished running the psychics and police subseries, which had already aired in Orange County.

At the condo, Cheri tried to keep the atmosphere light as they sat down at the glass-topped breakfast table to indulge in hot chocolate and coffee cake.

"You know, I've gained almost ten pounds since last summer," she said to break the silence.

"Where?" Sky cocked his head.

She wasn't about to point to specifics. "Everywhere."

"You were too thin." Sky popped another bite of coffee cake into his mouth. "Unless you're trying to stay at film weight?"

"I guess I was." Cheri hadn't consciously intended to keep on starving herself for the camera, but doing so had become instinctive after so many years. "I suppose I could lose this weight in six weeks if I really tried, but not if I go on eating so much."

"I suppose you could." He seemed to have lost interest in the subject. His eyes were focused somewhere beyond her right shoulder, on mental projections that only he could see. Then, suddenly, he said, "Are you positive you don't want to preview the show about the Granger house?"

"I'm sure it's fine." Cheri knew that Sky had control over the editing and she trusted his judgment. Besides, if she saw the program, she might get cold feet and insist it not be shown. That would infuriate Tad.

It might also embarrass Sky professionally. She wasn't ready to put their relationship to that kind of test.

"We haven't talked about New Year's Eve," she said. "How about Disneyland? Tad would love the fireworks."

"Oh." Sky ran his fingers through his already rumpled hair. "I'm afraid I've got to go to New York right after Christmas. There are some archaeologists who'll be in town from Egypt. I think it's a bit hokey, but Appleby wants me to look into exploring the mysteries of the pyramids.''

''The pyramids?'' She didn't mean to sound obtuse, but for some reason Cheri hadn't thought past Sky's trip to Russia. ''I didn't realize you'd be traveling so much.''

''There are a lot of places I'd really like to explore.'' A gleam of excitement lighted Sky's face. ''Places in Africa, South America, the Orient. Not that I want to be away all the time, but Cheri, this is what I dreamed about when I was starting out. Of having the freedom and the funding to examine belief systems and strange occurrences anywhere in the world.''

''That does sound exciting.'' *Don't you know you're breaking my heart? You haven't looked so keyed up about anything since you finished taping the Granger ghosts.* Well, you couldn't build a relationship on guilt. She had no intention of clinging to his sleeve, holding him back. ''I'm happy for you, Sky.''

He snapped out of his dreamy mood. ''You're being a good sport about this, Cheri. I know it's hard on you.''

Damn it, he didn't like the way she lowered her lashes, shielding the hurt he knew was hidden there. Why did the timing have to be so rotten?

It was going to complicate things even more when she went back to work. So far she'd shown no interest, but things were getting onto an even keel with Tad, and it wouldn't be long before she began feeling restless.

He'd known from the beginning that two demanding careers would be fatal to a relationship. On the other hand, he couldn't just throw away everything he'd worked for all these years. He didn't expect her to, either.

Damn common sense! Why couldn't he just stuff her and Tad into his BMW and drive off into the sunset? *Make that the sunrise,* he amended. The car wasn't amphibious.

"It's time to go pick up Tad." There was neither blame nor resentment in Cheri's tone. This was one strong, beautiful woman, and he knew he'd never find another like her.

Still wishing for a magical solution and knowing he wouldn't find one, Sky cleared the table and went with Cheri to pick up the boy who already felt like a son.

IT WAS A WEIRD IDEA for a New Year's Eve party, and the minute Cheri thought of it, she rejected it fiercely.

The problem was that Tad wouldn't agree to any of the other suggestions she came up with. He seemed to take Sky's leaving as a sign of abandonment. Two days after Christmas, when Sky left, Tad put the model antique cars away and sank into a sullen gloom for the first time since the day he'd run away.

No, he didn't want to go to Disneyland or Knott's Berry Farm. *No,* he didn't want to invite any of his friends over for the night. *No,* there weren't any movies he wanted to see.

He retreated into his earlier depression, closeting himself with his video games. Sometimes Cheri would hear noises in the wall and realize Tad was exploring the hidden passageway. He had taken refuge in the interior of things.

She had to do something, Cheri decided. She didn't want to confide in Kate; even though they'd become friends, it didn't seem right to tell Sky's own sister how his absence was hurting Tad.

The person Cheri felt like calling was Vinnie Dumont.

Somewhat to her surprise, she found that the psychic was listed in the phone book. It was three days before New Year, and Tad was upstairs, reading one of his Dr. Dolittle books.

Okay. It was worth a try.

Vinnie's voice had a dry, distracted tone when she answered. "I hope I'm not interrupting anything," Cheri said.

"Oh, I was painting." The other woman sounded disgusted with herself. "Frankly, I'm glad of an excuse to quit."

"I had a very strange idea—Tad's been so grumpy, and I was trying to think of something to do for New Year's Eve...." Cheri took a deep breath. "Do you think it would hurt anything if we threw a party for the Granger ghosts?"

"A party for the ghosts?" Apparently that was a new one, even in Vinnie's experience.

"You know, some old-fashioned music, tea cakes, champagne and grape juice, maybe a few streamers. So they wouldn't be lonely." Not wanting to sound like a kook, she added quickly, "I mean, it might bring Tad out of his blues."

"I see." There was a long pause. Cheri wondered if the other woman was trying to figure out a polite way to tell her to buzz off. Instead, Vinnie said, "Why not? Do I take it that I'm invited?"

"Of course," Cheri said. "We could ask other people too, I suppose, but they might think it was odd."

"It's up to you." Vinnie certainly didn't reveal much of her reaction over the telephone. "I'll be happy to help with the preparations. And we really don't need to include anyone else, unless you particularly want to."

"Actually, I don't." After making arrangements to get together a day in advance, Cheri said goodbye. She hung up wondering what on earth she'd gotten herself into.

SKY CALLED at dinnertime on New Year's Eve and seemed amused when Cheri told him what she was up to. "I wish I could be there." Was that a wistful note in his voice?

"Vinnie's coming over in half an hour." Tad had eaten quickly and gone upstairs to put on a suit, complete with vest and pocket watch, that she'd bought him for the occasion. "Tad's really looking forward to it."

"I was hoping to talk to him."

Cheri wished this whole situation weren't so awkward. She didn't want to tell Sky about Tad's moping. *I'm not going to pressure him. He's sensitive enough to guess what must be going on.*

There were so many other things she wanted to say, too. That the house felt empty and echoing at night, that frost had taken the bloom off her garden and left it skeletal in the early darkness. That she needed Sky's arms around her and his lips on hers, and his strength to get her through the winter.

She couldn't say any of those things. "How's it going with the archaeologists?"

His tone brightened as he told her about some new excavations in Turkey that he planned to look into next summer. He didn't want to focus too much on the pyramids, which had been overpublicized, but to look instead at such sites as Ephesus and, in Italy, Herculaneum.

"I talked with a psychic who claims he's had visions at both sites and, as a result, has been able to lead the excavators to some remarkable discoveries," Sky said. "It's great stuff."

"It sounds like it." She couldn't help adding, "Will you be back soon? It's just—I know you've got a convention in February, and then Russia, so I wondered . . ."

"Maybe for a few days." The regretfulness was quickly transformed into excitement. "My researchers have come across some interesting cases involving psychics and the police in Dallas and Louisville. You know, I wanted to expand the subseries, make it nationwide, and the only time I could squeeze these in would be January."

"Yes. Of course." To cover her dismay, she told him about her most recent meetings with Elaine, about a temporary setback in the schedule because an investor had pulled out, about the latest script changes and additions in casting. They had a couple of possibilities for Belle, maybe a big name if they could persuade her to accept a percentage of the gross in place of a large salary.

Then, a touch awkwardly, they wished each other a happy New Year and said goodbye. Cheri hung up feeling as if she'd been straining to keep the conversation going.

It was a relief when the doorbell rang and she went to let Vinnie in.

"Flowers." Vinnie presented her with a pot of rust-colored chrysanthemums. "I think Allie would like them. And some Godiva chocolates. I think *we'll* like those."

Instantly Cheri felt better.

Vinnie stepped inside, looking the picture of refinement in a high-necked shirtwaist dress which, except for its hemline, might have come from the Edwardian era. After some hesitation, Cheri had decided to wear Allie's white dress again. From Vinnie's smile, she knew the dress looked good on her and somehow it felt right, too.

Tad came skipping downstairs. "Hi! Is this okay?" He tugged on his bow tie.

"Perfect," Vinnie said.

From under his arm Tad produced a box of the miniature antique cars. "I thought maybe we could set these up, like the ghosts might enjoy them."

"Good idea." Cheri helped him find a likely spot on the coffee table. Maybe producing the cars was a sign that his resentment of Sky was waning. She hoped so.

Within a few minutes, the record player was piping out some offbeat hit songs from the twenties, a fresh lemon cake was retrieved from the refrigerator, and the air was full of gleeful shouts as Vinnie, Cheri and Tad battled it out over a game of Old Maid.

Afterward, they sang along with such twenties classics as "Does Your Chewing Gum Lose Its Flavor on the Bedpost Over Night?" and "I Scream—You Scream—We all Scream for Ice Cream." Cheri's personal favorite was

"When Banana Skins Are Falling, I'll Come Sliding Back to You."

The evening went more smoothly than she'd expected. Suddenly released from his depression, Ted chattered away almost nonstop, leaving no awkward silences. The ghostly guests behaved themselves, quite sensibly declining to interfere with the lights or scare Tad into throwing any more coats around.

It was a little after ten when Tad's eyes refused to stay open any longer. Cheri and Vinnie silently coordinated their efforts to carry him and his toys upstairs.

When he was tucked snugly beneath the covers with Buster, the women tiptoed down again.

"Well," Vinnie said. "Do you suppose it would be all right if I stick around until the New Year?"

"Absolutely." Cheri poured them each a second glass of champagne. When they were seated in the living room, she asked, "Are you going to Russia with Sky?"

Vinnie shook her head. "Oh, no. I've never been much for traveling. Besides, he won't need me; he'll be interviewing scientists, clairvoyants, people who've experienced various phenomena firsthand. Of course, I'll be helping out next month—I suppose you've heard about Dallas and Louisville already—and he's asked me about the Middle East next summer, but frankly I'm hesitant. I don't much like hotels, I hate muggy weather and I prefer shopping where the labels are printed in a language I can read."

That made Cheri stop and remember what mixed feelings she herself had about traveling. She hadn't done much of it; a few publicity tours, and once a TV movie on location in Montreal. She detested packing and unpacking, but she did enjoy seeing new sights, and it was easy to imagine that visiting some place really exotic would be even more challenging. She supposed she could cope with the weather and the language barrier, for a few weeks, at least.

"I suppose I'd like it, in moderation," she said. "Well, what shall we do for the rest of the evening?"

After some discussion, they decided to watch Cheri's tape of *The Sound of Music*. Like old friends, they settled down with a bowl of popcorn and sang along with Julie Andrews.

By the time the tape was done, it was well after midnight. "I suppose we failed in our duty," Cheri said. "Weren't we suppose to honk horns and throw confetti?"

"To hell with tradition." Vinnie had obviously sipped a bit too much champagne. "I had a wonderful time."

"I don't think you should drive home." Realizing that might not sound tactful, Cheri added, "There are too many nuts on the road. I can make up a bed in a spare room and lend you a nightgown."

Vinnie frowned. "I don't know. Marcella—you know, Allie's aunt—she's been troubling me. On the other hand, it doesn't seem to make much difference whether I'm here or at home, does it?"

Afterward it was hard to remember who got the idea first, but something about what Vinnie had said struck a chord in both of them.

"You know—" Cheri began.

"I don't suppose—"

The two women looked at each other.

"This is an awfully big house," Cheri said.

"My apartment is driving me crazy. I feel like I'm locked up in a chicken coop."

"There are three unoccupied bedrooms upstairs." The idea of having another woman in the house hadn't occurred to Cheri before, and she probably wouldn't have gone for it with anyone else. But somehow Vinnie felt like family. "Of course, I don't know what Sky will say when he comes back."

"I'm the soul of discretion," Vinnie promised.

"And it might make Tad feel better. We really do rattle around here, just the two of us."

By the time they finally settled down for the night, all but the details had been decided. Vinnie would move into the Granger house for a few months, until she found a larger apartment or made up her mind whether to buy a house. In the meantime they'd keep each other company.

And maybe, Cheri thought as she creamed off her makeup in the privacy of her bedroom, they would come to grips with the ghosts that refused to go away.

Chapter Sixteen

On a sunny Saturday in late January, Cheri had just finished showering off the dirt from a heavy-duty weeding session and was pulling on a silk sweater when she heard a car stop in front of the house.

It couldn't be Vinnie and Tad already. They'd left for the L.A. Zoo a few hours ago, to draw pictures of the animals. Tad was developing a considerable interest in art, stimulated by Vinnie's love of painting, and this was their first chance to be together since Vinnie's two-day trip to Louisville last week.

Vinnie, who seemed like the grandmother Tad had never known, was filling holes in their lives that Cheri hadn't even known were there. Not the great gap left by Sky's absence, but a hundred little chinks. Vinnie even seemed to surprise herself sometimes by the ideas she came up with for picnics and puppet shows and visits to art fairs. It was wonderful for Tad, and for Cheri, too.

But that didn't sound like Vinnie's old Buick station wagon outside. Stepping into her slacks, Cheri went to peer out the window.

The driver's door of a silver BMW was thrust open, and a familiar lean figure emerged. Why hadn't Sky told her he was coming back today? She could have changed her plans, but now...

Torn between eagerness and annoyance, she tapped downstairs in her low-heeled pumps and threw open the front door. Sky was coming up the walkway, carrying an enormous stuffed dinosaur and what looked like a bundle of sticks wrapped in plastic.

Before Cheri could speak, he said, "It's a rosebush. I couldn't resist. It's called *Mon Chéri*."

"I've got just the spot for it," she heard herself say. "I dug up a pitiful azalea bush this morning."

They stood on the porch after he set down the gifts, grinning at each other like two lovesick teenagers. *Oh, lord,* this wasn't how Cheri had expected their next meeting to go. She meant to act in a very adult, very sophisticated way, to show him that he needn't fear she would melt into a puddle of pleading, blaming it on her emotions. Even though that was sometimes how she felt.

Instead, here she was gawking like a schoolgirl. Sky seemed to shine in the sunlight, his gray eyes alight, his hair a bit unruly, his whole body radiating energy. It was obvious his work agreed with him very, very much.

He was studying her as if she were something so lovely and delicate that he was almost afraid to reach out and touch her. Which was laughable, considering what a grub she'd been half an hour ago.

"What's so funny?" he inquired.

"Us."

"Not funny. Hungry." Strong hands caught her shoulders and his mouth descended on hers with the confidence of a man who knows he's welcome. And he was. Terribly welcome.

Her whole body quivered with reawakening desire, with a sensual knowledge of his hands and muscles and skin, of the way his chest felt when it pressed against her breasts. *Oh, yes,* she knew how it would be, his hips mastering hers, his body demanding and taunting and teaching her how to give more than she'd ever known she possessed.

Cheri stepped back.

"What's wrong?" Sky asked quietly.

"I've—got an appointment in L.A. Elaine asked me to drop by a rehearsal for a play at the Theater Centre. There's an actress who's been recommended for Belle. She's got a movie coming out this spring." Cheri sighed. "I wish I'd known you were going to be here."

"Can't I come with you?"

It made such perfect sense that she didn't know why she hadn't thought of it immediately. Except that by now she'd fallen into the habit of considering their work spheres as separate worlds.

"Sure," she said. "Vinnie and Tad won't be back from the zoo until tonight, so we could have dinner together afterward. If you like."

"I like."

On the way to Los Angeles, Sky filled her in on his schedule. He'd wrapped up taping the rest of the psychics-and-police episodes and had a short break before heading for the station owners' convention next month. After that, he needed to prepare for the trip to the Soviet Union, and would be leaving at the beginning of March.

"I didn't expect to be quite this busy," he admitted as they parked the car in a downtown garage and took the elevator to the street. "Damn it, there isn't enough time for everything."

Cheri bit the inside of her cheek to keep from adding her protest to his. Instead, as they emerged and walked a few doors to the Los Angeles Theater Center, Cheri pointed out the renovations taking place in several aging buildings across the street. "This area was terribly run-down before the city started redevelopment. Now there are quite a few artists making their studios around here." She didn't mean to sound like a tour guide, so she added, "They're beginning to drive out the drunks, but I'm not sure where they'll go."

"Probably the beach. One man's solution is another man's pain in the neck." Sky held the door to the theater building and then walked beside Cheri through the vast lobby, which served the four theaters. It was a practical, large space with its own dining area and a high-tech feel that put her in mind of a train station.

Cheri led the way through a small entrance chamber into the steeply raked seating area of one of the small theaters. The director glanced up, nodded in recognition and went on giving instructions to the actors.

"Ever worked onstage?" Sky whispered as they sat down.

"Just scenes from acting class," she murmured back. It had been a dream of Cheri's once to star on the stage, but her agent had cautioned her against taking the risk. It wasn't likely to help her career much if she succeeded, but it could hurt a lot if she failed.

Right now she didn't have a career to worry about, but the idea of standing onstage in front of an audience was even more terrifying than going before a camera. What if nobody clapped? What if they walked out?

Cheri shrank into her seat.

The actors were ready to run the scene. The play was the eighteenth-century comedy *The Rivals*, and Angela Fry, the actress she'd come to watch, was portraying the heroine Lydia Languish. It took a minute to get used to the formal language issuing from a woman dressed in a sweatshirt and blue jeans, but soon the sheer delight of the scene carried Cheri with it.

Angela was good. Sly one minute, ingenuous the next. You could see her mind working, see a real personality taking over the role.

She would make a wonderful Belle.

There was a possibility Angela might have to spend the summer shooting a sequel to her new movie; an option had been included in her contract. If that happened, she wouldn't be available to Elaine.

Why am I hoping she can't do it? What am I, crazy? I don't want the part for myself. I'd have to be out of my mind.

Besides, Angela was a real actress. You could see confidence in every line of her body.

And what am I, a fake?

Cheri didn't like the thoughts that were coming to her: that Angela would do a better job as Belle, and that it would be a safe choice for Elaine, since the young actress was clearly up-and-coming.

Up to that point, Cheri had always known the part was hers if she wanted it. She and Elaine both seemed to assume that no one else could play it as well. Now she had to face the possibility that that simply wasn't true.

She waited, half hoping that Sky would say something as he had the night they'd gone to South Coast Repertory, insisting that of course Cheri was much better suited to play Belle. But he seemed absorbed in the scene before them, smiling at the appropriate moments and being swept away just as she had been by Angela's performance.

She's so much better than I could ever be. How could I have deluded myself all these years?

Pain clawed across Cheri's chest and twisted her throat. She'd been hiding from the truth by telling herself that she was choosing not to go back, that she needed time to live in the real world. The reality was that she didn't have the talent to become a major star.

Cheri inhaled deeply to still the trembling. It came from the void that had opened up inside her, an ugly vacuum in the place where her self used to be.

If she wasn't an actress, what was she?

The scene ended, and Sky turned toward her questioningly. Cheri nodded with a tight smile and walked with him out of the theater.

"She's good," she forced herself to say.

"Yes, she is." Sky stretched and gazed around the lobby with interest. How strange that he didn't instinctively feel the sharp twist her awareness had taken. But not strange at all, of course, Cheri reminded herself. He wasn't a mind reader.

"Maybe we could get a bite to eat." Sky took her arm as they stepped outside. "There's a restaurant right over there that looks promising."

"I'm—not very hungry." She couldn't eat now for anything in the world.

"Whoa." This time he had picked up the tension. Sky swung around and caught Cheri's hands. "What's going on with you?"

"She's—good."

"Ah." He lowered his forehead until it touched hers, closing them into a private space in the middle of the sidewalk. "And you don't think you are?"

"I know I'm not."

People were brushing by them, and Sky must have caught the glances of annoyance, because he took Cheri's elbow and led her toward the parking garage. "I hate to say I told you so, but I figured all along the real problem was you were scared."

"I'm not scared." Even as she said it, Cheri knew he was right. But not entirely right. "I'm also a realist. Sky, I'm a passable actress. My timing is good, I know how to relate to the camera. But I don't have the kind of talent she does."

They were alone on the elevator. "Excuse me," Sky said. "I think you should be talking in the past tense."

"I don't follow you."

"As a teenager, I'll agree, you weren't any Patty Duke." They stepped onto the oil-slicked concrete of the garage, into the heady vapors of auto exhaust. "As you've said, you were trying to please your mother, not yourself."

"There's no need to tell me what I already know." It might not be fair to sound so irritable, but she couldn't help it.

"All right, I'll tell you something new," he said as they got into the car. "Which is, you're not a kid anymore. Even in the time I've known you, Cheri, I've seen you grow more comfortable in your own skin."

She supposed that was true. "So what?"

"I'm not sure you even know how much talent you've got, or how much it's matured." He backed out of the space and wound down the tight turns of the ramp. "Maybe you ought to find out."

"Maybe I'm better off not knowing." The great void inside her had shrunk a little, but it wasn't about to disappear just yet. Grimly Cheri realized that this sense of empty space was going to become part of her life.

But it would be much, much worse if she went out there and failed again. Better to tell herself that she could if she would than to find out the hard way that she couldn't.

"It's your choice." Sky gave her a wry smile. "Frankly, it would suit me just fine if you'd been right all along. If what you really want is quiet domesticity, you and Tad can come with me to New York, and wherever else my work takes me. But the truth is that I'd only have part of you, and that isn't enough."

Most of what he said flowed past Cheri. There'd been something new and troubling in there. "New York? Does this mean you're moving to New York?"

"Miles is urging me to. He thinks it's a more practical base for the show than L.A., and besides, that's where his office is." Sky steered around a stalled car and swooped onto a freeway access ramp.

"Are you going to?"

"I haven't decided."

She bit back the urge to argue. All along, she'd told herself she wasn't going to hang around his neck like an albatross. This was Sky's decision, not hers.

This hollow space inside her wasn't empty, after all. It had teeth, and they were gnawing at her heart. Because she was about to lose two of the three pillars of her life. Sky and her belief in herself as an actress.

The only one left was Tad. But he was enough. He would have to be enough.

"Well?" Sky piloted them through the traffic with experienced smoothness. "Aren't you going to put in your two cents worth?"

"No. It's your life."

His mouth tightened. "That's all you have to say?"

"What do you expect from me?" The words bristled with hurt that quickly turned to anger. "This is everything you've ever dreamed about, right? Well, don't let me stand in your way."

She'd done it now. Cheri closed her eyes to contain the tears. He couldn't have missed the bitterness in her voice. All these months of holding it back had been wiped away in one resentful outburst.

Sky didn't say anything for a long, long time. The freeway miles ticked past as they glided by the flat endless stretch of warehouses and fast-food restaurants that made one Southern California freeway almost indistinguishable from another.

"We need some time to think this over." He was staring straight ahead. "I wish I weren't going to be gone for so long. I doubt if I'll get back to Orange County before April."

"Oh, Sky, it's just—" Just what? Just that she hadn't meant to fall in love with him?

She wasn't sure when it had happened. Love didn't really come all at once, the way the storybooks made it out. It happened a little bit at a time, shreds of your soul slipping away and clinging to another person, until suddenly there was a big part of yourself missing.

Unless the other person brought it back to you. And it didn't look as though Sky could do that.

"I don't know what to say." He coasted off the freeway and stopped at a signal light.

"I'm not—" Cheri cleared away the lump in her throat "—I'm not trying to push you into anything. We can just go on spending what time we can together."

But she knew, and sensed that he knew also, that the kind of love they had wasn't going to glide comfortably into a track. It had to keep on growing and deepening, forcing them to open themselves to greater and greater hurts, and neither would be able to tolerate that state of vulnerability forever.

Cheri wished that he would say something about love or about the future, some hint of a promise. But he didn't, and she understood.

When they got home, Vinnie's station wagon was parked in front of the house. "I'd better go see Tad," Sky said.

"He'd like that." They went in together, and didn't look at each other except when politeness demanded it. Cheri knew that Vinnie noticed, but thank goodness, Tad didn't.

"ANYONE FOR A MUFFIN? Cupcake? Cookies?" Kate gestured at the long paper-covered table, the row of paper plates mostly empty now except for crumbs and here and there a baked goodie.

Cheri huddled into her jacket, in the weak February sunshine. "No, thanks." It was getting nippy, and she was glad the bake sale was over. She hadn't seen much of the soccer game. In her brief breaks from helping raise money for the PTA, she'd been keeping an eye on Tad as he raced around with his buddies.

"Hey, seventy-eight dollars and thirty-seven cents!" called Andrea, bouncing up beside them. Since the night of the Halloween party, Cheri had gotten to know her and several of the other mothers on a casual basis, and to enjoy their comradeship. "Listen, you two look frozen. I've got to stick around for a while anyway, so why don't you go grab a cup of coffee? I'll watch the monsters."

"Sounds good." Kate shivered. "I'm sure they'll be glad to help with cleanup, since it means they get to eat what's left."

"Good idea!" Andrea waved her arms at the small figures that were darting about behind some trees. "Eats!"

"Let's get out of here." Kate directed Cheri toward her minibus. "Coffee sounds heavenly."

Cheri was about to protest that she didn't want to leave Tad, then remembered how much he wanted to be like "normal people." Which meant not hovering too much. "I always feel guilty when I complain about the weather," she said as she climbed in beside Kate. "But fifty-five degrees starts to feel like zero when you're out in it long enough."

"Windchill factor," agreed Kate, although the breeze was a light one. "And thin blood from living in Southern California so long."

They stopped at the first coffee shop they saw, and were served almost instantly. The place was empty at this predinner hour.

"I want to get your opinion on something," Kate said.

"Shoot."

"Well, I've been thinking of going back to school. Taking a class in desktop publishing. You know I've been putting out the PTA newsletter for two years—"

"It's stunning." Cheri had been impressed by the professionalism of the writing and layout, despite the amateurish look of the rub-off lettering and typed copy. "Are you going to buy a computer?"

"Frank suggested we get one for the boys, and you know him. He's got to get the latest state-of-the-art model." Kate smiled fondly. "We could use some spare cash, and I'm getting bored with nothing to do but housework and PTA. There's a lot of organizations that could use a sharp-looking newsletter, don't you think?"

"You'd be great." Cheri rested her chin on her hand. "I have to say it's been fun this year, but I can see how you'd go a little crazy after a while, chauffeuring kids around and organizing meetings of parents who can never agree on anything."

They chatted about the latest politics in the PTA, about the father who rarely showed up except to criticize and about the mother who often suggested complicated projects, but refused to volunteer for any of the work.

The topic drifted back to Kate's plans for desktop publishing. "Sky would have loved it when he was a kid," she said. "He used to put out his own magazine—hand-illustrated, banged out on a manual typewriter. He'd interview people around the neighborhood and then write them up."

It was hard to picture Sky as a child. "He sounds like the kind of kid who was shot out of a cannon."

"Eye on the prize." Kate nodded. "We used to say he'd either be a big success or kill himself trying."

"What else was he like?" Cheri paused as the waitress refilled their cups. "Interested in ghosts?"

"Not exactly." People were beginning to drift into the restaurant. "In things foreign, things unfamiliar, yes. Dinosaurs—well, weren't we all?—and space exploration. He used to read those books by Roy Chapman Andrews about hunting for dinosaur eggs, and what's his name, Halliburton, the explorer who swam the Panama Canal."

"Other cultures, other places."

"Why? What's going on with you two?" Kate hardly ever asked such a personal question.

"I'm not sure." Cheri tapped her fingers against the rim of her cup. "He's finally achieving what he's worked toward all his life, and I'm not sure how I fit in."

"He's a fool if he lets you go," Kate said. "One of these days he's going to wake up a very lonely man."

Cheri felt her throat thicken. It had become a familiar sensation, that nearness of tears. She liked to attribute it to her still-precarious emotional state from Donna and Jeff's deaths, but that had been almost a year ago. *Almost a year? Is that possible?* "We'd better go fetch the boys before Andrea self-destructs."

Kate refrained from adding any further comments, but Cheri could see she was concerned and thanked goodness for small, lively boys who demanded to pick up pizza for dinner and filled the empty spaces of the evening with their nudges and giggles.

Chapter Seventeen

"He ought to be here." Vinnie didn't often criticize Sky. In fact, she'd carefully avoided the subject since Cheri filled her in on the conversation in the car. Mention of Sky had been kept to impersonal contexts, and Cheri had done her best to sound cheerful whenever he'd called. As he'd said, there wasn't much they could do right now except try not to vent their frustration on each other.

"I agreed to the taping. I'm sure it will be fine." Cheri poured melted margarine over the huge bowl of popcorn.

"I'm surprised Tad isn't back by now." Vinnie carried a pitcher of lemonade into the living room. "Of course he knows you're recording it, but he wouldn't want to miss seeing the Granger ghosts live."

"He's probably rounding up his friends." Picking up the remote control, Cheri tuned the TV set to the right station. She'd tried not to think about the program, but her restless sleep last night was a sign that her unconscious mind wasn't about to be subdued.

In fact, her dreams had been troubling for weeks, filled with scenes of running through an airport, looking for Sky but not finding him, aching moments of staring at a bright star almost close enough to touch, only to watch it zoom away without warning.

"In here!" The front door banged open and in clattered Tad followed by a clump of tousled, gap-toothed friends, some with skateboards tucked under their arms. "You guys have to keep quiet now, or my folks will throw us out!"

My folks. Cheri loved the sound of it. She tried not to think about the one "folk" who wasn't here.

"There's plenty of popcorn, but you boys better wash your hands first," she announced. "Leave the skateboards on the porch, please."

In a surprisingly short time everyone was settled, if you can call it settled when boys keep poking each other in the ribs and thumping their jogging shoes against every available surface.

"Ssh!" Tad announced so loudly that Cheri missed the first bars of Sky's theme music.

There he was, standing outside their house, gazing straight into Cheri's eyes. Straight into the camera, she reminded herself firmly.

"This house in the Southern California town of Orange was built almost a century ago by a family named Granger," he began.

It seemed, as he outlined the story of Perry Dotson and ended with Allie Granger's death, that he was recounting the lives of people Cheri knew well. How quickly this house and its history had become a part of her memories. Would Sky someday be another figure in the past, someone to look back on with nostalgia and regret?

With a shock Cheri came back to the present at the sight of herself on TV, sitting here in this living room. She hadn't watched herself on-screen for over a year, she realized, scrutinizing her image carefully.

The soft dress she'd worn hid the slight increase in weight. Her face, she noticed, looked more inviting with a little extra roundness, but her voice, as always, struck her as a shade too childlike. It was hard to be objective; she could always find things to criticize. Did anyone ever really like to see her- or himself on camera?

It was Tad's turn to talk on the program, telling about his frightening dreams and the voices he'd heard. She turned to watch the real Tad, who was transfixed. Only three months had passed, but she could see that he'd grown in that time. Already his boyish chubbiness was giving way to a hint of the rangy adolescent to come.

He'd turned eight last week, a festive occasion for which Cheri had hired a clown and garnished the yard with paper lanterns and balloons. It seemed like only yesterday that he'd been a tiny infant cradled in his mother's arms, in Jeff and Donna's small apartment.

Before she knew it, he'd be a preteen, then a teenager, then all grown-up and gone away. To Cheri, motherhood had sounded like a lifetime proposition. But she was learning that you couldn't expect a child to fill up the rest of your years.

The blare of a commercial broke into her thoughts. Cries of approval went up from the ragamuffin audience, and wads of paper appeared from nowhere to fly in Tad's direction.

"Hey!" Cheri held up a hand for calm. "You guys better clean up the mess if you want refills on popcorn and lemonade."

The tactic worked wonders. The wads of paper disappeared and refreshments were eagerly grabbed. By the time the commercials ended, Cheri had been pulled away from her ruminations and was ready to focus on the program.

She'd forgotten how eerie that day had been with the wind howling and Vinnie picking up the personas of Jane and Perry Dotson. Even watching it on TV made her shiver.

Vinnie's explanation that most of the ghosts were gone reminded Cheri of their conversation afterward, in which she'd learned that Allie and Nora and Allie's Aunt Marcella were still around. But they'd been curiously silent these past months, as if the excitement of that day had tired them out.

As soon as the program ended, excited chatter filled the room. Tad's friends insisted on trooping up to the attic, where they spent close to an hour sneaking up on each other and making "Hoo-hoo" noises.

Cheri and Vinnie retreated to clean up the living room. "What did you think?" Vinnie asked.

"It was spooky." Cheri shuddered involuntarily. "If I were watching it, I'd be impressed."

"You were afraid people would think you were doing this to further your career," Vinnie reminded her as she plumped up the sofa pillows.

"What career?" Cheri shrugged. "I guess I'm not so worried about what people think anymore. It's what I think that matters, isn't it?"

"Mmm." Vinnie could be maddeningly noncommittal at times.

The phone rang. "That must be Sky." Cheri dashed into the kitchen and picked up the receiver. "Hi."

"Miss Louette? This is Sam Grotonski from *The Inside Story*. That was some program." The voice was smooth and impersonal, as if it came from an advanced type of robot. "Tell me what the ghosts are really like? Have any of them made any, shall we say, sexual advances?"

Stifling the urge to slam down the receiver, Cheri tried to answer in as dignified a fashion as possible. As soon as she managed to get off the phone, it rang again. This time it was a gossip columnist from one of the L.A. trade papers.

She'd thought that leaving the phone under Jeff's name would be as good as getting an unlisted number. Obviously she'd been wrong. It was going to be a long evening.

SKY SLAMMED DOWN THE PHONE in frustration. Busy again.

It was irrational, he knew, but he'd expected Cheri to be waiting eagerly for his call, not gabbing away with her friends. Of course, it might be Tad or even Vinnie on the phone, but couldn't they have the decency to get off for a few minutes?

It was almost 2:00 a.m. Chicago time before he got through. In the echoing silence, the hotel room had taken on a stiff, plastic feeling that made him uncomfortable. He'd trade it for a nice, haunted house any night.

"Hello?" Cheri sounded weary.

"It's Sky. I've been trying to get you for hours." Damn it, he hadn't meant to sound petulant.

There was a definite groan. "I've talked to at least two dozen reporters, Sky. I would have put the answering machine on, but I thought you might call."

His irritation vanished. "Can you handle it? I didn't expect this much reaction so soon."

"I don't know. If this is the worst, then I suppose I'm all right."

What more could there be? It struck him that he'd never really taken seriously her concern about the invasion of her privacy. A few questions—well, an experienced TV personality could handle that, couldn't she? Now he wasn't so sure.

"Maybe you guys ought to take a vacation for a few days." He was due in New York tomorrow, and leaving for Moscow in less than a week. If he could only change things around a little, swing a trip back to L.A. for a weekend...

"I don't think so," Cheri was saying. "Frankly, I'm apprehensive. There are tabloid reporters who wouldn't hesitate to break into this house and trump up some tale about what happens inside. I'd rather be here."

"Damn." It sounded like a siege; hell, it might *be* a siege. "Look, if you're worried, I'll hire a guard to keep people off the property."

"I've already arranged for that," Cheri said. "Vinnie suggested it. I don't want the garden getting trampled. Maybe I'm exaggerating things. I'm kind of tired right now. This may all blow over in a day or two."

"Look, I'll call you from New York. If things are bad, I'll put off the trip to Russia." Even as he said it, Sky knew that wasn't possible.

So did Cheri. "You can't do that. You've spent too much time getting it all set up. We'll be fine, Sky."

He hung up feeling unsettled and not very proud of himself.

Pouring himself a glass of wine from a previously untouched bottle left by the management, Sky stretched his feet out along the bed and tried to sort his thoughts.

He'd been concerned about Cheri's emotional reaction to the taping and to watching the broadcast, but he hadn't given much thought to her concerns about the press. Maybe, as she said, things would quickly calm down, but even being upset and hounded for a few days was a high price for her to pay for his ambitions.

Be honest with yourself. Did you really want to face the possible consequences of this program? Weren't you so damn delighted at scoring a coup that you were willing to let Cheri bear the burden?

One thing was sure: he didn't want to be leaving the country next week. He didn't want to be off in Moscow when he was needed in Southern California.

For the first time, Sky's ambitions were beginning to feel like a trap.

THE HOUSE HAD BEEN QUIET for hours now, and Vinnie still hadn't fallen asleep.

She closed her eyes in exhaustion. Maybe it would help if she just lay here without moving. Maybe...

She was standing in a room. This room, but not this room; the furniture was all different, and the wallpaper had ribbons and roses on it instead of tiny wildflowers. Through the lace-draped window, she could hear the solitary clop-clop of a horse-drawn milk truck passing in the predawn darkness.

There was a young boy lying in the bed, gasping for breath, his thin frame wracked with fever. He had to make it through the night. He couldn't die. Not her precious baby.

It brought back memories of her first husband—Marcella's first husband, Troy. Of that horrible night, only a year after they were married, when he went for a swim in the Pacific Ocean and never came back. Riptides, they'd said. Deceptive undercurrents that could suck a man out to sea before he knew it. She had waited on the beach, waited and waited, becoming anxious, then terrified. It was a night like this one, a night that went on forever.

Bending over to press a cool cloth to the boy's forehead, Vinnie saw that it was Tad. Not the sturdy boy of a few hours ago but a pale imitation in a white nightshirt, the kind boys used to wear at the turn of the century.

He was slipping away. Slipping past her. The night whirled and became day, a gray, dreary day. Every bone in her body cried out with weariness. The people around her were wearing black. So many people; why couldn't she remember their names? Her older boy was standing there with his head bowed, next to his father. Charlie looked lost, a child baffled by the realities of existence. He looked younger than his own son.

It was hard to remember now why she'd married Charlie. It wasn't a love match, not as it had been with Troy. But loneliness was a cruel mate. When the years began to run by and no other love came into her life, Marcella had chosen to marry for companionship and for children. Who could have foreseen the hollowness of her new marriage on the loss of her younger son?

Her love was bad luck, for Troy first of all and now for this child. She must try not to care about anyone anymore. That was the only way to protect them, and herself. The older boy would be all right; he'd always been strong.

She would do her duty, go through the motions. But she would never open her heart again. No one should be asked to endure such pain twice in a lifetime. Maybe this way he would be safe, this tall thin boy who was left, without the mother's heart that seemed to have the effect of a curse.

But she'll find out differently in a few years, when the war comes. She'll find out that withdrawal offers no protection.

Vinnie awoke with tears burning in her eyes. Why couldn't Marcella go away and leave her alone?

Vinnie sat up and tugged the quilt around her shoulders. She thought about Cheri, growing more brittle by the moment, and about Tad, who had endured so much. Right now they needed her, and she would stay here.

But they were both young, and they would eventually bounce back. Then Vinnie would have to decide whether to find herself another hole to hide in—or whether to go out and take chances. The kind of chances that Marcella hadn't dared face.

Chapter Eighteen

The call came from Tad's school while Cheri was preparing lunch for Vinnie and herself.

It was from the principal. "Miss Louette? There's a camera crew here creating a disturbance. We've called the police to keep them off school property, but I think you'll want to pick your nephew up yourself today."

"Of course." After she hung up, Cheri slammed her fist against the counter. "Damn them! Won't they ever quit?"

Vinnie came quietly into the room. She hadn't said much these past two weeks, as if sunk into some kind of reverie of her own. Which was just as well, because otherwise she'd have been going as crazy as Cheri.

Even Tad was getting tired of the harassment. After the initial interviews by phone, Cheri had turned down most requests, hoping the pests would get tired of bugging her and go away. Instead, half a dozen reporters had camped out in motor homes along the block and had made periodic attempts to sneak past the two guards she'd hired. One night, when she'd ordered a pizza, the delivery man had been bribed to lend his uniform to a reporter, and she'd opened the door to the flash of a camera.

It didn't help to know Sky was off in Moscow, safe from the intrusions of the tabloids. Not that she blamed him, but it would have helped to have him here.

Cheri had even granted two interviews, one to the *Los Angeles Times* and one to the Associated Press, so that the legitimate newspapers would have their story. But the bloodhounds hanging around her house—and now at Tad's school—weren't interested in mere facts. They wanted sensationalism.

She had no doubt they'd get it, even if they had to make up the stories. At this point she almost wished they would, so that they'd leave her alone.

"This can't go on," Vinnie said.

"I know." Cheri gestured futilely, not sure what she meant to convey. "Maybe we could get a court order."

"There has to be a better way." It was nice to have a level head around. "Why don't you talk to that friend of yours, Elaine? She might have some suggestions."

"I hadn't thought of that." If Elaine could make these reporters disappear, she'd have to be a real magician. But it might help to talk to someone with an inside knowledge of the media, if only to gain some perspective.

They couldn't stake her out forever. Could they?

She thought uneasily about Jacqueline Kennedy and Grace Kelly. Not that Cheri was in the same class, but the paparazzi had hounded those two famous women for years. Even a few months of such intrusion would be more than she could stomach.

Cheri put in a call to her friend, only to learn that Elaine was in San Francisco and wouldn't be back until tomorrow. "Well, I suppose one day won't make any difference," she grumbled.

A little after two o'clock, she pulled on a sweater—it was chilly for March—and faced the problem of how to get her car out of the driveway without a herd of reporters following her.

"I've got an idea." Vinnie studied her thoughtfully. "We don't look much alike, but we're only a few inches apart in height. Got a scarf and some sunglasses you can spare?"

"You're a doll!" The notion of a switch made Cheri feel like laughing for the first time in weeks. "I'll need to borrow one of your dresses."

A few minutes later Vinnie stuck her nose out the door. "I think I've been spotted," she called back. "Wait until we've vanished down the street."

Peering from behind the curtains, Cheri watched as Vinnie made a dash for the garage. A moment later she appeared at the wheel of Cheri's car.

There was a flurry of movement on the street, as idle reporters leaped into their vehicles. The front guard stood watching closely, in case anyone ventured onto the property, but apparently the bloodsuckers had learned better by now.

Then they were off.

Vinnie shot backward down the driveway, screeched around in a racing curve that would have done Mario Andretti proud, and zoomed down the street with five vehicles in hot pursuit.

I wonder where she's going to take them? Chuckling to herself, Cheri checked out the street. Two motor homes remained. She was almost certain their occupants had departed in cars, but she couldn't be sure.

Smoothing down the skirt of Vinnie's shirtwaist dress, she fixed her gardening hat firmly over her pinned-up hair and walked out, careful to maintain a leisurely pace on her way to Vinnie's station wagon.

The guard nodded distantly, then did a double take. A grin spread over his face. "Hey, you coulda fooled me."

"Good." Cheri got the engine started without any trouble, which was unusual for Vinnie's old tank, and headed for Tad's school. Watching her rearview mirror closely, she was relieved to see no one following. The car felt huge compared to her compact, and she knew the battered sides would have raised eyebrows in Hollywood, but right now she wouldn't have traded this old rattletrap for a Rolls Royce.

A sense of freedom surged over her. She'd forgotten how wonderful it felt to be an ordinary person, able to come and go unobserved.

On the other hand, she had to admit that she wasn't sure how she would have felt if no one had shown any interest in her after the program. But hadn't Emerson once said that consistency was the hobgoblin of little minds?

She was waiting in front of the school as children began pouring out, banging their books, shouting at each other, racing for the buses.

"Tad!" A bit embarrassed by the picture she must make in her droopy straw hat, Cheri stuck her head out the window and waved.

He didn't seem to notice her, and then the car caught his eye. "Vinnie?"

"No, it's me. We gave them the slip."

"Wow, just like on TV!" Joey cried from right behind his friend.

The boys piled into the car. Cheri discovered she didn't want to go home, back to that trap of a house. "Want to get something to eat?"

"Pizza!"

"Hamburgers!"

There was a pause as she edged around a parked car and slowly exited the school driveway.

"Doughnuts!" Tad decided.

"Yeah." Joey leaned over the seat. "You know the Doughnut Magic shop? It's right next to the Safeway."

Why was it, Cheri wondered in amusement, that kids always assumed everybody in the world knew exactly which Safeway they meant?

A few minutes later they rattled into the doughnut shop lot. Inside, Joey and Tad debated happily before settling on two doughnuts apiece.

Cheri was about to make her own selection when something stopped her. A trace of a thought that didn't dare make itself too clear.

"I'll just have coffee," she heard herself say.

The boys didn't seem to notice that she was abstaining, as they dived happily into their snacks. Sitting beside them, staring out into the thin sunshine, Cheri realized that subconsciously she was back on her diet.

Well, you never knew. Maybe she'd want to make some more television appearances or something. Besides, she'd never intended to let herself gain too much weight.

I could lose these ten pounds in about six weeks. Less, if I really worked at it.

Tad broke into her thoughts. "Could we have another one? Just one? It's only three o'clock, and we could eat dinner late."

"Okay." Cheri handed him a dollar bill and watched as the boys whooped their way back to the counter.

This was a very different Tad from the boy she'd come to know last summer. The shadow of his parents' deaths would never entirely disappear form his eyes, but more and more he was behaving like a normal eight-year-old.

Maybe she, too, was coming back to herself. It was no wonder the weight of such a tragedy, combined with the breakup of her first romance and the failure of her first major film, had dealt her a temporarily overwhelming blow.

Where, she wondered as the boys tumbled back onto the seat facing her, did her career fit into all this? And what about her commitment to be here for Tad whenever he needed her?

It was too soon to make a decision. Maybe a few months from now she'd be ready. But not yet.

By the time they got home after dropping Joey off, the reporters were back in place. Cheri and Tad had to make a mad dash for the protection of the security guard.

Laughing, they went into the house.

"Have a good time?" Vinnie was in the kitchen, stuffing a chicken for dinner. She and Cheri took turns preparing the meals.

"Joey and me had three doughnuts," Tad declared.

"Well, this won't be ready for an hour and a half, so that sounds about right." Vinnie washed her hands and gave Tad a big hug.

"Where'd you lead them to, anyway?" Cheri asked.

"I thought they might benefit from a nice tour around scenic Orange." Vinnie released Tad with one last squeeze. "They had quite a time getting out of the traffic circle. I think one or two of them may be going around there still."

Cheri grinned at the image. Tad frowned as if worried that the skeletal remains of a tabloid news hound might be discovered still circling endlessly, then realized it was a joke.

"You're real wicked, Aunt Vinnie," he said.

"I do my best."

The two of them had grown so close that Cheri could almost have felt envious—except that she knew Tad needed more of a family than just one person.

Perhaps Vinnie would be willing to watch Tad after school if I went back to work, Cheri found herself thinking. He wouldn't mind spending a few hours each day with his new friend.

She shook her head. Where were these ideas coming from, anyway?

After a minute, Cheri realized Tad had wandered away and Vinnie was speaking.

"...So after they figured out they'd been tricked and gave up, I went by to see a real estate agent I'd talked to a few months ago. He's going to check his computer and see what's available in that neighborhood I told you about. The old bungalows from the 1920s."

"You're thinking of buying?" Cheri began unloading the dishwasher. "Does this mean you're moving out? I hope those reporters haven't scared you away."

"Oh, no." Vinnie tucked the chicken into the oven. "You see, I've come to a decision. Something I'd been thinking about for a long time."

Cheri sorted the silverware into the drawer, feeling uneasy. Having Vinnie here with them gave her a sense of security, and yet she knew the other woman couldn't stay forever. "What's that?"

"Being a foster parent. Maybe I'll adopt later on, if I find a child I like as well as Tad." Vinnie folded her arms and stood in the doorway. "It's time I stopped running away."

"You're welcome here as long as you like. You could keep foster children here." Cheri wasn't ready for such a big change, not right now.

"I'd feel better having a place of my own," Vinnie said. "But that doesn't mean I won't be over here a lot. And I'll expect you and Tad to visit me plenty often." As tactful as ever, she didn't mention Sky.

"Is this—going to happen soon?"

"Oh, not for a month or so, I expect. Don't escrows usually take a while? Although I've still got all that money in the bank from Vick's life insurance, so I guess I won't need much of a loan." Obviously Vinnie had thought this through carefully.

Cheri sighed. "We'll miss you. A lot."

The rest of the evening passed in easy comradeship, enlivened by a game of Monopoly. But you needed at least three people to have any fun at it, Cheri realized.

Sky will be back from Russia in a few days. But he'd be stopping over in New York for a week, and she had no doubt that even when he returned he'd be swamped, editing the subseries on the Soviet Union.

They were drifting apart. She'd felt that the last time they were together, and when they'd talked on the phone. It wasn't something either of them could help. Maybe it was inevitable.

Not if they were both willing to fight, and fight hard. Surely something could be worked out if they would both make sacrifices, not only at the outset but over the long haul. But would he? Sky had made it clear from the beginning that his career came first. He'd said nothing since then to indicate a change of mind.

She almost wished she hadn't met him at all, Cheri told herself as she turned out the lights, tucked Tad into bed and went to her room.

No, that wasn't true. Undressing by the quiet glow of a single lamp, she thought about the nights she'd spent in Sky's arms. They had been times of discovery as well as joy, of learning about herself as a woman. The months that she'd known him had been an important part of the healing process, and of her own maturing.

He was right. She'd changed a lot since that sunny September day when he first turned up on her doorstep.

But part of the change was learning how to love. Really love. Her affair with Terence had been based on need, physical attraction, and a childish sense of romanticism. This was different.

I'm going to love Sky for the rest of my life. Whether we can be together or not.

The realization gave Cheri a sudden pang. It was a hurt only Sky could heal.

She climbed into bed and lay there for a long time before falling asleep.

"NORA." She hadn't expected to see Allie sitting in the living room this morning. Usually Allie stayed in the library, which had become her bedroom these past few months, since her hip had been acting up. "I need to talk to you."

"You shouldn't be up! You might have fallen!" Nora *hurried across the fraying carpet.* *"Now, you lie down and I'll fix you a hot cup of tea."*

"Sit down and stop fussing." Allie's *thick-veined hand pointed imperiously to a settee. Her white hair might be thinning, but her eyes were as fierce and commanding as ever.*

Reluctantly, Nora *sat. The habit of obeying* Allie *was an old one, even though they'd long ago ceased to be mistress and hired companion.* *"Well? Get on with it. There's breakfast to fix."*

"I read something in the paper last night that I hid from you. It was a selfish thing to do." Allie's *fingers drummed against the faded surface of the sofa.*

"Something in the paper?" Nora *shook her head in confusion.* *"What could that be?"*

"Bessie Severinson died," Allie *said.*

Bessie Brownlie Severinson. Hank's *wife these past thirty years, and the mother of his five children.* Nora *had seen them together at church, the family gradually expanding, then the children growing up. What contentment* Bessie *had radiated, and* Hank *too, after the first baby came.*

"I'm sorry to hear it," she said.

"Nonsense." Allie *gazed at her severely.* *"Do you think I don't know you were in love with* Hank? *That you turned him down for my sake? Well, it's not too late to make up for lost time,* Nora. *You're not such an old woman that you can't still marry."*

"And leave you?" Nora *was horrified.* *"Nonsense. Besides, what was between* Hank Severinson *and me has been over for thirty years."*

"Piffle," said Allie. *"That's your pride speaking. What you mean is, he hasn't asked you. Well, and he won't. Not unless you make a point of speaking to him. Take one of your lemon cakes over there. It's common courtesy to bring*

*food when someone has died. He'll make the next move,
believe me."*

"She's not even cold in her grave!" Nora protested. But
that wasn't really the problem.

What she'd wanted from Hank was a life together, children of their own, the kind of devotion that could only develop from surviving life's setbacks and unraveling its
complexities together. All that would be left now was companionship, and she had that with Allie.

"Go to him," her old friend said.

"No. I—"

"Listen to me." What effort it cost Allie to lean forward
and seize her hands, Nora could only guess. "I will say this
once, and only once, because I'm a proud woman myself.
But you listen, Nora Leeds."

"It won't change my mind."

"Be that as it may. I've been a damn fool, Nora. I can't
even remember what Jeremiah Hunt looked like. Do you
know, he's probably been dead for years? That or in jail.
Either way, I don't care. It wasn't for love that I shut myself up here. It was out of pure vanity. I've been the most
willful old coot that ever lived. And I've let you make a
mess out of your life for my sake, and never said a word."
Despite her frailty, fire blazed in Allie Granger's voice.
"Well, I'm saying a word now. You've got a few good years
left in you. Don't waste them."

A dark, bitter taste rose up in Nora's mouth. She had a
few years left, yes, but they wouldn't be good ones. Toler-
able, perhaps. Quiet, living on here after Allie was gone.
Because anyone could see that Allie was dying.

She didn't have the energy to start over again, to be a wife
now, even if Hank Severinson still wanted her. She would
stay on in this house, with her garden and that old pantry
full of vegetables canned in years gone by, smelling the
faded scents of a life that had passed both too quickly and
too slowly.

Something pressed down on Cheri's chest. Hot, unshed tears burned inside her as she floated upward through the darkness into the present.

She lay in bed for several minutes, not sure whether she'd been dreaming or remembering.

What a terrible thing, Cheri thought, rolling over and peering hopefully at the window, but there was no sign of dawn. Allie Granger's admission of a wasted life had been painfully real, and so had Nora's.

Cheri didn't want to grow old, never daring to take chances. With Sky she'd taken a risk that might hurt her deeply, but it was better than feeling nothing at all. Even if in the end he was going to drift away, she couldn't shut herself up here the way Allie and Nora had done.

It would be like suffocating.

Hugging her knees, Cheri sat in bed for a while, letting the early-morning air chill her shoulders. She was scared. Not frightened like an adult, but scared like a child. She wished Sky were there to hold and reassure her. But she couldn't go through life leaning on other people.

Finally she snuggled back under the covers, knowing that she'd reached a turning point—even though she didn't yet know which path she would choose to take.

CHERI FINALLY REACHED ELAINE on the phone in midafternoon. "Sorry to disturb you," she said, "but these reporters are driving me crazy. Any suggestions on how to get rid of them?"

"Sure." Elaine's breezy confidence flowed over the telephone. "Give a press conference."

"Right."

"I'm serious. Hire a meeting room—I'd recommend the Beverly Wilshire, it's got class—lay on a spread of pastries and coffee, answer their questions, pose for their pictures and tape-record the whole thing. Then if they make stuff up, at least you can prove it."

It would be like walking straight into the lion's den. "Excuse me, but I'm not real jazzed by this idea. For one thing, I wouldn't even know where to start."

"You start by hiring a publicist. Let him set the whole thing up. I've got somebody on retainer you could use."

The last thing Cheri wanted was a press agent, although she supposed one would come in handy if she really did intend to follow Elaine's advice. "Hey. Wait a minute." Something surfaced from the jumble of her conflicting thoughts. "Don't you usually give a press conference to make some kind of announcement?"

"Okay," Elaine said. "We'll announce that you're coproducing and starring in *Bonjour, Bel Air*."

"You never give up, do you?"

"Never."

"What about Angela Fry? Did they pick up her option to make that sequel this summer?"

There was a brief pause at the other end of the line. "Cheri," Elaine said with an edge of impatience, "I don't want Angela Fry. I want you."

She still believes in me. More than I believe in myself. It was as if Cheri had found a missing piece of a jigsaw puzzle lying on the floor and could finally put the picture together. She might not be sure she had talent, but Elaine was. And she respected Elaine's judgment as much as anybody's in Hollywood.

"I'll do it," she said.

"Well, glory be. You're coming to your senses at last." Elaine gave her the name of the publicist. "I'll have him set it up as soon as possible. You'll need a press kit, an up-to-date bio. When he calls you, Cheri, just act like the old pro that you are, okay? Don't put on your shrinking violet act."

Cheri wanted to give her friend a good thump, but she knew Elaine was right. She'd been nursing her self-doubts for far too long. "I think I've still got a packet of publicity photos somewhere."

"Great. I gotta go. Oh, who are you using for an agent these days? We've got to draw up some contracts."

"No agent." Cheri gave her the name of a lawyer who had reviewed several of her contracts in the past. "I'm sure he'll be fine."

"Okay for now, but find yourself a new one. You're going to be a busy woman after this film comes out. Ciao." Elaine rang off.

Too late to turn back now. I'd never be able to face Elaine.

Cheri sat down at the kitchen table and began making lists of things to do. That always seemed to calm her when she felt out of control. Right now, a roller coaster looked like an oasis of stability in comparison to what she was feeling.

She wished Vinnie hadn't gone out on a psychic consultation today. She wished...

Down the block the school bus pulled up. Cheri watched, frozen, as Tad pounded down the sidewalk before the reporters could stop him and raced up the walk. What was he going to think about all this?

She went to waylay Tad in the hall. As soon as she got him settled in the kitchen, she told him about going back to work.

"Fantastic!" His reaction was immediate and unreserved. "Wow, a real movie! The other kids have been asking me what you were doing next."

"It means I won't always be here when you come home," she warned. "I—I haven't made any arrangements yet. Maybe you could spend some time with Vinnie and some time at Kate's, or I could arrange with one of the neighbors. And maybe day camp this summer..."

"Sure." Tad shrugged. "We'll work it out." He sounded so much like Jeff that Cheri reached over and squeezed his hand.

"I love you," she said.

He wiggled. "Yeah. What about—I mean—" He looked slightly embarrassed. "Is Sky ever coming back, or what?"

"I don't know, Tad." She couldn't tell if he was upset or not. "I mean, of course he's coming back, but I don't know if he'll stay."

"Well, do you think he could come talk to my class at school? The kids think it's terrific about him going to Russia and they all watch his program."

"I'm sure he will." If there were dark undercurrents to Tad's thoughts, they didn't show. Kids were resilient, Cheri had heard, and she was beginning to believe it.

Somehow they were going to muddle through, she and Tad. Because they were a family.

Only there was someone missing, someone very important—but right now there was nothing she could do about that.

USUALLY the drone of an airplane made Sky sleepy, but despite his bone-deep weariness, he couldn't seem to doze off.

He wished he were going straight to California, even though it would add five hours to this already agonizingly long flight. It felt like years instead of weeks since he'd seen Cheri.

Being in the Soviet Union had been simultaneously stimulating and depressing. There hadn't been much time for taking in historic sites or cultural events, but he'd been impressed by the spires of the Kremlin and even more by the shining marble and mosaics of the subway system.

Right now, the findings of the researchers he'd met were all tangled up in his mind with the painfully slow task of communicating through translators, the awkward logistics of schlepping cameras around, and with the lively faces of young people on the otherwise gray streets.

The research they'd uncovered was exciting, although he doubted Western scientists would be willing to accept the evidence of psi powers even when demonstrated in the laboratory and shown on TV. It was a little frightening, too, to think of what military uses could be made of clairvoyance.

So much to think about. And he was much too tired and too homesick to sort it out now.

A stewardess bent over Sky, asking what he'd like to drink. Coffee, he said. Real American coffee.

Glancing past her, he saw that most of his crew members were asleep. Lucky people.

Adrenaline still coursed through his system. These past two weeks had been a tremendous challenge, exciting even when they were frustrating. But he didn't feel as elated as he might have a dozen years ago. Maybe it was because he was getting older; his stamina wasn't what it used to be. Getting older in more ways than one.

When he was younger, he'd felt like a snail that carried its home around with it. A suitcase, a notebook, a camera crew waiting downstairs in the lobby—that had been everything he needed.

Not anymore. He'd missed Cheri the whole time. Missed Tad, even the Granger ghosts. Wished he were there to help her fend off the press. Wished they had more time to let things unfold naturally between them, instead of being continents apart.

This wasn't the right time to fall in love. But it had happened, so now what?

Sky turned to look out the window. It was night, a very long night to compensate for the extrashort one on his way to Europe. In the cloudy darkness he could make out a few stars, but the ocean below was invisible. He felt suspended here between worlds, in a hidden pocket of time that belonged only to jet travelers.

He'd had one phone call from Appleby last week, to tell him the ratings were outstanding. Ten more stations had signed up. The show on Cheri Louette's house had turned the corner for them.

He closed his eyes, remembering his first sight of her, clinging to a pillar on the front porch. Wild-eyed, as delicate and as tough as a doe. Not what he'd expected.

Caught between worlds. Both of us.

He wished he weren't obligated to spend the next few days in New York. Besides which, Appleby was pressuring him to move there full-time.

Sky leaned his head back against his seat and wondered why the ratings didn't mean nearly as much as he'd expected. But of course, he already knew the answer to that.

What he didn't know was what he was going to do about it.

Chapter Nineteen

"Checklist." Vinnie waved the sheet of paper from where she sat on Cheri's bed. "Ready?"

"Uh-huh." *Darn it,* if she was this nervous already, how was she going to feel tomorrow? Setting her jaw firmly, Cheri pointed at the closet. "Gray suit, cleaned and pressed. Purse already packed. Shoes shined. Matching stockings."

Vinnie made little check marks on the paper. Cheri could have done it herself, but it calmed her to lean on someone else for the moment. She was glad Tad had already gone to bed. His blind confidence made her feel inadequate.

"Next?" Vinnie prompted.

Cheri moved to her dressing table. "Makeup ready to go. Earrings, necklace, hair clip. Do you think I should have arranged for a hairdresser? I prefer to do my own hair, but what if it comes out wrong?"

"You'll probably have time to work in a hair appointment if you need to." Vinnie was doing her best not to look amused.

"But Elaine and I are having lunch at the Ivy, and I'll have to leave here by eleven to make it." Cheri chewed on her lower lip as a new thought occurred to her. "I should have had my car tuned! What if it won't start?"

"You'll take mine."

"But—" She didn't want to insult Vinnie's car, but the old station wagon would stick out like a sore thumb.

Vinnie didn't need her psychic ability to figure out why Cheri was hesitating. "Or I could drive you up, and you could take a cab the last two blocks to the restaurant."

The absurdity of it made Cheri smile. "Oh, who cares? I'm not applying for *Life-styles of the Rich and Famous*, right?"

Vinnie tapped her finger against the checklist. "Let's get on with this."

"Okay." Cheri lifted a briefcase from the floor and opened it. "Publicity photos, check. The publicist has the press kits. Here's my notes about the Granger house, in case my mind goes blank. Also a tape of Sky's show. Anything else?"

"If there is, it's not on your list, so don't worry about it." Vinnie handed the piece of paper back to her. "Now, let's go downstairs. I've got something to show you."

Cheri realized guiltily that she'd paid hardly any attention to Vinnie this week. Arranging the press conference had taken all her spare time, along with contacting the lawyer and making an appointment to talk to an agent she'd heard good things about.

The problem was that she didn't just need an agent. She needed somebody she could work with, who would understand that sometimes Tad came first and that Cheri wouldn't take a role she didn't believe in.

Most of all she needed someone who believed in her as an actress. Which might not be easy, given her reputation as a lightweight TV child star whose only major film had flopped.

Pushing the thoughts away, Cheri followed her friend downstairs.

"Now." Vinnie picked up an envelope from the hall table. "These aren't very good. They're just instant pictures, but they give you the idea."

The photos she handed Cheri showed a tidy cottage vined with climbing roses. The house must be a good sixty years old in the traditional California bungalow style, judging by its old-fashioned porch, peaked roof and double-hung windows.

"It's charming." She turned so she could see better in the hall light. "Is this one of the houses you've been looking at?"

"Actually we opened escrow this morning," Vinnie said.

It took a moment for the news to sink in. "You bought it?" Cheri didn't know whether to laugh or cry. This was an important step for Vinnie, she knew, but already the Granger house felt achingly empty. "But—when do you move in? I don't know what we're going to do without you."

"It's only a ten-minute drive from here." The suspicious brightness of Vinnie's eyes belied her matter-of-fact tone. "And next week I start my foster parenting classes. We have to go to four, you know. At least I've had practical experience, living with Tad. That ought to help my case."

"They wouldn't dare turn you down!" Cheri bristled at the idea. "They'll be lucky to get you!"

"Well, there is a crying need for good foster parents," Vinnie agreed mildly.

The phone rang in the kitchen. "Probably Elaine, calling to see if I've got cold feet." Cheri went to answer it.

The sound of Sky's deep voice sent a chill through her. So much had happened these past weeks. For him, too, she was sure. She didn't want to think about the gap that might be growing irreversibly between them.

She tried to keep her tone light. "Welcome back! How was Russia?"

"Fascinating." Sky sounded tired. "And exhausting. Are those reporters still driving you nuts?"

She told him about the press conference. "I'm kind of nervous."

"Elaine's a sharp lady," he said. "It'll take the wind out of their sails."

"That isn't all."

"Isn't all what?" His voice had a hoarse rasp to it. She realized it must be after midnight in New York.

"Well, you—you usually call a press conference to make an announcement, so Elaine suggested I announce that I'm starring in her new film, and I decided to do it." The words tumbled out more bluntly than Cheri had intended. "So I'm going back to work."

Her heart thudded loudly in the silence that followed. Was he angry? Disappointed? Or maybe relieved that she wouldn't be tugging at his sleeve, demanding attention? Cheri felt their future together hanging in the balance. If only he'd tell her how he felt.

"When do you start?" he asked quietly.

"Probably the end of April or the beginning of May," Cheri said. *And then you'll be going to Turkey this summer. Is this the way it's going to go, one of us always rushing around, never any time for being together?*

She waited, her throat tight, for him to respond. It seemed to take forever. Finally he said, "I'm pleased for you. I think that's the right decision, Cheri."

"You aren't going to say I told you so, are you?" They were being so damn civilized. Why couldn't he yell at her if that was how he felt? Maybe they both ought to face the truth that sometimes love wasn't enough, not if one person was off flying around the globe and the other needed an identity of her own. Instead, here they were making polite chitchat. Cheri's teeth ached with the effort of holding back her feelings.

He'd said from the start that ambitions and relationships were a losing proposition. Did he always have to be right?

"I knew you couldn't shut yourself up in that house forever," Sky said. "Listen, I'm really wiped out. It was a long flight and—I'm not thinking clearly. Good luck tomorrow."

"Thanks." So many things she wanted to say, and it wasn't the right time for any of them. "Get some sleep."

They wished each other a good night like two casual acquaintances. Cheri hung up, feeling as if she'd just run a marathon race backward.

He hadn't said anything about the future. What was there to say, anyway?

Vinnie came in from the other room. Cheri appreciated that her friend had given her privacy for this conversation.

"Anything I should know about?" Vinnie said.

If she broke down and cried, Cheri wasn't sure she could stop. The last thing she needed was to have red eyes and blotchy skin in the morning. "Not—particularly."

The older woman looked as if she wanted to find something reassuring to say but couldn't. "Try to get some sleep."

Cheri nodded and went upstairs. Tonight, for the first time since the weeks after Jeff and Donna died, she forced herself to take a sleeping pill.

AMAZINGLY, Friday dawned bright and clear. Tad didn't come down with the measles, Cheri's hair didn't self-destruct and her car even started on the first try. Except for the shadow of pain across her heart, she felt fully functional and almost calm.

This time, Cheri reluctantly agreed to a table set prominently on the Ivy's patio dining area, where she and Elaine would be noticed by everyone who came in. At least she hadn't been dogged by reporters this morning; since being handed their invitations to the press conference, her usual entourage had decamped.

"You've got to start courting attention," Elaine reminded her after they ordered a light lunch.

"I suppose—"

"Cheri! You're looking wonderful!" A character actor who'd had a recurring role on *Young and Eager* stopped by to exchange cheek kisses and superficial compliments. Cheri remembered to praise his latest stint on a cable TV series.

"Good. You're getting your feet wet," Elaine said after he left.

"It's so hard to think of what to say. I guess I'll have to start reading *Variety* more closely." She knew Elaine would take her grumbling in the right spirit. "I'm going to see that new agent on Monday. Wish me luck."

"You don't need luck. You've got talent," Elaine said. "And it looks like you've already taken off a few pounds."

"A couple." It was harder dieting now that she had Tad, Cheri had discovered. Cooking meals for a hungry eight-year-old made it difficult to content herself with a small salad. And sweets of one kind or another seemed to migrate into the house of their own accord. But she was managing.

"Oops. Don't look up," Elaine said.

Cheri ducked her head. "Who?" Her old agent? The director of her bomb?

"Give me an *O* for obnoxious, give me an *M* for Me First...."

Terence Omara. "Where?"

"Coming up the steps with a bimbo on his arm."

Cheri peeked sideways through the screen of her fingers. Two tall figures were strolling toward the host's station with studied aplomb.

They didn't seem to be looking her way, but other people might. Cheri carefully kept her expression bland even as she continued to study them surreptitiously.

It had been a year and a half since she'd seen Terence. He wasn't quite as thin as she remembered, but otherwise he'd stayed fit. Handsome, yes, in a slick leading man way. Thick eyelashes, piercing blue eyes, photogenic cheekbones. There might be a few more wrinkles at the corners of his mouth from excess sun, but men were allowed to look craggy.

The difference was in the way she felt about him.

Cheri could see the calculation behind his every move, how he scanned the room—passing over her as if she didn't exist—to check out those present who might be able to help his career. How he ignored the young blonde at his side, not even bothering to introduce her when he greeted a film studio executive. All this she could observe objectively. The electricity she'd once felt radiating from him had disappeared. He was just someone she used to know.

It was hard to believe she'd been so blindly enamored of him two years ago; but then, he'd taken care to shower her with attention during the early stages of their romance. She would never be so easily fooled again.

Because she knew now what a real man was like, and how genuine affection and concern grew between two people. She knew the difference between a deep, irresistible drive to achieve something that mattered to you, and shallow ambition based on egotism and greed.

But all that wasn't much of a consolation right now. It made her miss Sky with all her soul, in a way she'd never missed that popinjay Terence.

Wow, she thought with a smile. *Poor old Terry. He's only a passable actor. He needs to play the game for all it's worth, or he'll sink like a stone.*

"I don't believe it." Elaine was watching her approvingly. "You're actually grinning. What gives?"

"I never thought I'd feel sorry for Terence," Cheri sa
"But I do."

Elaine didn't need to ask why. Elaine had never liked Terence. "I hear he just got beat out for a Steven Spielberg film he thought was going to turn him into the next Harrison Ford."

"No comparison," Cheri said.

"Of course not. But you don't expect Terence to see that, do you?"

A waiter was seating Terence and his companion at the far side of the patio. On purpose, Cheri was sure. Hollywood waiters knew better than to put ex-lovers too close to each other.

"The only thing that bothers me," she said, "is that everybody else is going to think I'm upset."

"Well," Elaine said, "I did hear he's up for a supporting role in a new police series."

Without thinking twice, Cheri stood up. Instantly she felt dozens of pairs of eyes focus on her. Carefully maintaining a pleasant expression, she made her way between the tables and crossed to where her former lover sat.

"Terence!" She knew how to give his name exactly the right cheery, impersonal tone. "You're looking wonderful. I hear you're up for a terrific part—good luck!"

After a split second of baffled confusion, he rose to the occasion. "Rumor has it you're getting back into harness. Way to go, Cheri."

They shook hands. "Hi," Cheri said to the blonde, who looked very young and somewhat intimidated. "I'm Cheri Louette."

"I know." The girl accepted her handshake hesitantly. "I—I've been a fan of yours for years. I—that was a wonderful program about you and the ghosts."

"Thank you." *Time to cut off this encounter.* "Nice to meet you. See you around, Terry." She knew he hated the ickname, but she couldn't resist.

"Bye." Momentarily at a loss for words, he sank into his as she departed.

When Cheri returned to the table, their lunch was being served. She and Elaine said nothing until the waiter was gone.

"That should give everybody something to chew over," Elaine said.

"Had to break the ice sometime." Cheri dug into her salad. "You never know when we'll run into each other."

"A lovely performance." Elaine smiled over her forkful of fish. "I give it two thumbs up."

"Save it till after the press conference." But Cheri didn't feel nearly as apprehensive as she had a few hours ago.

VINNIE COULDN'T RESIST driving by the cottage on her way back from the bookstore. It needed painting; she was tending toward blue and gray, but that combination was being a bit overdone these days. Yellow might be nice, too, and cheerful for the children.

Already she could imagine them playing in the yard, shouting as they kicked a ball or zoomed around on skateboards. Skateboards. She shuddered. Now there was something Marcella Granger hadn't had to worry about.

It felt a bit odd that she hadn't heard from Marcella in quite some time. Maybe the woman had finally gone to her rest, but Vinnie didn't really think so.

She drove on past the house that was going to be hers, though she should really have spent her time today at a furniture store, picking out the new sofa and beds she would need. She'd discarded the worn-out items from the apartment when she moved into Cheri's house.

It would be nice to buy new towels and sheets, too, though no doubt grimy little fingers would quickly re them to rags. But that was a minor problem.

As she drove, Vinnie felt her doubts creep back. indulging too much in romantic fantasies ab children and happy homes? Most foster child abused or neglected, and their lives would rupted by being placed in care. No doubt they'd be difficult, sometimes aggravating, even destructive.

She had a feeling that the prospect ought to bother her. But it didn't.

The thing is, Vinnie admitted as she halted at a stoplight, *I'm bored with being too comfortable. I could use a little chaos now and again.*

The light changed, and her station wagon chugged forward. It had seen better days, but the vehicle she'd bought to cart easels and art supplies around would serve well for carrying children. And groceries. And toys.

Books, too. She carted the bag of them into the Granger house, nearly tripping as she went up the steps and fumbling with her keys. She really shouldn't have bought so many books.

Inside the front hall, Vinnie dumped the sack onto the table with relief. She'd only gone into the store to look for guides on foster parenting, and instead she'd been seduced into the children's section. Having heard a lot about Judy Blume, she'd felt obligated to buy one of her books, along with a guide to computer games that would appeal to Tad.

Then, spurred by Kate's recent enthusiasm about learning to use a computer, Vinnie had been seized by the urge to buy one of her own. A check of the computer store had been enough to intimidate her. So many models, and so much software! She would need to do some research, she could see that. No doubt Tad would be glad to help.

Standing there in the hall, Vinnie became aware of how ~~e~~mpty the house was. Usually Cheri stayed home; espe- ~~cial~~ly these last few weeks, when she'd hardly gone out at ~~all. T~~here were an awful lot of creaks, considering there ~~wasn't~~ any wind today. And rustling noises from the back ~~of the hou~~se.

~~"Cheri?" s~~he called. No, he wouldn't be home yet. It was ~~only four-~~thirty.

In the months she'd lived here, the Granger house had come to feel like home. Vinnie hardly noticed the wisps of perception that wafted her way these days; Allie and Nora were simply two more rather faded members of the family.

Something thumped in the library. A book, falling off a shelf.

"Oh, Marcella," Vinnie snapped. The spirit was back, no doubt moping about, mired in her own self-pity. Just as Vinnie used to be.

Irritated as much with her former self as with the restless ghost, Vinnie strode into the library. As soon as she entered, she knew the room was empty.

Why had Marcella come and gone so quickly?

A volume lay open on the floor, face down. Vinnie picked it up, noting that it was part of a set of Shakespeare's plays. Turning it over, she was about to smooth out a dog-ear when she saw that it appeared to point to one particular speech. The play was *As You Like It*.

"Well, well," Vinnie clucked under her breath as she read the exiled duke's words.

Sweet are the uses of adversity, Which, like the toad, ugly and venomous, Wears yet a precious jewel in his head; And this our life exempt from public haunt Finds tongues in trees, books in the running brooks, Sermons in stones, and good in everything.

She closed the book gently. Was it a simple coincidence or a message? Vinnie was inclined to believe the latter. Marcella had found consolation in seeing the lessons own tragedies turn Vinnie's life around. A jewel h from adversity, and Marcella, it would seem, h last to accept the beauty that lay everywhere

Now she can be at peace.

The realization left her strangely sad. Annoying as Marcella could be, she had also come to feel like a part of Vinnie, and it was hard to let her go.

Just as it had been hard to let go of her own self-pity, her own futile dreams of establishing a career as an artist, her own cloistered but unsatisfying life. Now Vinnie had shaken herself free, and so had Marcella.

"Hi! I'm home!" The bang of the front door emphasized Tad's words.

"In the library," Vinnie called, not sure she was quite ready for the boy's rambunctious presence.

"What are you doing in here?" Galloping through the house, Tad burst into the room like a spurt of fireworks. "Hey, I got an A on my math test!"

"That's wonderful. You worked hard for that." Vinnie dragged her thoughts out of their introspective spiral. "You know, I could use a little advice."

"From me?"

"Yes." All of a sudden the air smelled fresher, and she noticed that sunlight was pouring in through the windows. "I've been thinking about buying a computer. What would you recommend?"

She barely had time to call and leave a message for Cheri before they were out the door, heading for the nearest computer store.

THE FIRST PART of the press conference went smoothly. At her publicist's suggestion, Cheri played the tape of Sky's show on the large monitor, then, with Elaine, announced that she would star in and co-produce *Bonjour, Bel Air*.

e first few questions she'd prepared for. They had to her feelings about returning to Hollywood after nspicuous failure, and Cheri was proud of the which she acknowledged her conflicting feel-

"I've got to find out sometime whether I can handle it," she said.

Before she could call on another questioner, a reporter from one of the tabloids stood up. She recognized him, because he'd been staking out her house for that past two weeks.

"Miss Louette." He somehow infused the name with sneering innuendos. "This business about your house being haunted—that was a sham, wasn't it? A gimmick to get your name back in front of the public. There's a rumor you've been dating this guy Sky Welton. You cooked this up between the two of you, didn't you?"

Half of her wanted to crawl under the podium. The other half wanted to throw a cup of hot coffee at the creep.

Her publicist and Elaine both started to speak at once, but Cheri held up her hands. She'd called the press conference, and it was up to her to handle this.

"Let me address your points one at a time." Cheri took care to refrain from mirroring his insulting tone. He might behave like a jerk, but she didn't have to.

"First," she heard herself say, "at the time I agreed to tape that program, I had no intention of returning to acting. The legends about the Granger ghosts date from long before I moved into the house. You don't have to believe them. I sometimes have doubts myself."

Several reporters nodded. She hoped that meant they'd checked out the Granger legends for themselves.

"As for Sky Welton, he and I have become friends." Let the questioner read into that whatever he wanted. "We r___ when he came to ask me if he could tape a show o___ Granger house. So much for your absurd suggest___ he and I cooked this thing up."

With a calmness that was hard won, she p___ other raised hand, this one belonging to a re___ of the respectable trade publications. "Y___

"Is your move into co-producing an attempt to gain greater creative control?" Now they were back on a professional plane.

"In a way. I certainly don't want to go through another experience like my last film." She didn't cite the director or her co-star, but people in show business would draw the right conclusions. "Up to this point, I've let other people run my career. Well, I'm a big girl now. If I fall on my face this time, I'll have no one else to blame."

There was a ripple of sympathetic chuckles from the ladies and gentlemen of the press. By this time most of them were on Cheri's side. She suspected their articles would reflect that.

An adrenaline high surged through her. She was facing down the lions in their den and coming out unscathed.

Was this really Cheri Louette, the submissive child, the uncertain teenager, the gawky young woman who'd fallen hook, line and sinker for Terence Omara?

No, she realized as she fielded the last questions with ease. This was Cheri Louette, mother of Tad, who knew what it was like to love a mature man with all her heart.

If she could handle this press conference, then she could work out her life with Sky. It wouldn't be easy. What marriage ever was? There would be countless issues to resolve, scheduling problems to overcome, minor and major crises arising unexpectedly.

But she could weather it, if Sky was willing to meet her halfway.

The only problem was, she couldn't be sure he would. After their abbreviated conversation last night. Not this time they were spending apart, and the way were changing.

ren't on the opposite side of the country. But real problem. The real problem was that be exactly where he was.

As she stepped down from the podium and obligingly posed for photographs, Cheri knew that she couldn't leave the next step to chance.

She was going to have to confront Sky. Fly out to New York, if that was what it took. She'd have to be prepared to accept whatever response he might give.

It was going to be a whole lot harder than facing up to this press conference. But she was strong enough now.

At least she hoped she was.

Chapter Twenty

Cheri navigated the freeway interchanges automatically, scarcely noticing the thickening late-afternoon traffic. Her thoughts flew ahead of her.

Book a flight to New York. Call Sky and make sure he had time to see her. Arrange for Vinnie to watch Tad, maybe with some help from Kate.

Pack her clothes. Pack her feelings, fears, hopes. Cart the whole mess to the East Coast.

Cheri frowned as a red Camaro cut in front of her. Another overeager Southern California driver, risking life and limb to get home five minutes sooner. Why couldn't people have more sense of perspective?

Perspective. Maybe that was what she'd been gaining during the last year. Maybe that was what Sky had been referring to when he told her she'd matured.

Well, okay, she could see things clearly now. That she ¹dn't need to lean on anybody, that she wasn't cut out to ɔme quietly snuggling up to her vacuum cleaner and cookies all day.

ǝt she loved Sky with all the depth and strength of

¹ was still in turmoil as she turned off the ¹sed home. She was glad Vinnie and Tad

had decided to go shopping. It would be nice to have a little time alone, time to calm down.

The funny thing was that in a way she felt terrific. She'd handled the press conference like a pro, as Elaine had been quick to point out. She wasn't even nervous about seeing the new agent next week. If he didn't meet her standards, she didn't have to sign with him.

The agent worked for her, not the other way around. How she'd ever put up with that jerk she used to have, Cheri couldn't understand, except that she'd been a different person at the time. An insecure girl instead of a woman.

She turned the corner, relieved that her street was no longer lined with campers full of snoopy tabloid reporters. But there was a car parked in front of the Granger house. A silver BMW.

Sky? He was supposed to be in New York until next week.

Cheri pulled up behind the car. Yes, she recognized the license plate. Unless Sky had loaned his car to someone, he was here.

A wave of apprehension washed over her. She wanted so much to see him, but she wasn't ready to do it now. They were at a turning point. What if he wasn't willing to make compromises for the sake of their relationship? How would she rein in her pain, hold back the tears and recriminations? The last thing she wanted was a bitter scene.

Trying to stiffen her resolve, Cheri tilted the rearview mirror and freshened her makeup, smoothing on the pow der and lipstick, then ran a brush through her hair. Th were a few small lines at the corners of her eyes th hadn't noticed before, she realized with a start.

They would disappear under the right kind c of course. She was still more than two years No need to worry. Except that the years v wait for her. The problem with maturin to grow older in order to do it.

There was nothing to be gained by sitting here and thinking philosophical thoughts. Any minute she'd start playing out scenarios, imagining what Sky might say, and torment herself to exactly the state of near hysteria she was trying to avoid.

Cheri reluctantly opened the car door and walked up to the house. It was locked. Taking a deep breath, she went around to the garden.

The roses that she'd pruned last winter had burst into their first, most glorious spring bloom. Bright red and pink blossoms starred the dark green bushes and wove upward around the newly repainted trellis. The air quivered with their sweetness.

On the stone bench, Sky sat staring into space. Unnoticed, Cheri paused as a memory stabbed through her. Hank, waiting for his Nora, only to be sent away.

Does the history of this house have to keep repeating itself?

Sky looked up and saw her. "Cheri!" He rose and moved forward, then stopped. Had he seen the trepidation in her face?

Neither of them spoke. Cheri couldn't tear her eyes from his face. He looked different—not older, really, but his skin had a ruddy cast that spoke of long hours and hard travel, and there was a trace of sadness in his eyes. It was a face she had come to know as well as her own.

"How was the press conference?" Sky said.

"Not bad." She caught her breath. "It was—well, they ˺ˑed the kind of questions I'd expected. Nothing I ˈn't handle."

˹y you decided to go back to show business?"

˹he said. "Are you?"

˹ expecting it." He walked slowly toward her, might startle away like a frightened deer. ˹cited about playing Belle. From what ˹art sounds perfect."

She didn't want to talk about acting. "Sky, I've been thinking."

"Wait." He caught her hand. "So have I."

Her knees began to tremble. "Maybe we should sit down." As he led her toward the bench, she said, "Not there."

"Why not?"

"That's where Nora..." *No.* She wasn't going to start talking about the ghosts as if they were real. "I mean, I had a dream...."

"Still?" Here in the garden it was cooler than she'd realized, and when Sky's arms encircled her, Cheri leaned into his warmth.

"A while back. Vinnie's been dreaming too, about Marcella. It's made her come to terms with some things she's unhappy about." Chattering about Vinnie felt safe. "She's buying a house. She's going to be a foster mother. Don't you think that sounds wonderful?"

"I love you," Sky murmured.

"What?"

"I love you."

It had come out of nowhere. "Yes, but—I mean—why are you telling me this?"

"Because you're so frightened." Sky moved back a little, so he could look at her fully. "Aren't you?"

"Yes, but—"

"Last night, after we talked, I did some heavy thinking. Which is why I'm here."

A cool breeze blew over Cheri, raising goose b...
"Could we go inside?"

"Of course." He seemed to understand that ...
to delay a little, that she wasn't quite ready ...
ever he had to say. They went into the hou...
coffee, and then they sat down in the li...

It was here that they'd first made love, here that they'd taped that fateful program. And here, appropriately, that they should say the things that had to be said.

"Okay," Cheri said. "Shoot."

"Why do I get the feeling you mean that literally?" Sky said, smiling but with an edge of strain. "Well. You remember what I said when we first met, about marriages between ambitious people not working?"

She nodded.

"I've been thinking about that." He sipped his coffee gratefully, and Cheri realized that he must have gotten up early to catch a flight to L.A. Which meant he was even more tired than he'd been last night.

"What's occurred to me," Sky went on, "is that in marriages like that, both people have to make sacrifices. That's easy to say; it sounds like something out of a marriage manual. But as you know, when you've worked for something all your life, it's not easy to give it up, even part of it."

She felt she ought to say something. "I've been thinking about that, too." *It is possible, if you really want to. But I won't push.*

"It seemed to me that after a while, both partners would start to feel resentful." He was looking down at his coffee cup, as if it held something of intense interest. "There's a measure of frustration and conflict in any long-term relationship. Add extra stress, and things can deteriorate quickly."

"It wouldn't be easy," Cheri said.

~~ky slanted a look at her. "No, it wouldn't. Being apart ~~ enough, when there aren't children involved. I know ~~ few months have been tough on Tad already. But ~~aste of success, and it isn't enough."

~~n't have spoken then, even if all the Granger ~~d in a conga line through the middle of the

"What I'm trying to say—" Sky took a deep breath "—is that I'm willing to make the effort. Compromise doesn't threaten me anymore. I don't think I'd miss whatever it was I gave up, not nearly as much as I'd miss you if you weren't around."

"What about—moving to New York?" Right now Cheri needed to focus on specifics. "And Turkey?"

"I've already told Miles that he has to accept L.A. as my headquarters if he wants my show," Sky said. "He wasn't crazy about the idea, but we're a big hit, so he could hardly refuse. If the ratings slip, he might have my throat, but I'm not going to worry about that."

"I don't want you to feel later that you gave up too much." She hated to say that, but didn't want any lingering doubts.

"To hell with it." Sky glared at her, then smiled. "I'm not angry at you, just at—at myself, I guess, for being so cautious in the first place. As for Turkey, we'll put that off until you've wrapped your film. It may still be summer vacation, but either way, Tad will come with us. Travel is educational, right? And a family should be together."

"There'll be times when we can't." Cheri was talking to herself as much to him. "I used to think I couldn't handle long separations, but...I'll miss you like fire, but that's better than missing you all the time."

"Your turn," he said.

"For what?" Then she remembered. "Oh. I love you, Sky."

Before she realized what he was doing, Sky had scoop___ her up from the couch and was kissing her very, very ___ oughly. After a stunned moment, Cheri wrapped h___ around him and kissed him back.

In a rush of heat, her body reminded her how ___ missed him, missed the masculine scent o___ hardness of his chest against her soft b___ roughness of his jacket under her hand___

Together they sank onto the couch, a little self-conscious at first, but quickly forgetting it as they explored each other with long-suppressed hunger. Cheri needed Sky with every inch of herself, her skin, her mouth, her soul.

And he needed her. That was the marvelous, unbelievable part. Whatever he might be giving up, he was doing it with joy.

They had to force themselves not to proceed too quickly, to savor each caress. When finally they were one, Cheri's body quivered with the throbbing awareness of love.

This sense of completion was more than she'd dared dream of. The self-doubts of her past melted into nothing and her fears for the future wisped away like fog on a bright morning. The present became an endless circle of infinite richness.

When the lovemaking ended, they lay together for a while, listening to the now-familiar creaks of the house and the soft whisper of wind outside in the trees.

"I want time." Sky's voice seemed to come from deep inside him. "Time to be with you, time to relax. And I'm going to make that time."

"Me, too." She knew that filming would be an intense process, and that as co-producer she'd be involved with pre- and post-production. But really, it didn't take that long to make a film. Not nearly as long as it had taken them to build this precious closeness.

"I suppose—" He sat up and began pulling on his clothes. "We ought to talk about where we're going to live. ᵥote for the Granger house."

"It does feel like home," Cheri said, lazily following suit. "e could turn the attic into a rec room," Sky said. d. Then you and I could share the library as an of-

ve to settle all this right now?" Cheri chuck- ᵤess. "Once you make up your mind, you do you?"

"Absolutely not." He fumbled with his shoes. "We can have a big wedding if you like, but I suggest we take Tad with us and elope. That way we can have our privacy until after the honeymoon."

Cheri had forgotten about the reporters. They'd love this story. "They asked about us at the press conference," she said. "I hemmed and hawwed."

He shrugged. "They'll get used to us. We'll have one of those boring marriages that lasts forever. There are more of them than you'd think, even in show business."

Suddenly she had a lot to tell him. About how she'd handled the meeting with Terence, and Kate's excitement over her computer classes, and Tad's new circle of friends. But it could wait.

"We ought to go break the news to Tad," she said. "If I know him, he'll keep Vinnie at the computer store until it closes."

"Good idea. Then we can go out for pizza."

"Like normal people." She grinned, remembering Tad's remark.

"Like normal people."

They walked out together to Sky's car. As she waited for him to open the door, Cheri glanced back at the house. Maybe it was a hint of movement that had caught her eye.

Yes. Upstairs in her bedroom the curtains were billowing slightly. The windows didn't fit tightly, so she wasn't surprised.

But there was an odd, oval shadow on the window. *No.* Not exactly a shadow. It looked like a frost tracing, so thing Cheri had seen once on a skiing trip to Big Be most like a face.

"What the—?" Sky had noticed it, too.

It looked like an old woman's face, Cheri could make out two eyes with pouches und nose and a sagging chin. Like Allie G dream. Was that Nora just behind her

"She's smiling," Sky said.

Not smiling, exactly, but the face had softened suddenly, as if in approval.

"You don't suppose—" Cheri bit her lip. It was absurd. There were no such things as ghosts, not really.

Yet the impression came to her that Allie finally *was* happy. The cycle of lonely women in this house had been broken.

"I'll be damned," Sky said as the images vanished. "That's the first time I've ever seen a ghost."

"I don't believe in them." Cheri turned firmly and slid into the car.

"Of course not." Sky closed the door and went around to the driver's seat. "Neither do I. But I'm glad they approve of us."

They drove off to get Tad and Vinnie and break the good news.

Epilogue

"It's too long again this year," Sky grumbled as he reached for another handful of popcorn. "Why can't they cut the production numbers?"

"Yeah, and who wants to see all those old people that nobody watches any more?" Tad chimed in from where he and Joey were sprawled on the floor, playing Uno.

"The Oscars wouldn't be the Oscars if they weren't long and boring." Cheri, her sneakered feet propped up on the arm of the couch, felt warm and cozy and was in a highly tolerant mood.

"Besides, who cares?" Tad said. "You shoulda been nominated, Cheri." He'd dropped the "Aunt" some months ago; she couldn't precisely remember when.

Sky nodded gravely. "Next year, Tad. The film wasn't released until last month."

"Well, then they shoulda had you be a—whattaya cal-lit?—a presentator."

"Presenter," she corrected automatically. "They we' mostly lined up way ahead of time, Tad. Until *Boni* came out, nobody was paying any attention to me."

"Oh?" Sky cocked an eyebrow.

"We're speaking of my public life." She shift ing her head against his shoulder. It was a r she'd discovered in the eight months they'd

It had been a busy, satisfying year since that agonizing press conference that was already fading into a distant memory. Shooting the film had been exhilarating and challenging; Elaine had turned out to be a dream of a director. And Cheri had found she liked being part of the production team. For the first time in her career she'd felt like one of the grown-ups.

After a whirlwind wedding, she and Sky and Tad had taken a working honeymoon in Turkey, Egypt and Israel. The only link missing had been Vinnie, who couldn't come along as a consultant because she was now responsible for three foster children.

Two of them, a brother and sister, had been neglected, and another little girl had been seriously abused. She'd made a remarkable recovery, though, in the months she'd been with Vinnie, and there was a possibility she might be freed for adoption.

It had occurred to Cheri that she might like to have a baby of her own. Sky obviously loved children, but the time wasn't right yet. Well, maybe in the years ahead.

"Hey, look." Sky pointed as Angela Fry stepped up to the podium as one of the presenters. "Her career has really taken off."

"Mmm." There was a twinge of envy—but just a twinge—in Cheri's throat as she watched the stunning young woman exchange scripted repartee with her co-presenter. Angela was tremendously talented, and she didn't have any flops to make the critics hesitate about praising her. On the other hand, she didn't have a beloved husband and son, either, Cheri reminded herself.

"Didn't you say you nearly hired her to play Belle?" Tad ᵃ good memory, although it wasn't always evident from ᵈes. "She wouldn't have been as good as you,

ou got two thumbs up on that TV show," Joey like those guys, but Mom and Dad do."

"All the reviews say she's the best," Tad informed him softly. "They said she's a—a revolution."

"Revelation." His fierce loyalty sent a glow through her. "But I think I like revolution better."

Sky was staring at the screen. Cheri turned to watch. The winner of the Best Supporting Actor award, a sleek young newcomer, was grinning from ear to ear as he thanked his agent and his director.

"Isn't he the one you might be acting with this summer?" Sky reached around for his lemonade glass, nearly knocking it over before his hand closed around it.

"My agent says they're very interested in me." The offers had come trickling in at first, then flooding as the reviews for *Bonjour, Bel Air* hit the trades. "I like the role, but the script as a whole needs work."

"They could take out the clinches," Sky grumbled. "I hate love scenes."

Sitting up, she swung around so that she could see his face. "You never told me that!"

"That guy in *Bonjour* was a clown," he said. "It only bothered me a little."

"Yeah," Joey piped up. "Do you really kiss those guys, or do you just make it look that way?"

"Big ears," Sky whispered, adding aloud, "She just makes it look that way, Joey."

Not until later, after the last sequin-gowned actress had choked out her grateful acceptance speech and the last round-faced comic had cracked a semblance of a joke, did Sky and Cheri take up the topic again. By this time, both boys were sacked out in the bunk beds that now occupied Tad's room.

"Do you really mind about the love scenes?" asked as she pulled a nightgown from her closet and off her sweatshirt.

"Wasn't there a scene in that script where be in your lingerie?" Sky demanded.

"Oh. I plan to insist on a slip." She took off her jeans

"Do you suppose they'd settle for a suit of armor?" F was only half joking.

Cheri poked her head through the neck hole of th nightgown. "Sky, I don't have to do this particular movie

"It's a good role."

"There's nothing sexy about shooting one of those lo scenes." Surely he knew that intellectually, but feelings we harder to control. "I mean, you've got zillions of camer, men, gofers, directors and assistant directors and script gir and whatnot all hanging around. Who could take it ser ously?"

"Me," Sky admitted. "Damn it, Cheri, I'm proud c you. You're terrific. And you've never tried to hold m back. I don't want to put a crimp in your style, either."

She sat next to him on the bed. "Sky, I don't want an of those actors. Sure, when I'm acting, I sort of feel wha my character would feel, but that isn't me."

A sheepish look came over his face. "I don't believ we're even discussing this. It's not that I don't trust you Cheri. But you're so beautiful and sweet. I don't know how those guys could help falling in love with you."

"Most actors are only in love with themselves." She gav him a light punch in the side.

"How about talk show hosts?"

"Them, too," she teased. "There's one good thing abou your line of business, though."

"What?" He eyed her suspiciously.

"Most of the women you interview are either too youn too old for you," she said. "Or just plain weird. Onl e you like 'em weird. After all, you're the ghost bus

ack from a pillow caught her off guard. In sec d Sky were tussling across the bed, a matc d into love play.

"Well?" he said when they were lying breathlessly side by side.

"Well what?"

"Did it feel like you were really making love, without all those cameramen looking on?"

"I'm not sure," she said. "Maybe we ought to run through it again to make sure we got it right."

So they did. Afterward, in the quiet-alert state that comes just before sleep, Cheri noticed how still the house was— except for the soft breathing of Sky beside her and the faint snores of the boys down the hall. There wasn't even a creaking board to break the silence.

The ghosts had found contentment. And so had she.

Harlequin American Romance

COMING NEXT MONTH

#281 ONE WHIFF OF SCANDAL by Judith Arnold

For weeks Griff had been on the trail of the worst sex, money and power scandal ever to hit sleepy Rhode Island towns. Then Jill Bergland stumbled onto the story and made Griff wonder—could love survive scandal?

#282 KISSED BY AN ANGEL by Kathy Clark

Guilt had changed Kristi Harrison's life and made her seek solitude at a Florida beach house. When nightmares drove her from her bed to the quiet of the moonlit beach, she met Scott Sanders, who was driven by his own midnight demons. They each had their secret guilt—but could they find peace in each other's arms?

#283 SIDE BY SIDE by Muriel Jensen

As children, Janessa and Clay had promised to be united forever. It was a bond they vowed would never be broken. But could their childhood dreams anticipate their adult realities?

#284 LADY'S CHOICE by Linda Randall Wisdom

Whoever called it "midlife crisis" was right! At forty, Abby's life had gone haywire. Her grown children continued to give her problems, and now her best friend suddenly decided he wanted *more* than friendship. Zach's timing was perfect, for they would need their combined strength to weather the crisis to come.

Harlequin Temptation dares to be different!

Once in a while, we Temptation editors spot a romance that's truly innovative. To make sure *you* don't miss any one of these outstanding selections, we'll mark them for you.

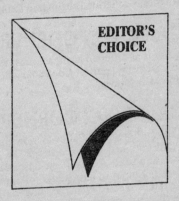

EDITOR'S CHOICE

When the "Editors' Choice" fold-back appears on a Temptation cover, you'll know we've found that extra-special page-turner!

THE

Temptation

EDITORS

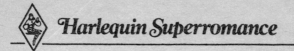

CALLOWAY CORNERS

Created by four outstanding Superromance authors, bonded by lifelong friendship and a love of their home state: Sandra Canfield, Tracy Hughes, Katherine Burton and Penny Richards.

CALLOWAY CORNERS

Home of four sisters as different as the seasons, as elusive as the elements; an undiscovered part of Louisiana where time stands still and passion lasts forever.

CALLOWAY CORNERS

Birthplace of the unforgettable Calloway women: *Mariah*, free as the wind, and untamed until she meets the preacher who claims her, body and soul; *Jo*, the fiery, feisty defender of lost causes who loses her heart to a rock and roll man; *Tess*, gentle as a placid lake but tormented by her longing for the town's bad boy and *Eden*, the earth mother who's been so busy giving love she doesn't know how much she needs it until she's awakened by a drifter's kiss . . .

CALLOWAY CORNERS

Coming from Superromance, in 1989:
Mariah, by Sandra Canfield, a January release
Jo, by Tracy Hughes, a February release
Tess, by Katherine Burton, a March release
Eden, by Penny Richards, an April release

Harlequin Superromance

Here are the longer, more involving stories you have been waiting for...Superromance.

Modern, believable novels of love, full of the complex joys and heartaches of real people.

Intriguing conflicts based on today's constantly changing life-styles.

Four new titles every month.
Available wherever paperbacks are sold.

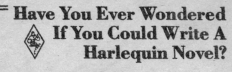

Have You Ever Wondered If You Could Write A Harlequin Novel?

Here's great news—Harlequin is offering a series of cassette tapes to help you do just that. Written by Harlequin editors, these tapes give practical advice on how to make your characters—and your story—come alive. There's a tape for each contemporary romance series Harlequin publishes.

Mail order only

All sales final
